The Hɪᴛ Lɪsᴛ

By
Frank Malley

First published in 2023 by Sharpe Books.

For Carole and Michael

When you have to kill a man it costs nothing to be polite.
Winston Churchill

THE HIT LIST

1

On the day of the shooting she could not have been happier, or any sadder.

Emily Stearn's life was full of such contrasts, but in the back of the white van, empty crisp packets and old paper coffee cups feuding for space with the latest computer technology, she felt a sudden tranquillity.

The moment caught her by surprise. After all, four hours trapped in a confined space with three middle-aged men in the summer heat, ambient air less than fragrant, waiting and watching but experiencing nothing more exciting than a traffic warden pinning tickets to illegally-parked cars, was not her usual idea of a good time. But this was different.

"How long do we wait? Are we sure they'll show up today?" asked Emily.

"They'll be here. Our man in Moscow's rarely wrong." Mason Jones, a round-faced Welshman with a permanently cheery smile, handed Emily a cup of muddy coffee from a thermos. Warm and wet, she accepted it gratefully, even though it tasted rough and smoky.

She took a few generous slurps before raising her binoculars, spying the warden ruining more people's days in the distance, along with a lad carrying a skateboard. She thought nothing of him. Teenagers with skateboards were like black cabs on the streets of London. Part of the scenery.

"Here we go." A sudden tingle of excitement in Emily's tone as she trained the binoculars on two black 4x4s as they slowed to a halt in Portland Place in front of the Chinese Embassy.

She nudged Jones. He sat up straight, or as straight as confined space allowed in the back of the van, parked across the road at a distance calculated to afford maximum visibility but evade routine detection.

The vehicles promised action at last.

"Okay, Emily, remember the drill. Short and sharp." Jones's voice was warm, his smile encouraging and his wink to the others designed to enlist their support.

All four members of the unit wore white boiler suits with the words *Gas Engineer* emblazoned in red letters on the back. Bob Wilson, a former field officer with an acid tongue and a droll sense of humour, also wore a set of headphones, pen and notepad in hand, poised to scribble. The team leader, Luke Scafell, sat back, arms folded, the epitome of experience and composure, studying flickering images on several computer screens.

"Two men exiting front vehicle. Black suits. One with an arm across the front of his coat possibly concealing a holstered weapon. The other, a finger to his ear. FSO (Federal Protective Service, Russia) lapel badges. Dark glasses. Eyes left and right. Bodyguards giving the street the once-over." Emily's commentary was calm, measured and precise, a hint of anticipation giving the end of each sentence an upward lilt. She had yearned for a piece of the action and the thrill of her first time in the field did not disappoint. She continued, clipped staccato phrases tripping off her tongue. "Two men alighting from second vehicle. First one, short, stocky, youngish. Crew cut. The second, tall, silver hair, blue suit, around fifty, carrying a black briefcase. Confirmed. He's our man."

The two men strode past the sculpted pillars at the embassy's ornate portico, eager to escape the midday sun, disappearing into the cool of the building. A short time later the vehicles moved off.

"Well done, Emily." Scafell voiced encouragement as he stretched a leg to relieve a muscle cramp. "Good, swift spotting, especially the lapel badges. Excellent communication. We'll make a watcher out of you yet."

Jones nodded in agreement, a gesture that caused Emily to experience a glow of warmth. It was the first time the office had trusted her to take the lead during an operation, even if it was little more than a training exercise. She could hardly believe her good fortune. Two years ago she worked in an insurance call centre, each day a mirror of the one before. A job devoid of mystery, intrigue, or even basic interest. Now she was a cog in a team evaluating why a Russian delegation was visiting the Chinese Embassy in London. Watching and listening. A spy in the making.

Scafell shifted in his seat, glanced at his watch and turned to face Wilson, who stroked a scruffy brown beard, tenderly, in rhythmic fashion, as if it were a cat. Wilson looked bored with life. For good reason. He *was* bored with life. At least life in white vans watching and waiting, never doing or experiencing the thrills that once lured him out of bed in the morning.

"You look knackered." There was a disparaging edge to Scafell's tone.

"Yeah." Wilson yawned, oblivious to any implied criticism. "Time for lunch? Nothing's likely to happen for a few hours. May as well while we can."

Scafell agreed. "Back in half an hour. You two can take a break then. Message me if anything happens in the meantime. We're only around the corner."

Scafell and Wilson clambered out of the vehicle, each carrying a bag of tools to suit their cover story. Watching them through the one-way back window panels as they sauntered down the street in their grubby boiler suits, Emily thought they made convincing tradesmen. Lumpen gaits and lazy demeanours. She saw Scafell pluck a hammer from his bag and twirl it above his head as if loosening neck and shoulder muscles stiffened by inactivity before turning left into a side street and disappearing from view.

"What's going on in there?" Emily floated the question, gesturing towards the embassy.

"No idea," said Jones. "But you can bet your life, nothing pretty. The Russians don't do social calls. There was a time …" He trailed off. He was about to say the department would have moved heaven and Earth and everything in between to listen to what the Russians were hatching in the building opposite. They would have found a way, through an agent, a bug, or whatever it took, to burrow inside. Modern technology meant satellites could detect a pin landing on a fluffy mat, if required. But the anything-goes spy fever of the Cold War was long gone. These days, everything bowed to accountability and transparency. These days, parking on the street needed signed permission from the minister-in-charge. Booking a satellite probably required a full meeting of the cabinet.

"You were going to say it was better in the old days, weren't you?"

"No … well, yes, probably I was. It's frustrating, that's all. What's the use if all we can do is watch what's going on, but do nothing to influence events?"

Emily enjoyed Jones's company. She liked the sing-song lilt of his accent. Even when he whinged it sounded like he was having fun. She also appreciated the way he had helped and encouraged her, bringing her up to speed with technology and the politics of Intelligence. She loved talking music with him, even if his taste was disappointingly mainstream. There were times when she thought him inclined to the odd bout of self-absorption, but his tales of mischief and magic with his two-year-old son were always a joy. When she joined up she had been warned there was no room for friends in the Secret Intelligence Service, but she regarded Mason Jones as a friend as well as a colleague and hoped he viewed her the same way.

Emily reached for the binoculars again. "At least we don't have to live in fear all the time," she said. "I don't think I could exist like some of the field guys. In Afghanistan or Iraq, or Moscow. On their own. In danger. Not knowing who's friend or foe from one day to the next. All we do is use their information and work out what's going on from a safe distance."

"There's no safe distance in this business, Emily. That's the number one rule."

Emily could always rely on a gloomy riposte from Jones to keep her focused. In jest, some of the team had nicknamed him Jonah, but it was all in good humour. They continued their conversation, light and frothy.

"What are you planning on eating tonight, Emily?"

"I'm not really into planning where eating's concerned. Whatever takes my fancy at the time. Smoked salmon. Beans on toast. Something simple."

"Not much of a cook then?"

"Hardly. The joy of cooking is when I'm not doing it."

Jones chuckled, while Emily tweaked the focus wheel on her binoculars, studying the ebb and flow of traffic in the distance. She spotted the skateboard lad again. On the opposite footpath, 250 yards away, maybe more, but heading towards them. He wore a grey hoodie over a peaked navy cap. Not that unusual, if the temperature hadn't hovered around 28 degrees centigrade.

He no longer carried the skateboard but rode it, coasting at a steady pace towards the embassy from the direction of Regent's Park. The street was unusually quiet, thought Emily, who as a Londoner found the incessant bustle and noise of the capital comforting.

"Everything okay?" said Jones.

"Yeah, think so."

The lad skated on, flitting in and out of Emily's vision behind the pitted trunks of high-hanging trees lining the road's central reservation. As he passed the entrance to the embassy, his knees bent hard and the skateboard swivelled, making an unexpectedly tight turn to cross the road at the junction of Portland Place and Weymouth Street.

Emily heard the cough of a motor, followed by the roar of an engine revving. A powerful engine, the vibration rattling the van's metal casing like a fast train rushing through a station. When the vehicle reached the junction, the car touched 60mph, maybe more. Hard to tell in the black blur that followed.

A shiver ran up Emily's spine. She expected a squeal of breaks, but none came. Instead, the car hit the skateboard lad head-on, his body bouncing on the bonnet, smashing against the windscreen, cartwheeling high in the air, legs and arms whirling, before slumping to the ground in a heap. The car sped off.

For an instant, Emily and Jones did nothing, staring at each other with numb expressions, trying to make sense of the recklessness. Then adrenalin kicked in and Emily made for the van doors.

"No." Jones grabbed her upper arm, forcing her back, pinching the skin so hard he drew a sharp yelp. "We can't get involved."

"The lad could be dying. Of course we can get involved. I'm not leaving him there."

5

Jones tightened his grip, but still Emily struggled to wriggle free, her eyes fiery, jaw determined. Jones's gaze alternated between her and the stricken lad as he weighed up the next course of action. Protocol v principle. "Okay, I'll go. Stay here, we can't leave control unmanned. Warn Scafell, and call an ambulance."

As Jones scrambled out of the van, Emily dispatched a WhatsApp message and snatched her binoculars.

The skateboard lad lay motionless, his face turned away from her. She saw Jones reach him and fall to his knees, checking for signs of life. A line of cars crawled past on the opposite carriageway, drivers gawping, but no one stopped. Emily fiddled with her phone, punching in 999, relaying their location, urging the ambulance service to hurry. Through her binoculars she could see Jones talking, asking for the lad's name but receiving no response, before gently manoeuvring him into the recovery position. Jones had medical training. Emily was glad he'd gone. He'd know what to do.

She was feeling calmer when she detected a sudden stiffness in Jones's demeanour. Through the restricted lens of her binoculars, she saw him turn from his kneeling position and a grimace, laden with astonishment, set concrete firm on his features. For a moment, Emily too was bewildered before a black-clad figure wearing a balaclava, pointing a gun, slid into view.

Jones raised his arms, maybe in capitulation, perhaps to protect himself, she couldn't tell. He mouthed, "Don't," followed by a shot, like the sharp snap of a Christmas cracker. The rest was little more than a blur in Emily's consciousness. Someone screamed. The skateboarder sprang to his feet and sprinted away. She heard two more shots and saw Jones collapse backwards onto the tarmac, all the while her world spinning in slow motion. A curious trick of the mind.

Nothing made sense. The skateboarder vanished around the nearest street corner, as if he'd never existed. The shooter disappeared too, in which direction Emily had no idea. Her brain wouldn't work. She'd always had problems with stress and while training had instigated coping strategies to stem the panic, this was different, this was industrial-grade stress.

THE HIT LIST

She sucked in a deep breath, dug her nails into fleshy palms, forcing paralysed limbs to work. Throwing the van doors open with disregard for anyone who may care to view the spy booty within, she jumped out, the physical effort supplying the shot of adrenalin required.

By the time she reached Jones he was gasping and gurgling. Blood poured from holes in his chest and exit wounds in his back. His eyes flickered, then closed.

She cradled his head. "Stay with me, Mason. For God's sake, someone help." Her scream, desperate as it was, went unanswered. Ramming her hand into Jones's chest, she pressed hard to try to stem the bleeding, but it was no use. Blood pumped out, leaking wet and warm, dripping through her fingers, spraying in a fine red mist, staining the front of her white suit. She looked around for help and spotted a few frightened bystanders on the opposite pavement.

She heard the scuffle of running feet as Scafell and Wilson sprinted around the corner, Wilson several paces behind, extra pounds around his midriff taking their toll.

Emily felt Jones squeeze her hand. She looked into his eyes, pupils dilating, eyeballs rolling, life ebbing. He pointed upwards to his right, in the direction of the Post Office Tower. "She ran …." He gasped out the words, slurred, indistinct, the effort forcing a thick projectile of blood to splatter onto the road.

"Never mind Mason … stay with me … please stay with me." Her voice tremulous.

He tried to point again. "She ran …"

Those were the last utterings of Mason Bryn Jones, before his body flopped, head lolled back, and he died in Emily's arms.

For a moment, she contemplated CPR, but swiftly realised his wounds were too catastrophic. Instead, she sat on the warm tarmac cradling Jones's head, rocking back and forth as a mother comforts a baby, a distant siren wailing.

2

She watched the big pleasure cruiser chug its way up the river, a choppy wake bullying smaller boats on either side. Revellers on board sipped from champagne flutes despite the early hour, while others danced to the thump of music deadened and distorted by the armoured glass compulsory at HQ.

The Thames rolled on, the city going about its business as usual, but as she gazed out of the office window Emily wondered whether life would ever be quite the same. She wasn't the reflective type. She had learned to live with difficulties that genes and nature had thrown her way. An obsession for routine, a compulsion for numbers and solving riddles as well as a struggle to feel socially accepted even in the presence of friends and colleagues.

She always knew her new job would prove challenging despite the training, even though she had been hand-picked. But there was no preparation, no handbook, for witnessing a friend and colleague assassinated in ruthless fashion. Maybe she should have stayed in the insurance call centre, or taken the further degree in mathematics she had set her heart on. Perhaps she wasn't cut out for the real world with all its dangers and uncertainties.

The door opened, the welcome draught sweeping away introspective thoughts.

"Ah, Miss Stearn." The thick-set frame of Dougie McBride filled the doorway, his deep, sonorous Scottish voice resembled the slow tuning stroke of a double bass. Lots of rolling Rs. "I trust you feel up to a few questions."

Emily nodded. She saw Scafell and Wilson shuffle in, heads bowed like schoolboy truants entering the headmaster's study. Two other men she didn't know followed them. The unknown pair had pale demeanours, carried clipboards and briefcases, exuding the pen-pushing anonymity of civil servants who wait for others to make decisions. Scafell and Wilson took chairs either side of Emily at the conference table while the others sat opposite.

McBride motioned for everyone to stand and nodded to one of the briefcase men, who clicked a keyboard. A picture of Mason Jones, fresh faced, wearing his cheery grin, appeared on the wall-mounted monitor. "First, let us remember Mason. A first-rate professional and a fine man." They stood for around a minute, the silence solemn and respectful, the only sound the wheezy rasp of Wilson's chest.

"Thank you everyone," said McBride, before his Ayrshire brogue transformed into a gravelly growl. "Now, what the hell were you all playing at? Do you realise the shit-storm you've unleashed?"

McBride was chief of the recently created Section X, specialising in intelligence evaluation and surveillance, charged with adding extra value to clandestine missions. It was the morning after the Portland Place killing. Doctors had checked out Emily at St Thomas's Hospital, treating her for shock. Scafell and Wilson had liaised with the Metropolitan Police, packed up the white van and informed McBride of the incident. Scafell had collected Emily from the hospital, informed her parents, before taking her home to her flat in Archway where she lived with her boyfriend, although he was away on an academic course for a few days. Scafell offered her a bed for the night at the cottage he shared with his partner, but she refused. She wanted to be alone with her thoughts.

One thing, in particular, puzzled her. There was no mention of the incident on national or local television, or radio news. Not a line in the Evening Standard. That was odd, even for an incident involving the Intelligence services.

McBride was giving nothing away. He had forged a reputation for ruthless efficiency during his three years in charge of the section. Mistakes did not happen on his watch. Operatives certainly did not get killed, at least not a short Tube ride from the office. A dent such as that could end a section chief's career. Which explained why his mood was mad as hell. He signalled to the civil servants sitting either side of him. One, wearing thick-lensed glasses that gave his eyes the appearance of a permanent squint, reached into a briefcase and took out a recording device, placing it on the table, setting it in motion. The other opened a large notebook and sat poised, pen in hand.

"Very well, Miss Stearn," growled McBride. "Take us through the incident from the start."

Emily's many talents included a photographic memory. It made for meticulous descriptions of the timeline, the arrival of the Russian delegation, the skateboard lad and the shooter.

McBride sensed her precision and desire to be thorough. He remained patient, refraining from interrupting until she reached the moment the skateboarder apparently collided with the car.

"Tell me, Miss Stearn, why did Mason leave the van, blowing your cover on a busy London street when others, bystanders, potential helpers, were around, when the fate of the so-called skateboarder was unknown? Why would an experienced operative do that?" One of McBride's eyebrows lifted as if supplying the question mark.

Emily fiddled with her hands on her lap, eyes lowered in a gesture of submission as if the fatal error resulting in Jones's death was suddenly dawning. It wasn't sudden, of course. She'd thought of little else since paramedics had prised Jones's blood-soaked body from her grasp in Portland Place. If she had thought and reasoned, instead of reacting, perhaps Jones would still be alive.

"I made him leave the van. He didn't want to. But he stopped me from going to help the lad. He held me back. He went in my place. It should have been me. I should have been shot." A tremor resonated in Emily's voice. She thought she was about to cry, a rare occurrence in Emily's existence. She didn't. Instead, she threw out a question of her own.

"Why would anyone want to kill Mason? He was a sweet, family man. He did no one any harm. It doesn't make sense. It was a routine operation."

McBride banged a fist on the table and his brown eyes smouldered, although his words were cold. "There's no such thing as a routine operation in our line of business. Thanks to your routine operation I've got MI5 on my back for treading on their patch, the Chinese and Russians accusing us of an act of aggression, the Home Office doing its nut, the Foreign Office threatening to close down one of our sections, and the Prime Minister fuming that we've put a vital trade deal with China in jeopardy."

That explained it, thought Emily. That's why no reports surfaced in the media. The news blackout made sense. It was inconceivable Chinese security forces had not tracked the incident on their doorstep. They knew all right, but the last thing Downing Street wanted was an embarrassing spy scandal with a potential trade deal worth billions at risk.

As if to stress the seriousness of the incident a gentle knock sounded and the door swung open. Emily had seen, read about, but never met the man who entered. He wore a dark suit, sharp enough to convey class and authority but not too snappy to be considered ostentatious. His wire-rimmed glasses gave him the bearing of a professor, silver hair slicked back, his features relatively unwrinkled. Emily thought she could smell the woody scent of his cologne. His status as Service chief was confirmed when McBride rose swiftly to his feet.

"Thank you for coming, 'C'," he said with a deference at odds with his previous growls. "We're due to hear about the shooter."

'C', for that is how a century of tradition dictates the main man is addressed, sat at the foot of the table, and gestured for McBride to continue.

"Miss Stearn, take a wee moment if you like, but if you could run us through the actual shooting."

This was the part Emily had been dreading. The problem with owning a photographic memory is that it confers the rare ability to retain vivid images in the mind for a prolonged period, months, years sometimes, in the same intricate detail as first seen. It meant the final horrific moments of Jones's life remained stored in sharp focus in Emily's brain, undimmed and undiluted by time or the shock of her ordeal.

Scafell tried to intervene on her behalf, but McBride waved away his protestations.

"I didn't get a good view of the shooter. It all happened so fast. I was watching through binoculars so I didn't pick up the seriousness of the incident until it was under way, but she was definitely left-handed." Emily's tone was confident.

"She?" said McBride. "You're sure it was a woman."

"Not certain, but there was a lightness to the shooter's gait, and I'm sure Jones said, 'She ran', and pointed in the direction of her escape route. He said it twice before he …" She trailed off.

"What about the bogus skateboarder?"

"I didn't get a good look at him. He was wearing a hoodie. When he was lying in the road his face pointed away from me and he jumped up and sprinted away as I was clambering out of the van."

'C' had been listening in studious silence but cleared his throat to address McBride.

"Surely we must have pictures, video of the incident. Satellite imagery. It's one of London's main roads."

McBride shuffled papers nervously. "I'm afraid not. The only public CCTV camera pointed at the junction was temporarily out of order. Maybe coincidence, maybe not, and none of the private ones in range caught the incident. Nothing via satellite either."

"But what about our own pictures?" A perplexed grimace formed deep, wavy lines of confusion on 'C''s brow.

"Erm … I'm afraid Miss Stearn was the only operative on duty in the van at the time. The others were taking lunch. Miss Stearn deemed it more important to go to her colleague's aid than to take pictures."

"Christ, and we call ourselves an Intelligence service." 'C' stood. His knuckles white, his jaw jutting. An uncomfortable silence filled the room, McBride squirming along with those around him.

"Could it be Tinman?" The Chief's question hung in the air.

Eventually, McBride answered. "It seems certain the shooter was left-handed, and obviously there were Russians in the area. Both of which could point to Tinman, but Jones appeared certain the shooter was female. Miss Stearn is also convinced. We'll know more when we get the ballistics report. We found one casing at the scene."

"Only one? I thought the shooter fired three times."

"That's right. We think the gun was wrapped in a plastic bag to catch the casings. An old professional's trick to conceal evidence."

"But one escaped? That doesn't sound very professional."

McBride shrugged.

"Any communications intercepted?" asked 'C'. "We know the Russians like to crow." This time McBride shook his head.

'C' scanned the table as if gauging the trustworthiness of the disparate characters, before addressing McBride. "Get on to the guys in Moscow. I want a report on my desk first thing in the morning. A list of suspects and some clue as to what's behind this nonsense. Is that clear?"

McBride nodded.

"And Intus will be in touch as usual in these cases," said 'C'. "They'll want to speak to everyone at the scene, as well as those who authorised this operation."

Intus represented the informal title for the internal investigation unit. The name derived from the Latin for *inside*, the unit pressed into action as a matter of course when a mission went wrong, an agent went missing, an operative injured or killed, or whenever a department was deemed insecure. The idea was to keep the Service neat and tidy, above suspicion. No one liked internal investigations. No operative welcomed being snooped on or interrogated by the Service's own officers. Everyone was suspicious of Intus, especially the bosses. If Intus sprang into action then something had gone wrong, someone was not doing their job. Ultimately, that was 'C''s responsibility.

The Chief left.

When the door closed, McBride's gaze fixed on Scafell and his growl returned, even more menacing.

"Okay, you heard the man. I want reports from you all and we need answers to two obvious questions."

"Such as," said Scafell.

"How did the shooter know we were outside the embassy? We planned the operation only a few days ago to keep an eye on the Chinese. It was supposed to be a training exercise to give Miss Stearn experience of work in the field. Hardly weapons-grade spying. Outside the people in this room, who knew the time and location?"

"And the other question?"

"Why would a professional killer take out an anonymous operative in what appears to be an elaborate, planned execution, with the skateboarder and speeding car driver as accomplices? Mason wasn't a spy. He was a desk jockey. He didn't have access to sensitive information, at least not the sort anyone would want to kill for."

"Could it be Tinman?" said Scafell. "Feels like it could be. It's the way he operates."

"Unlikely. He's after bigger fry than Mason. But speak to Moscow. Find out the word on the street."

McBride picked up his folder and strode out of the room, the two admin personnel scampering in his wake. Scafell and Wilson discussed the presence of 'C' for a few minutes.

Emily gazed out of the window at the boats riding on the river, her heart heavy, her mind numb, trawling through random notions. She replayed the events at Portland Place over and over, desperate to reveal some miniscule clue that could make sense of the futile loss of life. She recalled Mason Jones and his cheery smile. She thought of his wife and little boy, and wondered how deep the Thames was at high tide.

3

That evening Emily visited her parents in Highgate. She couldn't tell them about the shooting or discuss work. But she needed the familiarity and warmth of the family home.

She ate dinner and pored over some old photographs with her mother. They enjoyed an hour's reflection, smiling at memories of a seaside holiday in Brighton and a trip to the New Forest where pictures of Emily riding a pony at around eight years old brought a nostalgic glow to her mother's face. There were also snaps of Emily and her father at Felixstowe watching the container ships dock.

Such trips punctuated her childhood, although Emily's fondest memories remained noting the registration plates of cars on a pad as they passed the house. Her mother had worried about her back then. Emily never cried. Not even when sustaining the bumps and bruises that are part and parcel of growing up. Did she reside on the autism spectrum? That was the concern. Doctors never reached a diagnosis, while Emily grew proud of what her mother deemed her *special qualities*.

Emily accepted she was different, which certainly applied to her relationship with her boyfriend. Like her, Al Andrews was a mathematician, a mature student cum algebra teacher, currently taking a further degree at University College London, having transferred from Bristol when they became an item 18 months ago.

They were opposites, Emily socially tense and anxious when consumed with work, Al laid back, confident, a font of knowledge on music and most other subjects. It should not have worked but somehow it did. Emily yearned to tell Al about the shooting. He always knew what to say, always cheered her up when she was down, putting life and work in sharp and mostly humorous perspective. But while Al knew where she worked, she could not divulge details. Anyway, he was away for a few days. She decided to call him later that evening. As she strolled home down Highgate

Hill a car pulled into the kerb with its passenger window rolled down. The driver called her name. Scafell.

"Hi, Luke," said Emily. "What are you doing here?"

"Thought I'd call to make sure you were all right. Jump in, I'll give you a lift home."

Emily slung her bag off her shoulder and slid into the passenger seat. They made small talk for the few minutes it took to reach Emily's flat before she assured Scafell she was fine and wanted an early night. She opened the car door and made to exit, then changed her mind, snapping it shut, a sudden lurch of curiosity prompting her to pose the obvious question since the office meeting that morning. "Who's Tinman?"

Having still to complete two years' probationary training, Emily's security clearance barely extended beyond the pass required to enter HQ. She could accompany senior personnel on missions such as the embassy stake-out, but was not yet privy to sensitive information and Tinman right now was the hottest security news in town.

The mention of Tinman seemed to provoke a reaction in Scafell. His neck and shoulder muscles tightened and Emily sensed tension in his eyes. He killed the engine.

"I probably shouldn't be telling you this, but 'C' mentioned Tinman this morning while you were present, so I'm guessing there's no harm in you knowing." He paused.

"Knowing what?"

"Do you recall the news last week about the Army general killed at his holiday home in Devon?"

"Of course, it was all over the papers and TV. General Parker, wasn't it?"

"That's right. Everything points to it being the work of Andrei Reblov. Our man in Moscow is sure of it. The general was shot multiple times and only a professional hitman of the highest order could have breached his security and escaped without leaving a trace."

"Where does Tinman come in?"

"Tinman and Reblov are one and the same person."

"Why Tinman?" Emily was engrossed, her eyes bright, dancing with curiosity, her questions fired swiftly.

"For Tinman, read Putin's man. He's a former bodyguard of President Putin. For years, he was close to Putin, checking his mail, tasting his food. If you watch videos of Putin when crowds were around, you'll see Reblov right beside him, always carrying a suitcase. He's been known as Tinman in the Service ever since."

"What was in the suitcase?"

"An armoured shield. At the touch of a button Reblov could deploy a large, umbrella-shaped Kevlar sheet. It wouldn't stop an RPG, but would save Putin from small arms fire, unless the shooter got lucky."

"Did you meet Reblov?"

"No."

Scafell smiled and licked his lips. Emily could tell he was enjoying imparting information. Everyone knew Scafell had clocked up 20 years in the Service, eight in the Moscow station. He spoke fluent Russian. More important, he understood the Russian psyche, reciting it like a mantra to anyone in the office with the time and inclination to listen. His considered insight into the population of the largest country on Earth boiled down to the willingness of the masses to accept the rule and fabrications of autocrats. Fear played a significant part, he would say. But it relied on admiration too. For strong and ruthless leaders, who wouldn't hesitate to kill enemies, friends also if required, to realise ambitions. Years ago, when Russia annexed Crimea, the Service had asked Scafell to monitor Russia's intentions. He'd told them Putin planned a full-scale invasion of Ukraine. He warned of the president's mood swings, increasing intransigence and suspect decisions. But did they listen? No, they filed his report in the Amazonian cloud that harboured the Service's innermost secrets, pulling it out too late when Russian tanks were rolling towards Kyiv.

"Why would Reblov kill General Parker and, more to the point, why kill Mason?" asked Emily.

"I've no idea about poor old Mason. In my opinion, he was in the wrong place at the wrong time. Simple as that. Maybe the

Russians received spurious information. But General Parker fits the Tinman criteria."

"Criteria?" Emily's eyebrows met. She wasn't following the line of reasoning.

"General Parker. A crucial defence chief, an Army big wig and a confirmed hard liner. He would have had NATO's entire battle force camped on Russia's borders all year round if he could. He thought putting tanks up Putin's backside was the only way to get his undivided attention. He's the third general in Europe in less than a month killed in suspicious circumstances. One in Poland, another in Spain and now one in the UK."

"And your point is?"

"Revenge, Emily. Pure and simple. Russian revenge for all the generals killed in Ukraine. Killed by weapons supplied by Poland and Spain, the rest of Europe, the United States, and, in particular, the UK. We believe Tinman has a hit list and is on a one-man vigilante crusade to avenge the deaths of Russia's top brass. If I've come to know anything about Russian leaders, it's that they hold grudges and lash out when they feel wronged or betrayed."

"Have you told McBride?"

"Yes. Of course, he knows. We all do. Tinman's the most wanted man in Europe. Agents across the globe are working night and day, searching for clues to his whereabouts. But that's easy to say, catching him is the hard part." He turned and peered into Emily's eyes. "Are you sure whoever shot Mason was a woman?"

A video flickered deep in Emily's brain. She saw a slender left arm extend, heard three tight shots, followed by the elegant movement of a compact figure. No, not compact. Slight. Womanly slight. And then Mason's two words. "She ran." Emily shivered, her eyes still and distant, as if in a trance. A photographic memory was a curse as well as a charm.

"Emily," said Scafell, a concerned frown lining his face. She shook her head.

"Sorry. I was thinking … never mind. Yes, I'm pretty sure the shooter was a woman. Not certain, everything happened so quickly, but almost sure. Call it a gut feeling, not just from what Mason said, but from the sway of the hips, the way she moved."

Emily stepped out of the car. "Thanks for the lift, Luke. See you tomorrow."

4

Emily rose early next morning. She caught an underground train to Blackfriars and walked the rest of the way. It was cold but bright, one of those mornings that confers a smug feeling of nuanced superiority, as if experiencing a thrilling dawn fulfils one of life's labours.

She paused on Blackfriars Bridge to take in the vista. On one side the capacious dome of St Paul's Cathedral dominating the skyline along with the regal framework of Tower Bridge. On the other, the Big Ben clock tower in the distance, marking the Houses of Parliament and the seat of power beside the impressive sweep of the River Thames. This was what had clinched the deal for Emily when the Secret Intelligence Service came calling. Not the spectacular view, although that helped, but the lure of working where powerful people prowled and big decisions were made. Where, in some small way, she could make a difference.

By chance, she had met the man who offered her a job two years ago. David Stephens had attended the funeral of her Uncle Sebastian, a Cambridge history professor who turned out to have a much more interesting past than she had first given him credit for.

Following Sebastian's death, Emily's father tasked her with cataloguing belongings at his seaside home. She discovered an encrypted journal. With help from Al, she deciphered the code to reveal Sebastian was not only a professor, but also a spy, recruited as a Cambridge undergraduate and pressed into service, many years later, when he thought his usefulness must surely have expired.

The journal revealed his mission involved travelling to Soviet Moscow during the Cold War in 1981 to help eliminate a Russian assassin by the name of Igor Kalenkov, deemed to be one of the biggest threats to the West.

The sensitivity of the journal's information attracted the attention of the Intelligence Service, who monitored Emily and Al, impressed by their powers of deduction. A few months later Emily received a call from Stephens, a director of operations at MI6 with old school charm, who had sat unannounced at the back of the crematorium at Uncle Sebastian's funeral. Stephens was a former case officer, now responsible for the Service's smooth running of foreign agents. He offered her a job. Emily's first reaction was to tell him she had no intention of killing people.

Stephens smiled. "My dear, our Service is not about killing people. It's not about racing around roofs with guns or endless car chases. That's for film directors. Our job is, in the main, mundane, but no less important for that. We provide protection by being one step in front of our enemies. Here at HQ, as much as in the field. These days we are the front line in the fight against global terrorism. We need bright, young minds. Like you, Emily. Problem solvers. People capable of cracking codes, assessing risk and reward ahead of the rest."

Emily liked the sound of that. It appealed to her mathematical mind and was also a way of honouring her late uncle's legacy. She felt flattered. It helped that she had recently walked out of a dead-end job in an insurance call centre and dumped a cheating boyfriend. She was ready for a change, a challenge, a job with purpose and intrigue. Which is how she came to accept a post at HQ, negotiating the induction course, brushing up her French, learning the rudiments of Russian, finding herself fast-tracked into the Service's acute Intelligence section as an analyst where she mixed and learned with seasoned professionals such as Scafell and Wilson. A sense of purpose and achievement filled each day. It wasn't work, rather it felt like destiny.

When she reached the office, McBride was already there. She made herself a coffee at the little kitchenette in a zone concealed from the open-plan floor and as she carried her cup through to her desk he beckoned her into his glass-panelled cubicle.

"Miss Stearn."

"Call me Emily, please. Miss Stearn sounds so formal."

He neither confirmed nor denied her request, a mere flick of an eyebrow revealing her comment had registered. She found that irritating and disconcerting, which perhaps was the intention. As far as Emily could work out, McBride called everyone else by their Christian names. One of the Service's core principles ruled there should be no 'Sirs' or 'Maams'. No formal signs of deference, apart from 'C'. The rule extended loosely to surnames in the interests of team bonding, as well as having the additional benefit of masking identity to anyone who may be listening or watching. At least that is what Emily had deduced from her induction course. In her case, maybe because she remained a trainee, McBride had clearly made an exception.

McBride scribbled something on a pad before swivelling in his chair to give Emily his full attention. "As you know, we need to report to 'C' this morning. Can you compile a list of women capable of Mason's assassination? It can't be a very long list."

"Will do," said Emily, bristling slightly at McBride's dispassionate tone, although she did not think he was being intentionally uncaring. McBride wasn't old. Perhaps late forties, although he had the gruff insensitivity of an older man. Maybe the scar tissue sustained dealing with life and death issues on a daily basis piles up over the years. Thickening the skin. Layers of emotional detritus dulling sensitivity and perception. Maybe he regretted his decision 20 years ago to choose the grey government building and Whitehall hypothesising of his desk job over the chance of an operational life in the field.

"Intus have asked to see you this afternoon," added McBride, turning to scroll down his computer. "Can you ring them to set up a time?"

Emily nodded. "Is the ballistics report available?"

"Not yet." McBride's eyes remained fixed on his computer screen. Emily ambled to her desk.

For the next two hours she trawled the department's files, sifting through the world's most wanted female assassins. It made disturbing reading. Activists, terrorists and freelancers prepared to murder to order for a suitable fee. A longer list than Emily anticipated, but she whittled it down to half a dozen as some were known to be in hiding, some protected by rogue states, while others had alibis provided unwittingly by the department as they were under constant scrutiny, tracked by satellites and known to be thousands of miles away from Portland Place at the time of the shooting.

Emily created a picture presentation and when the call came she was ready.

The team met in the conference room, McBride leading proceedings with Scafell and Wilson, as well as Emily, among 10 people present.

McBride reminded everyone of the top secret nature of the case. Because of the proximity to the Chinese embassy, the sensitive trade negotiations and the potential risk to national security, the Foreign Office were taking the lead in the inquiry. Which perhaps explained why the Metropolitan Police so far kept their own investigations low key, although McBride said they were abreast of all developments.

McBride spent the next hour combing the minutiae of Mason Jones's existence. Three operatives assigned to the task had discovered nothing more unusual than Jones once played the French horn in the South Wales chamber orchestra.

He was married to Imelda, had a two-year-old son, Archie, lived in Camden, and supported Cardiff Blues rugby team, although he made time to watch them no more than three times a season. He didn't drink, smoke, or socialise with dubious characters. His work assignments over the past six months had been routine to the point of tedious, a fact Wilson could vouch for as he had teamed up with him on numerous occasions. There was nothing, private, or work related, to suggest why he may have been a target for a professional killer.

"Sounds like bloody Saint Mason," growled McBride, who detected the odd eyebrow raise. He covered up swiftly. "Nothing wrong with that, of course, but it's not exactly helpful when it comes to solving matters. Okay, Miss Stearn, what do you have regarding potential suspects?"

Emily opened a file on her computer. Her research had thrown up more potential female assassins than anticipated. Mostly affiliated to terrorist groups, such as Chechen suicide bombers and ISIS. She included other secret services in her search, but had narrowed down her suspects to three.

She clicked her computer and a figure appeared on the conference TV screen. The image of a beautiful young woman with cascading curly black hair drew knowing glances from several around the table.

"This is Mossad operative Erika Rodgers, known as Agent Annabelle. In her twenties and renowned as a crack shot." said Emily.

McBride's nose wrinkled. "Why would Mossad be interested in Mason Jones, or in shooting anyone on the streets of London right now? The Israelis have their hands full in so many other places. Besides, they're precise. They're not mavericks. They kill the enemies of Israel or those whose work carries danger for Israel."

Emily shrugged. "The facts match. The manner of the shooting fits. Black balaclava. Left-handed. Always three bullets."

"Go on," said McBride.

The next picture flicked up, an older woman with peroxide blonde hair and thick dark eyebrows. Emily rattled off the details. "Ruth Grossman. Forty-two. Born in Venezuela. On the FBI's most wanted list as a female gun for hire. Graduated from the University of Miami's Institute of Marine Science. Known as Miami's Mistress of Murder. Thought to be living in Saudi Arabia but wanted for several recent shootings in America."

Scafell interjected. "Is she left-handed too?"

"Ambidextrous, actually."

McBride nodded. It was the first time he had observed Emily in action and he was impressed, as much by her confident delivery as the substance of her information.

The third picture appeared on the screen.

"Here is the West's most wanted terrorist. Samantha Webb. The subject of an Interpol Red Notice and a member of a Somalia-based radical group. Thought to be responsible for assassinations in Mombasa, Istanbul and Paris."

"Does she have any connection with the UK?" The presentation had grabbed McBride's attention. Those who knew him could tell by the way he rocked his right cheekbone with a forefinger, an unconscious habit, as if adjusting the contrast or volume on his concentration.

"Yes. Her father was a British Army colonel. Served in Northern Ireland."

"He must be very proud of her." Wilson stroked his beard, his deadpan aside sparking a collective snigger around the table.

"The family are no longer in contact."

"Is she left-handed?" Scafell repeated his earlier question.

"That isn't recorded, but while she has been off the radar for a couple of years, she's thought to be the group's main operative in Europe."

The images cleared from the screen. McBride caught Emily's eye and nodded his appreciation. She felt a warming infusion of elation. Not only due to the recognition of an efficient job, swiftly compiled, but mainly because she was doing something tangible to track down Jones's killer. At last McBride appeared convinced Emily was right. The killer was a woman.

McBride set about organising the plan of attack, assigning the workforce in pairs to investigate the recent movements of Emily's female suspects. He authorised contact with the CIA, Interpol, and use of satellite technology.

As the meeting broke up into little huddles, a secretary knocked on the door and passed a note to McBride. He studied it for a few moments, before motioning for everyone to retake their seats.

His tone grave. "This, I think, changes everything. The Met have released the initial ballistics report. The bullets that killed Mason most probably came from an SPS pistol, a gun with armour-piercing SP10 bullets."

"And?" Wilson was eager for the explanation.

"A gun favoured by the Russians," said McBride. "In fact, the same type of bullets used to kill General Parker last week."

"Tinman." Scafell drew the obvious conclusion.

"Yes, Tinman."

A voice screamed in Emily's head. She wanted to tell McBride he was making a mistake. That the image ingrained in her mind was of a woman, with multiple characteristics confirming her gender. Narrow shoulders, trim waist, dainty movement. But she detected the high tide of popular opinion racing in, running up the shore of her logic, rinsing her confidence.

"Is he left handed?" she asked.

McBride's ego answered. "He most certainly is, Miss Stearn. Ever since he lost his right thumb protecting Putin during an assassination attempt at a rally in Ekaterinburg. Tinman, or Andrei Reblov to give him his proper name, threw himself at the gunman, deflecting the shot but also injuring his right hand in the process. Most men in his business would have retired. Not Reblov. He set about teaching himself to shoot left-handed. If anything, became even more ruthless. He is thought to be the FSB (Russian Federal Security Service) man behind several recent killings. All with Moscow's consent."

"But why kill Mason Jones? It doesn't make sense."

McBride considered the question before replying. "Assassins are not perfect. They mess up like everyone else. Remember the Moroccan laddie, that waiter killed by Mossad agents in Norway some years ago. They thought he was the leader of a Palestinian terrorist group when really he was merely good at laying tables. Mistakes happen. There are far more cock-ups than conspiracies in life. But the facts are the facts. And forensics don't lie."

Yes, they do, thought Emily. They lie all the time. No test, no information, no DNA sample, no ballistics report, is 100 per cent accurate. Everything is subject to the laws of probability. The first rule in the murky world of Intelligence is as simple as it is stark. Accept nothing at face value. Rarely is anything what it seems.

5

Emily arrived on time for the meeting with Intus that afternoon. Unpunctuality offended her sense of order. Not that she was early. In her book, that was almost as rude and uncultured as being late, creating a vacuum, giving her time to ruminate. In this case, time to explore the graphic details that inhabited the dark corners of her memory.

A secretary with a charmless demeanour and long lank hair to match her personality pointed to a plastic chair in the corridor where she could wait. One of the Intus panel members was late.

Ten minutes went by, then 20. Emily fidgeted in her handbag, looked at her watch, frustration growing. She was ready to suggest rescheduling when the secretary took a call and motioned for her to enter the interview room.

A middle-aged man in a dark suit with a straight back, the sort of ramrod spine routinely on parade at Buckingham Palace, stood gazing out of the window. He signalled for Emily to take a seat and paced the room behind her for half a minute, creating an air of uncertainty, which doubtless was his aim. Finally, he sat behind a desk, two younger colleagues either side of him, a man and a woman. No apology for the late start. Instead, he introduced himself as Savage, the unit chief, with those either side referred to as his *secretary* and his *eyes and ears*. He mumbled their names, but Emily's thoughts were racing and she didn't catch them.

A rush of nervous tension saw Emily bite one of her nails. Savage missed nothing. His squinty blue-grey eyes studied her in silence for a few moments, as a poker player might read an opponent's intentions. What may she know? Would she tell the complete truth? Why was she anxious? Would she protect or betray her colleagues? Savage thought the former. He knew Emily was inexperienced, naïve, stubborn but competent, that much he had gleaned from her resume. But there was an uncomplicated innocence about her demeanour. The sort to believe the best in her comrades. A commendable trait in any normal business. But this wasn't a normal business. This was a business which on occasions asked men and women to bury their anxieties and fears so deep they could never surface. That asked people to take the most heinous risks for the sake of their country. Those demands pushed people to the edge of their sanity. Sometimes, for Savage had known it, those same splendid people had woken up, minds in a dark alcove of the night, and decided to betray their families, their colleagues, their country, their vocation. Some for money, others for ideology. He had confronted such traitors in this very room and now brought the experience gleaned from such treachery to every interview he conducted. If you work in a factory that teaches people to lie and deceive, you must expect nothing less in return. From such a platform, Savage began his questions.

His first request was the one Emily dreaded, but she steeled her mind and related again the events of the day of the shooting. On automatic pilot, still with instant recall, although repetition over the past 48 hours was beginning to blur the edges. Adhering to her training, she forced herself to remember what she saw, rather than merely to repeat what she had said previously.

The panel listened without interruption, the secretary, a petite lady of exquisite neatness, scribbling notes in beautifully aligned shorthand. When Emily finished, Savage sat in silence for a few moments, his head nodding as if in contemplation. When he spoke, his question surprised Emily.

"What do you think of Wilson and Scafell?"

"I don't understand." Emily's brow knitted.

"Do you know them well?"

"I've worked with them for the last three months, that's all. So the answer's no, I suppose."

"Do you get on?"

"Yes, they've been very supportive. I don't know what you're getting at."

"I'm not getting at anything. I'm trying to determine why the killer struck while they were absent and you, the most inexperienced of operatives, were in the van by yourself. Don't you think that was rather convenient?"

"I guess it was by chance. It all happened so quickly. It could easily have been me and Mason who'd gone for lunch."

"Whose idea was lunch?"

"I don't recall."

"Don't recall? Emily, it was a small van, there were four of you, two went for lunch. Who suggested that? Was it you?"

"No."

"Was it Mason?"

"No."

"Only two left."

"I don't know. I think Luke and Bob agreed between themselves. I can't remember whose idea it was. It seemed innocuous."

Savage rocked in his chair. He had a pedantic delivery, but a hectoring tone and a confidence that warned Emily to be wary. "How long have you been with the Service?"

"Eighteen months."

"I'd say that was long enough to realise that nothing we do or say is innocuous. Much of the Service's purpose entails sifting through a minefield of chitter-chatter, part of which you may class as innocuous, some of which may be just that. But distinguishing the truly innocuous from the seemingly innocuous is what we do. It saves lives. We have to get it right every time, and we're pretty good at it."

A sudden urge tempted Emily to remind Savage that wasn't always true. She had done extensive research before joining up, learning the Service was instrumental in providing the world with intelligence that former Iraq president, Saddam Hussein, possessed weapons of mass destruction. That he could strike on London and other European capitals within 45 minutes. Specific intelligence that led to the invasion of Iraq in 2003 resulting in thousands of deaths, including British and American troops and Iraqi civilians. Except the intelligence was bogus. There were no weapons of mass destruction. That's what Emily wanted to say, but she was too inexperienced, too respectful. Instead, she said, "I don't recall who brought up lunch. All I know is that they went."

Savage ambled over to the window and for a few moments gazed at the familiar view. His arms hung limp behind his back and he

29

twiddled his thumbs. An innocuous act, thought Emily, before he turned and fixed her with cold eyes.

"Emily, who may you have alerted to the operation in Portland Place?"

"No one."

"A friend maybe?"

"No."

"Family?"

"Definitely not."

"How about Mr Andrews?"

The mention of her boyfriend struck like a physical blow. A griping nausea mixed with acid anger coursed through her stomach.

"No. I never discuss anything about work with Al."

"But he knows you work here."

"Of course, but that's allowed."

"I believe his full name is Andreyevich, Alexei Andreyevich."

"Yes, he's from Latvia."

"But with Russian connections."

"You knew all about this when I joined the Service. Al was checked out and interviewed. He's a sweet guy whose family had good reason to hate the Russians." Emily spat out the information and could hear her voice rising, affronted by Savage's insinuations. She could tell he was gauging her reaction, playing games. She sucked in a deep breath to compose herself. "He's the last person the Russians would try to recruit."

Savage's eyebrows raised. "You're getting ahead of yourself. No one is accusing Mr Andrews of anything. We are merely exploring where information may have been leaked."

"If you're after a mole then look elsewhere, because it hasn't come from me, or Al."

"A mole? How nineteen sixties. But, you're right, we have to rule that out. There are many avenues down which information could have leaked. The man who provided the van, the operative in charge of itineraries. A careless secretary. It's our job to find out, because someone who shouldn't, knew your van was parked outside the Chinese Embassy that day. I don't believe in chance."

He strode back to his chair and sat down. "Thank you, Emily, that will be all for now."

As Emily left the interview room, thoughts dancing a sullen tango, she spied Wilson in the corridor, perched awkwardly on the same chair where she had waited. Emily couldn't work out Wilson. She had solving puzzles in common with Scafell. He had also helped with her Russian studies and welcomed her to the analysts' team. Wilson was that bit older, probably early fifties. More distant. He dressed shabbily, carrying more than a few extra pounds as men with nothing, or no one, to care for, tend to. Sometimes, she thought he smelled of whisky and neglected his personal hygiene. He also seemed to regard everyone with suspicion. Doubtless that came from his time in the field when wariness of friend and foe was paramount. She had never indulged in meaningful conversation with him outside that required in work, but she detected sadness in him. Resentment, too, as if, as he slowed down, he believed the Service had treated him harshly. He beckoned to her and she ambled over.

"Did they ask about me?" he said.

"Not directly."

"What does that mean?"

"They wanted to know whose idea it was to go for lunch that day?"

"Bastards."

"Pardon."

"They've been trying to get me out for years. Without a pension if they can. What did you tell them? Did you say it was my idea to abandon ship?"

"No, I told them I couldn't remember, but thought it was a mutual decision. I don't see that it matters."

"Of course it matters, they're in the blame game. And I've got a bloody big target on my back."

A beep sounded and the secretary waved Wilson into the room. As he grabbed the door handle he turned and mouthed something, although the muttering was lost in his beard. Emily was sure it wasn't complimentary.

6

It was a warm evening and as Emily left HQ she decided to stroll along the south bank to clear her head. Take in the sights. Watch the sun glinting on the river and pretend she hadn't a care in the world, like revellers on the cruise boats, even though the opposite was obviously true.

She'd walked no more than 50 yards, weaving through the commuter ant circus that constitutes rush hour, when she heard her name called from behind. Scafell, arm-in-arm with his partner.

"Thought it was you," said Scafell. "You've met Leanne, haven't you?"

"I don't think so." Emily and Leanne swapped diffident glances before shaking hands.

"What are you doing for dinner?" asked Scafell.

"I hadn't thought."

"That settles it. Come with us. We're off to Primrose Hill." He gestured at the rucksack on his back. "Leanne's packed enough picnic food in here for a week."

"I'm not sure …"

"I'm not taking no for an answer. I'm the boss. Literally. Consider it an order. You could do with some downtime to take your mind off things."

"Okay, if you insist."

"I do."

When they reached Blackfriars Bridge, Scafell hailed a cab. Forty minutes later they were perched above the city, enjoying panoramic views over Regent's Park and the capital beyond, the jagged blade of the Shard puncturing the bluest of skies. More than a few Londoners had the same idea and dozens of little picnic groups grazed on the scrubby grassland, dotted around like sheep on Exmoor.

Leanne unpacked the ruck sack. Scafell had not been exaggerating. There was a selection of sandwiches, pork pies, hunks of cheese and bottles of craft beer. He opened three and passed them around. They made small talk, Leanne extolling the virtues of living in London, pointing out the best gastro pubs and clubs in Camden Town. The conversation light and frothy, if a little stilted, as it tends to be among people who hardly know one another. Emily wasn't sure what to make of Leanne. She wondered what it must be like to live with and love someone in the Intelligence Service, always on guard, unable to talk about work or reveal true emotions. Leanne, however, seemed measured and carefree. Younger than Scafell, late-thirties maybe. Her long brown hair and warm eyes gave her a welcoming demeanour, although her features were on the large side, hovering between pretty and plain. But she looked physically fit, pert figure, flat stomach and healthy glow suggesting she frequented the gym.

Emily appreciated the way she steered the conversation, light and easy, scolding Scafell if he dared mention anything remotely to do with politics or sport.

"We're not here to talk boring or heavy stuff. We're here to talk books, theatre, music and all the other things that London has to offer. What's your favourite show, Emily?"

For half an hour they debated the best Lloyd Webber musical, although Emily admitted she had only seen one at the theatre, The Phantom of the Opera.

"Well, you've seen the best one," said Leanne.

"No, you've not." Scafell put the case for Evita, but was clearly losing the argument when Leanne needed to break off to visit the toilets. They were located further down the hill and meant Leanne would be gone at least 15 minutes.

Scafell offered Emily another beer, but she declined. He seized his chance to talk shop.

"How did it go today in the interview room?"

"Okay, I suppose. I don't really know what they were after."

"Wilson told me they asked why we'd gone for lunch and left you on your own."

"I wasn't on my own."

"That's right, Emily, you weren't."

A playful black spaniel from a nearby group wandered over, wagging its tail, in search of a treat. Emily patted its head and

Scafell offered a small piece of ham from an unfinished sandwich. The dog made short work of the morsel, begging for more, until, on hearing a sharp whistle, it scampered back to its owner.

Emily didn't know how to play the conversation. The interview panel's line of questioning intrigued her and she found the mention of Al disturbing. Likewise, the reaction of Bob Wilson. But she remained unsure she should discuss any of the substance, even with Scafell. She regarded him as a man with few distinguishing characteristics. A stable temper, a standard frame, a pale, pleasing, but unremarkable complexion. The sort of man who could go unnoticed in an office or crowd. Yet he always seemed abreast of the latest news, especially adept at handling the politics of any situation. Good spy material, she thought.

After a few moments, Emily said, "Bob seemed to think they were out to get him."

"Bob thinks everyone's out to get him, he's a glass-half-full type of chap. Infamy, infamy, they've all got it in for me. That's Bob in a nutshell. A grumpy old sod, if truth be told. Perfectly good at his job, though, even if pushing a pen is a come-down from what he once did."

"What did he do?"

Scafell tapped his nose. "Never mind. Official Secrets Act and all that."

Emily spotted Leanne trudging her way back up the hill. "It must be hard for Leanne, not being able to discuss the day with you. What does she do?"

The subject had not arisen when they chatted earlier. Leanne seemed that sort of person, full of interest and informed questions for other people but reticent to speak about herself. Emily thought it a sweet trait.

"She's a teacher," said Scafell. "Does supply teaching, here and there. A freelance, if you like."

"I've always thought teachers were worth their weight. They can make or break people's lives. Everyone remembers at least one teacher who inspired them. Pity they don't get the recognition or the pay they deserve," said Emily.

"Did they ask about me?" Scafell returned to shop talk, asking the same question as Wilson, knowing Leanne would return soon.

"No, not directly, only in relation to whose idea it was to go to lunch. They seemed to think someone in the department may have leaked information. Should we be concerned?"

Scafell plucked a strand of grass, twisting it in his fingers, taking several moments to answer. When he did his voice was almost a whisper, his manner considered. "I've seen it before. Someone gets an inkling there's a leak in a department. They start laying traps, and making unsettling noises. They know they can't accuse a whole department, so they ask questions and hope someone breaks cover. If they seriously thought anything was amiss about the Portland Place job they would have suspended us all by now. I'm seeing the panel tomorrow. Chances are they'll back off after that. Go chasing some other poor sod who has lost his security pass, no doubt."

Leanne returned, insisting she and Emily must meet again soon for a girly chat. Half an hour later with the sun dipped, a slight chill descending, they packed up, winding their way down the hill. Emily thanked Scafell and Leanne for the impromptu treat before catching a cab home. On entering her flat she heard a scraping noise emanating from the kitchen, triggering a brief moment of concern. A figure appeared in the doorway. Al, wide toothy grin, mischievous glint in his eye.

"What a surprise. What are you doing here? You're not due home until next week." Emily danced over to him and they embraced.

"Thought you sounded as if you could do with a hug when we spoke on the phone."

"Lots of them, please."

7

The next day Al and Emily drove to the family seaside home in Weymouth on Dorset's Jurassic coast. Emily hadn't wanted to leave London. The Portland Place incident occupied her every thought and she was reluctant to miss any development. Now the department had debriefed her and Intus had conducted the obligatory interview, McBride had other ideas. He phoned her that morning, ordering her to take time off.

"Get the whole messy business out of your system for a few days," he said, with a caring tone Emily had not anticipated. She argued with him, insisting she wanted to work on the ensuing investigation, reasoning it made sense for analysts abreast of the facts to be utilised. McBride remained unmoved. "It's not a request, Miss Stearn."

Uncle Sebastian's bungalow seemed the perfect bolthole. The iodine aroma and salty taste of the sea never failed to invigorate Emily. She had grown to love the hilltop bungalow with its panoramic views of the Isle of Portland, Chesil beach glinting in the distance. To Emily, it constituted a place of calm and wonder. It was also where she met Al.

He had been house-sitting for a couple next door, while she sorted Uncle Sebastian's belongings at the bungalow following his sudden death. They shared a love of maths and when Emily found the encrypted journal they relished the challenge.

The story they unearthed on deciphering the code proved barely believable, the stuff of fiction, except that it was true. Uncle Sebastian, a seemingly boring if highly regarded Cambridge history professor, a man who wrote books and taught the lessons of the past for a living, was also a member of the Intelligence Service. Back in 1981, tasked with eliminating one of the Kremlin's most-feared assassins.

Emily and Al's friendship had blossomed over the month or so they worked on the journal, although Al quickly realised that Emily wasn't like any of his former girlfriends. She didn't wear make-up. Not that she needed to. With cascading brown hair, pert figure and fine features, she was naturally pretty but she didn't act as if she was. A permanent frown knitted her brow and she held herself in a gawky fashion, reluctant to make eye contact, as if clothed in awkwardness. Once, Al had caught her looking at him from a window as he dug the garden, stripped to the waist in the summer heat, and she had recoiled with such force that he worried she may have done herself an injury. Yet, little by little, their bond tightened. She laughed at his corny jokes. She confided the embarrassment of her first date with a boy from the same school class who, unknown to her, had accepted a dare to ask out *the strange girl who couldn't cry*. Never was she more comfortable, however, than when she and Al were sitting opposite each other at the office desk, deciphering, analysing, inhabiting a world of random numbers and equations requiring solutions. Their first kiss had been a disaster, a mistaken lunge, a faint brush of lips, followed by a jab in the ribs and confused apologies. Yet, as the weeks went by, Al persisted and Emily had come to trust the man with a Latvian father and a mother who suffered hardship and tragedy in the crumbling final throes of the Soviet Union. They were good together.

"Great to be back, isn't it?" said Al, placing a comforting arm around Emily as they gazed at the little white sails jagging randomly in the distance.

"I'd forgotten how peaceful this place is. Pity we only have a couple of days"

"Better make the most of them."

Which is exactly what they did. Strolling along the promenade licking ice creams and watching fishing boats unload at the quaint harbour with its lifting road bridge. Wandering around Nothe Fort, exploring its maze of underground passages, flinching at the boom of cannons fired for the tourists from high on the ramparts. Drinking wine on the bungalow terrace as the sun went down and the lights flickered across the causeway.

They had bought supper one evening, eating fish and chips out of paper cartons by the harbour, a flock of seagulls squawking and screeching in anticipation, when Al tackled the unspoken subject that had seen him abandon his recent course early.

"Something's happened Emily, hasn't it? Something at work you can't tell me about."

Emily lowered her head, peering into the shallow sea water, watching minnows darting back and forth, a shoal of larger fish on the prowl.

"I can't talk about it."

"I know, but you're going to be all right, aren't you?"

"Al, remember the day that old guy collapsed in the street with a heart attack?"

"Yes."

"You went to his aid and I froze?"

"You didn't freeze. You called for an ambulance."

"I did freeze. I was useless. Zoned out. My mind was mush. But, afterwards, you held a glass of water above your head, and showed me how I was holding everything in. You said the glass was easy to hold at first but the longer you did so the heavier it seemed to get and eventually you would have to drop it."

"I talk a lot of mumbo-jumbo, don't I?"

Emily smiled. "That's true, but I've never forgotten that story and it has really helped me these last few days."

"How big is your glass?"

"More like a bucket, Al, but I'm okay. I'm letting the water out, drop by drop."

"That's my girl. If you ever need to talk, you know I'm here. No pressure, no details, just mumbo-jumbo."

They finished their meal, Al lobbed their rubbish into a waste bin from an impressive distance, and they walked back up the hill to the bungalow, spending the rest of the evening listening to music and solving Emily's Rubik's Cube. Emily carried one with her at all times. She believed it helped with problem-solving skills and improved concentration, although Al disagreed, convinced it was a monotonous and solitary hobby that only increased frustration. The fact that Emily was a speedcuber, capable of solving the puzzle in fewer than 10 seconds, and Al wasn't, probably accounted for the discrepancy in their views.

The next day they were heading back to London when a news item on the radio caught Emily's attention. She twiddled the volume button in time to glean a German defence minister had been involved in an incident in the heart of Berlin, not far from the Brandenburg Gate.

The newscaster's voice was dispassionate. He could have been reading a fast food menu as he revealed a jogger had found the official slumped in the back of his car with his driver shot dead in the front. "According to German police the killings have all the hallmarks of an assassination." The announcer moved on to financial news and Emily flicked over to a music channel. But she wasn't listening.

"Tinman," she muttered.

Al didn't hear.

8

The following day Emily reported for duty as normal, the clinical surroundings of the office building in stark contrast to the quaint beauty of her holiday bolthole. A secretary intercepted as she walked to her desk.

"Mr McBride would like to see you."

A shiver of apprehension ran up Emily's back, wondering about her meeting with Intus and worried about their interest in Al. She caught a glimpse of McBride in his glass-panelled office where he appeared in earnest conversation with Scafell. After dumping her bag and folders on her desk, she ambled over.

The door was slightly ajar and she could hear McBride's gruff tones, so she knocked lightly and entered.

"Ah, Miss Stearn," said McBride, beckoning her to take a seat at the desk alongside Scafell. McBride rose from his own chair, closed the blinds, shutting off the room from the main office. He also closed the door. Simple acts, but ones which conferred instant gravity.

"I trust you had a tranquil wee break."

"Yes," said Emily, glancing at Scafell, whose neutral gaze offered no clues.

"Would you like to nail the man who shot Mason?"

A strange question, Emily thought. Not because it was delivered in the matter-of-fact tone someone may use when asking if you'd fancy a particular cocktail, although she found that disconcerting, but because it was obvious. Of course she wanted whoever had pumped three bullets into Jones's chest to face justice. The question didn't need to be asked, and certainly didn't require an answer. She also clocked the reference to *the man*. Emily had absorbed the ballistics report and understood the connection with Reblov, but the picture stored in her brain didn't fit. Her image was female. It persisted, however hard she tried to shake it off.

Her answer, however, was pragmatic. "Of course."

"Good. Then welcome aboard Operation Tinman."

McBride went on to explain that, while the investigation was at an early stage, the killings in Berlin were thought to be consistent with Reblov. Johannes Berendt, the German defence envoy, had been shot three times and his driver once through the head. Berendt was responsible for pushing through Germany's increased defence budget, much of which was aimed at securing the country's borders against potential Russian aggression. He had also diverted millions of German Euros to send air defence and tank-busting missiles to Ukraine. Crucially, the Service's man in Berlin had heard chatter. The word on his informed street, for some time, fingered Berendt as a Russian target.

Scafell jumped in, fixing eyes on Emily. "Tinman is the obvious suspect. He's out of control. Berendt's another notch on his belt. Where will Tinman strike next? That's the question we need answered, and we want you to help."

"How?"

"When I was asked to name our sharpest analyst. I didn't need to think twice. You've not been with us long, Emily, but you have a capacity for absorbing information and solving conundrums which is second to none at HQ. This operation requires swift and detailed analysis. It needs people who can recognise connections, link events, spot patterns, compute probability, work with numbers, and predict outcomes."

Emily's mind was spinning. Scafell was describing her dream role, but she didn't understand how sitting in an office by the River Thames was going to trap Reblov. She squirmed in her seat.

McBride sensed her concern. "We're assembling a team. A team that'll work with our own agents, but also alongside Interpol, national agencies, and with the help of our American friends."

"The CIA," said Scafell.

McBride continued. "We'll have satellite back-up. An around-the-clock operation, potentially involving special forces. The fear is that Reblov has only started. More attacks are likely and that means no Army chief, no politician in Europe, is safe. Tinman's an obvious foreign threat to the UK, for which Intelligence is imperative. That comes directly under our sphere."

Emily interrupted. "But I'm still on probation. My security …"

McBride waved a dismissive hand. "Don't worry about security clearance. You'll be upgraded from this afternoon. Luke will take you through the procedures. The team will work from the operations room on the third floor. Any problems, come directly to me. Reblov must be stopped."

Three hours later Emily was at her new desk in a room brimming with hardware. An array of monitors adorned one wall, displaying live feeds from airports, train stations, and government buildings in major European cities as well as the UK. A row of clocks displayed different time zones in a selection of European cities and American states. One big screen dominated the wall, although it was blank. Computer keys clacked. A hum of technological devices filled the air. Three young men and two women sat in a corner booth, headphones in ears, listening to chatter, possibly from phones identified as suspicious. Emily had witnessed a similar scene on a visit to GCHQ in Cheltenham earlier in the year. Had the Service recruited their help, or was this all in-house? Whatever the answer, it was impressive.

McBride entered, carrying an armful of folders that he placed on the main desk in front of the monitors. "Okay, gather round for a wee chat." His Scottish boom demanded attention, everyone obeyed, the room suddenly quiet. He nodded to a woman sitting at a computer terminal and the picture of a man appeared immediately on the big screen. A man with close-cropped dark hair, long face, wide shoulders, wearing a dark suit. He could have been a funeral director. Bordering on handsome, but with eyes that disturbed Emily. Dark pools of sullen menace, she thought.

"This is Tinman, or Andrei Reblov to use his real name." McBride slid a sheet of paper from one of his folders and read off a list of particulars, his curt manner defying any interruptions. "Aged 42. Orphaned as a child. Brought up by grandparents. Divorced. No children. Graduated in engineering science from Moscow University. Former bodyguard to Vladimir Putin. Master of disguise and deception. Currently an officer in the FSB. Identifying marks, right thumb missing, cross-like scar on left cheek. Weaknesses? None, other than an allergy to shellfish and a passion for vodka, although he keeps his alcohol intake under strict control."

McBride continued for 10 minutes or more, building the profile, highlighting Tinman's mastery of languages, revealing he spoke fluent French, German and Italian, as well as his native Russian.

"What about English?" Scafell spotted the omission.

"Yes, sorry, must be the Scottish chip on my shoulder. Of course, he's fluent in English also."

The next 10 minutes concentrated on Tinman's expertise in weaponry, his knowledge of Europe's train networks, including the short, trundling, cross-country lines often overlooked by security forces but which presented unlikely routes to evade detection. And the fact that the CIA believed he carried out at least 12 assassinations over the past decade.

When McBride finished, he invited questions, sparking 20 more minutes drilling into Tinman's past and his relationship with Putin. It emerged that Tinman was considered responsible for the brazen shooting of former Russian deputy prime minister Boris Nemtsov in 2015 outside the Kremlin, as well as linked to the poisoning of opposition leader and anti-corruption activist Alexei Navalny. Emily took notes until McBride wrapped up the meeting.

"I needn't impress upon you all how important this is," he said, a grave catch to his tone. "Operation Tinman is top priority. As well as the shooting in Berlin, we believe Tinman killed General Parker in Devon and was responsible for the shooting of Mason Jones, one of our own and a dear friend to some of you, in Portland Place last week."

He paused to let his words sink in before sweeping up his files, adding a parting growl. "Launching manhunts is not the way we usually do business. Not routinely in our sphere of operation, but this is an Intelligence matter as much as a security one. More than that, this is personal."

9

The bar in Soho was Al's idea. He knew if Emily stayed home she would work all night. She couldn't help it, obsession forming part of her nature. Al had no clue about Tinman, but he knew something or someone occupied Emily's every thought. Which is why he suggested a relaxing drink in one of her favourite cocktail bars. Gin's Joint. Reluctantly, she agreed.

Al ordered her a pink gin, a beer for himself. It was early but the bar filled up slowly, enough customers to draw in passers-by looking for life and energy, not yet too many so no one could hear themselves speak. Al and Emily sat on stools on the popular side of the bar where a jazz musician was setting up a keyboard and microphone. Two couples were arguing about football, but the debate seemed friendly enough.

"Thanks Al, this is what I need. The real world." Emily raised her gin in a toast and they clinked glasses.

"The real world," said Al. "That's something worth drinking to."

They had a discussion about the ordinary things in life.

"Life's not about landing on the Moon or becoming President of the United States," said Al. "Too many people think happiness comes from extraordinary moments and achievements. It doesn't. The trick, as someone once said, is finding the extraordinary in the ordinary. That's why we should celebrate the ordinary. Too often ordinary is looked upon as mediocre. It's not. It's like blood pressure."

"Blood pressure?" Emily wrinkled her nose. She wasn't following this line of thought.

"You don't want high blood pressure, nor do you want low blood pressure," explained Al. "You want average blood pressure, because average is normal and normal means healthy. It's the same with …"

A commotion on the far side of the bar interrupted his thought. The sound of breaking glass and raised voices as the barman struggled to reason with a customer.

"I want a large whisky. Give me a whisky." Hanging glasses obscured the customer's face and the light was dim but Emily and Al could see he had a big frame and his hands clutched the bar counter as if steadying himself. The barman's voice sounded patient but contained a steely edge, as if accustomed to such confrontations in the heart of the capital.

"You've had enough, mate."

"You're not my mate. My only mate's Johnny Walker."

"Very good, pal, but it's time you and Johnny were leaving."

"Just cut the shite and pour me a drink." The words slurred, spat with venom.

"Go home, buddy. Look after yourself."

"Don't patronise me. I could have you killed. You don't know who I am."

Al and Emily glanced at each other. A hush descended, customers straining necks to check out a confrontation taking a sinister turn.

"That's enough." The barman scuffled around the bar. As he did so, the customer leaned forward, snatched an empty wine bottle from behind the counter and smashed it against the bar top, the resulting jagged shard forming an evil makeshift weapon.

As he stretched, the man looked up and Emily caught a glimpse of his face, eyes wild, bushy brown beard unmistakeable.

"Oh God, no." She shrieked across the bar. "Bob."

The shout registered somewhere in the drunken fog of Wilson's brain. His features crumpled into a perplexed frown, his mind struggled to clear, and in that moment of confusion the barman was upon him, pinning the arm holding the broken bottle. Stocky, though by no means a big man, the bartender was probably half Wilson's age, stronger, fitter, with the poise and instant authority of someone used to dealing with physical danger. Ex-military, Emily guessed.

Help swiftly arrived in the burly shape of the doorman, responding to Emily's shout and shattering glass. Together, the two men grappled Wilson to the floor, the barman aiming a vicious kick at his unprotected groin. Wilson screamed as the blow struck its target. Another kick would have done more damage if Al had not left his stool and grabbed the barman's arm, spinning him around.

"Pack it in, he's an old man, he's had enough," said Al.

"Are you his mate?" Fire glinted in the barman's eyes. Al suspected he was enjoying the aggravation.

"No," said Al, swiftly accompanied by a "Yes" from Emily, who by now had joined Al.

"He's a friend of mine," said Emily. "I saw what you just did."

"Serves him right for trying to glass me. Get him out of here before I change my mind and call the cops." The barman stood over Wilson, boot at the ready.

Emily motioned for Al to take one of Wilson's arms, she grabbed the other. With a helpful lift from the doorman they half pushed, half dragged Wilson outside.

They managed to reach the nearest corner before Wilson slumped to the ground, back scraping against the brickwork of an old Methodist chapel, his trousers soaked, a sharp stench of urine invading Emily's nose. He wailed something incomprehensible and Emily dropped to her haunches to shake his shoulders.

"Bob. What's the matter? What's going on?"

"They think it's me."

"What's you?"

"They think I killed Mason. They're sure I told someone. They think I'm the leak."

"Who thinks that?"

"That Intus bastard."

"Are you sure?"

"I'm suspended."

That explained why Emily hadn't seen Wilson on her return to the office and why he was not involved in the Tinman operation. But she thought it odd that neither McBride nor Scafell had mentioned him.

"Bob, look at me." Emily grabbed his face with both hands, her fingers tugging at his beard to gain his attention. Wilson's eyes rolled, eventually focusing. "It will get sorted. You're not a killer. You were friends with Mason, I know you were. I was there, remember"

"They want me out, want shut of me. But I know things … I know things." Wilson's eyes were drifting again, his words slurring as he fell into a drunken stupor repeating the same depressing mantra. "I know things."

Al helped Emily to her feet. "Should we call him a cab?" said Al.

"We'll have to see him home. No cabbie would take him alone in this state."

It took around five minutes for Al to grab a cab, another two for him to persuade the driver that Wilson wasn't going to leave an unwanted deposit on the upholstery, yet more time, accompanied by vigorous shaking, to coax the address out of him.

When they arrived at the basement flat in a terraced house overlooking Clapham Common, Al dug in Wilson's pockets and found his keys. An odour slapped them across the face as they opened the door. At first Emily couldn't place it, but in the kitchen she spotted sour milk, the remains of several meals, mostly takeaways, on the worktop. Empty whisky bottles spilled out of a big cardboard box. The rest of the flat appeared equally uncared for. Paint peeled from the lounge ceiling, old newspapers littered the floor, a huge damp patch in the shape of Africa, accompanied by dark mould, dominated the bedroom wall.

They half-threw, half-dragged Wilson onto his bed and spread a blanket over him. Johnny Walker did the rest. Within seconds he was snoring loudly.

Al glanced around the apartment, nose wrinkling. "I've seen tidier rubbish skips. Does he really work in your office?"

Emily nodded. "You probably weren't supposed to hear most of that tonight, Al, but I'm glad you were there. He'd have taken a beating otherwise."

"What's going on, Emily? I know you can't do details, but he was talking about his friend being killed, leaks, and being suspended. It all sounds …"

"Unbelievable?"

"Well, yes. Like something out of one of those spy thrillers. Who is Mason?"

For a moment, Emily hesitated. She heard Savage's jibes about Al and his Russian connection in her head. But that was a matter of record. Agents had monitored Al and Emily around the clock for more than a month when they deciphered Uncle Sebastian's coded journal. Even listened in to their conversations. They knew all about Uncle Sebastian's relationship in 1981 with Anna, his minder in Moscow, who turned out to be Al's grandmother.

Al was the shrewdest, most resourceful person Emily knew. He'd worked out something devastating had happened at work. Now he knew someone killed Mason Jones. She decided to tell him about the Portland Place incident. No mention of Tinman and the ongoing investigation. Instead, the bare bones of the hit-and-run, the bogus skateboarder and the murder of Jones.

Al knew better than to press for more details. He pulled her close. They hugged tight. "You poor thing. It must have been terrifying."

"I can't get it out of my head."

"What about Bob? Is he going to be okay?"

"Don't know. He may be right. They seem out to get him. Perhaps they're after a scapegoat. I'm worried he's going to say something he shouldn't."

"Should you report him, tell your bosses about tonight?"

"That doesn't feel right, Al."

"No, but you heard him in the bar. What if he blurts out some sensitive information? That would be worse."

Little worry lines creased Emily's forehead. "Some relaxing evening this has turned out to be."

They caught a cab back to Archway.

10

Everything considered, it was a wonderful evening.

A little too much alcohol perhaps but Claudio Mantelli could hold his drink and you only turn 60 once. Anyway, he didn't suffer hangovers. Don't pump poison into your bloodstream. Drink only fine Barolo wine, he'd tell his recruits. The king of wines. Made from the purest Nebbiolo grapes from Piedmont, the region of his birth. He'd go on to recite drinking escapades from his youth in the hills on the outskirts of Turin before he had learned the art of sobriety, knowing that his charges would laugh but pay no attention. No man, he knew well enough, ever learned from another's experience.

By way of celebration, he had taken Sophia this night to see Puccini's Tosca, his favourite opera, at the magnificent Theatre Palazzo Santa Chiara, near Rome's Pantheon. The romantic score and sweeping tale of passion and jealousy had moved her to the point where she actually cried on his shoulder.

They'd gone on to La Pergola, a Michelin three-star restaurant in a little side street off Via Veneto which reserved a table for Mantelli whatever the day or hour. The maitre d' looked after him, the waiters referred to him as Generale, and the food proved as enchanting as the service. They even sang Tanti Auguri to him and served up a cake with snow white icing and a single candle.

He blew it out and made a wish. Mantelli was lucky in life. He'd risen to Generale di Brigata in the Italian Army and acted as chief advisor to the government's defence department. A respected figure in military circles, relied on by ministers for his advice and experience. Wealthy too. He was not so lucky in love. Two marriages had failed, although a son and daughter were gifts from each.

Sophia was his latest love interest and for the first time it felt uncomplicated. Unlike the others, she demanded nothing from him, except tasty food, a good time, and the occasional fringe benefit. He was happy to oblige.

After dinner, at Sophia's urging, they embarked on a drive-by tour of Rome's famous sites, most illuminated for tourists on a warm, still, evening. They took in the Coliseum, swung by the ancient ruins of the Forum, visited the Spanish Steps and Trevi Fountain, Mantelli's chauffeur easing his way where most vehicles were prohibited. A perk of Mantelli's rank and position.

When they reached Piazza Navona, Sophia suggested they take some fresh air, walk off the evening's excesses. The chauffeur cautioned against it, but the silver crescent moon beckoned, Sophia was persuasive, and Mantelli did not want to disappoint her. Despite the late hour, small huddles of holidaymakers still toured the area, snapping photographs, random flashes piercing the night sky.

They arranged to meet the car at the far end of the square and sauntered arm in arm, savouring the lingering smell of pizza mixed with ground coffee and cigarettes. Familiar and comforting. The unmistakeable aroma of Italy. Mantelli experienced an infusion of pride for his beloved homeland.

He pointed out the famous Fountain of Four Rivers, delighting in informing Sophia it was designed by Berlini and constructed in 1651 for the Pope. Somehow the weathered stone and gentle sweep of history seemed to caress the moment. They kissed, slow and tender, in the middle of the square by the ancient obelisk, stopping for a few moments to listen to an Italian-style mariachi band playing to the few restaurant tables still occupied, the beat of a drummer pounding in their ears.

Reaching the far end of the square, they entered a narrow passage leading to the point where their car waited. Dark as pitch, the camera flashes had compromised Mantelli's night vision. A damp smell of urine stung their noses while the drumming in the square echoed around the tall buildings either side. As they walked further along the passage, Sophia's head resting on his shoulder, Mantelli glimpsed a shadowy figure emerge from behind a buttress.

He sensed an arm raise, a gun point, the professional soldier in him recognising in a final moment of terrifying clarity that fine wine, rich food and the attentions of a beautiful woman had rendered him vulnerable.

Pushing Sophia wide of the firing line, General Mantelli thought of his children and hoped for salvation.

Three shots rang out in rapid succession before Tinman strolled back to the square where the band and the drummer played on.

11

Emily was late. Crammed as always, the underground train to Blackfriars had slowed to a halt in the tunnel after leaving Farringdon station. It remained motionless for what seemed to Emily like most of the morning but was probably around 20 minutes.

The driver apologised over the intercom in a robotic voice that chewed vowels as if coated in caramel, but conveyed not a shred of concern for the delay. Tempers frayed as the temperature rose. Some commuters even considered prising the doors open and walking back along the electrified line to Farringdon. Emily closed her eyes and worried about Wilson. She had decided not to inform McBride or Scafell. It was a calculated risk but she knew reporting Wilson for his bar room brawl would end his career and probably cost him his pension. He was desperate enough without that.

At last the train lurched forward, wheels and axles moaning and groaning. As it crawled towards Blackfriars, the driver offered an explanation. A passenger had been taken unwell.

"Another bloody jumper," muttered a man in a pin-striped suit, recognising the driver's preferred staff euphemism when informing the public of a suicide.

A cold shiver caused Emily to gasp as an instant vision of Wilson swigging from a bottle of whisky before leaping into the path of a speeding train invaded her thoughts. She vowed to check in on him. Al would help, she was certain.

When she reached the office it was obvious there had been a development. A current of excitement percolated amid little pockets of animated conversation. Most of the analysts were gathered around the central desk while McBride and Scafell spoke with two men in the glass-panelled cubicle on the far side of the room.

Emily dumped a bag at her station, making her way to the central area as McBride and Scafell emerged.

"Gather round, everybody." McBride's voice boomed above the chatter. Silence descended as Emily slid into a seat at the back of the throng.

McBride stood alongside one of the men Emily had seen him talking to. "First, let me introduce Jack." A flourish of McBride's palm. "Jack's an expert at tracking terrorists and foreign special forces. Knows how they think and are likely to react. He's here to offer advice and guidance."

Jack Easton acknowledged the group with a curt nod. Something told Emily his skills extended far beyond advice and guidance. He had the practiced gaze of a man accustomed to weighing up danger. Not overly tall, but he held himself tall, making every inch count. His shoulders were broad, frame firm, stomach flat. His arm muscles weren't big but they rippled beneath his short-sleeved shirt as if accustomed to physicality. Emily thought late thirties, but he could have been older. Steady blue eyes promised wisdom while a black mole on his cheek ruined the symmetry of his fine features. He didn't speak.

McBride allowed a pause as the group greeted Easton with murmurs of approval before continuing. "I won't beat about the bush. For those of you catching up with the news from Rome, we believe Tinman struck again last night."

He proceeded to describe the manner of General Mantelli's execution, revealing the location, the fact the shooter fired three bullets and that Mantelli's female escort was unharmed.

"General Mantelli was instrumental in leading Italy's commitment to NATO, responsible for a hard-line approach to Russia over Ukraine. In recent times he'd become even more vociferous in his opinion that Russian aggression had to be stopped."

One of the analysts raised a hand. "What was he doing strolling around a tourist location late at night without protection? Isn't that asking for trouble?"

"Good question," said McBride. "I've no idea. We're in touch with the Italian police as well as Interpol. The General wasn't gung-ho. Our man in Rome insists that normally he kept a low profile. He was security conscious but we all make mistakes. His official car would have made him visible."

Another hand shot up. "Are we certain there was only one shooter and did the lady friend get a good look at him?"

McBride glanced at Easton, the slightest raise of an eyebrow inviting him to answer. Easton considered for a moment.

"Nothing is certain when bullets are fired, people killed and witnesses in a state of shock," he said. "But it appears the gunman was masked and no cartridges were found at the scene. Everything points to a professional hit. Given the current climate it's logical to assume it was Tinman operating alone."

"Alone?" Emily hadn't intended speaking, but her question, loaded with puzzlement, escaped involuntarily, a hint of derision in the upward lilt.

Easton fixed his gaze upon her and he seemed amused, as if relishing a challenge.

"Alone, as in there was one gunman. But if it's Tinman, he's never alone. He's the tip of a spear that leads all the way back to the Kremlin. He can call on agents in every country in Europe and beyond. Agents with eyes on the ground, embedded in all manner of organisations. Spies, to you and me. Chances are Tinman knew General Mantelli's itinerary that evening, knew he was going to the opera and where he would be dining. It's unlikely he knew he would be strolling in Piazza Navona, but the general was travelling in his official vehicle. Easy to follow. A sitting duck. That was the fatal error. When he got out for an impromptu stroll, Tinman seized his opportunity."

Easton glanced across at Emily. "You still look puzzled."

"That all makes perfect sense," said Emily. "I'm just wondering how he moves so quickly, jetting around Europe, picking targets, seemingly without anyone laying eyes on him. I'd have thought we'd have spotted him at an airport or ferry terminal by now. We know what he looks like. Why hasn't anyone picked him up?"

Easton grabbed a briefcase and strode over to a big white board where McBride had scrawled the details and aims of Operation Tinman. He pointed to a row of pictures of Andrei Reblov. As a young man studying at Moscow University, watching a football match with friends. At work as a bodyguard with a crowd and limousine in the background. "This is the Reblov we're looking for," he said. He paused for a few moments to allow the image to sink in.

Fishing in the briefcase, he pulled out a picture of what appeared to be another man. He held the picture aloft. "This is also Reblov." The difference was striking. A long, blond ponytail replaced the close-cropped dark hair. The face was craggy, eyes blue and smiling, not dark and sullen. He looked 20 years older, but meeker, milder, like an easy-going but ageing rock star in a tribute band. The cross-like scar on the left cheek, an obvious identifying mark, was gone.

"This was taken a couple of years ago," said Easton. "We didn't know it was Reblov at the time, but it became apparent later that this was how he escaped surveillance. He's a master of deception with the skills of a professional make-up artist. He can assume any persona. With his connections, passports matching that persona aren't a problem."

Easton paused again to allow the group to absorb the information, a murmur resounding in appreciation of Tinman's attention to detail.

Easton continued. "I don't want to build him up. He's only human, but Tinman knows how we think. He's steeped in espionage and the tricks of the special forces' trade. We need to think outside the box. Get one step ahead of him. Spot the pattern. There's always a pattern."

He slid the picture back into the briefcase and signalled to McBride that his contribution was done.

"Any questions?" McBride threw out the invitation more as a nuanced full stop to the meeting than a genuine offer to extend proceedings. Emily ignored the subtlety, Easton's mention of a pattern pricking an open sore.

"What about the shooting in Portland Place? How does that fit into a pattern? I get the executions of General Parker and the killings of defence chiefs in Berlin and Rome. As horrible as they are, we can all see the logic. But why would Tinman want to kill one of our colleagues?"

McBride scowled and looked at Easton, who shrugged. For a moment Emily wished she could flick her tongue and snatch back the question. Like a chameleon captures its prey, she thought. Come to think, didn't that sum up Tinman? A chameleon. Changing his appearance at will. Blending with his surroundings. A master of the invisible.

Easton eventually spoke. "I'm struggling to answer that question. The likes of Reblov don't make mistakes. Not on the streets of London in broad daylight. It may not be obvious yet how the death of Mason Jones fits into the pattern, but the killing has all the hallmarks of Reblov. The reason behind it is the missing piece in our jigsaw. Find that piece and everything will become clearer."

12

Easton didn't appear in the office again that day, nor did McBride. Scafell was tasked with splitting the group into sections, each concentrating on a different aspect in the search for Tinman.

Emily was assigned to study the pattern of his known movements. The job involved sifting through airline routes connecting Warsaw, Madrid, London, Berlin and Rome, searching the manifests of flights within the appropriate time frames, looking for anything that may progress the investigation. Logic told her to concentrate on male passengers travelling alone, without hold baggage. Hanging around an airport carousel waiting for lost suitcases did not fit the profile of a would-be assassin on the prowl. When she identified a possible flight, a colleague retrieved the relevant video footage, applying facial recognition technology. It was laborious work, requiring meticulous attention to detail.

Following Easton's warnings of Tinman's deception skills, Emily also insisted on viewing still photographs. Tinman could change his features at will. Changing his frame, the way he held himself, may not prove so easy. She concentrated in particular on anyone wearing gloves, reasoning Tinman would endeavour to disguise his missing thumb.

She worked two hours past her scheduled finishing time without identifying anything of note and would have continued if Scafell hadn't insisted she leave.

"Go home, need to be fresh and alert tomorrow. Plenty more to do then," he said. His tone was warm and protective. Emily stood up, her legs stiff. Engrossed in her work, she had barely moved for hours. She grabbed her coat, phoned Al on the way out and agreed to meet at Trafalgar Square.

She arrived first and amused herself watching the eclectic life of one of London's most famous landmarks. Tourists snapped the four Landseer Lions on their plinths and attempted, with varying success, to take selfies with Nelson's Column in the background. A busker with a pitiful voice mutilated *I Will Survive* while a street performer dressed as the Statue of Liberty stood and did nothing quite brilliantly. Whenever someone dropped a coin in the box below, the statue turned, jerking sporadically but elegantly in robotic fashion, nodding its head in gratitude. Emily watched entranced.

"They say it's art." Emily recognised the pitch of the voice behind her, although at first she couldn't place it. She spun around. McBride.

"Oh, hello, I was miles away," said Emily.

"Always thought they'd do well in our business," said McBride, nodding towards the statue.

"Why?"

"Self-discipline. Imagine the control of mind and body one must have to stay still as a statue in front of this lot for hours on end."

"I'd not thought of that. I don't think I'd be very good. My legs were stiff as a board after sitting down all afternoon."

"Exactly, Miss Stearn. It calls for inner calm at all times. They can't even scratch a wee itch. Wouldn't do for me, but what a brilliant way to watch the world. I think we'd call it hiding in plain sight, wouldn't we?"

"I suppose so." Emily felt uncomfortable making small talk, especially with a boss who refused to use her Christian name. She didn't know what to make of McBride. In the office he owned a fearsome turn of phrase, didn't suffer fools, by preference taking the way of pragmatism. The office juniors mischievously called him 'M', after the head-of-missions character in the James Bond films, but would not dare address him as such to his face. McBride didn't do frippery, although on occasion, a softer side emerged. According to Scafell, McBride hailed from Donegal, occasionally sank a Guinness or two, which invariably led him to express pride in the lush countryside and polite little villages inherent in the Irish roots on his mother's side, although his father was a noble Scot. A complex Gaelic mix. Perhaps that explained the contrasts.

"Got to go. Due in Whitehall to joust with the Foreign Office," he said.

Emily watched McBride disappear into London's teeming theatre throng before her gaze returned to the statue. A young boy dropped a few coins into the box and the statue bowed. It moved as if made of stone. That, she mused, was the art of disguise. The illusion had to be subtle and complete. Always in character. Never betraying the secret, regardless of interaction or surroundings. Her thoughts turned to Reblov. Maybe that was how he appeared to have freedom of movement, even though police and security agencies throughout Europe searched for him. An assassin posing as a pillar of the community perhaps. Someone ordinary, yet extraordinary.

Al's arrival interrupted her thoughts.

"Hi, good day?" he said

"Long day."

"Fancy a plate of pasta and a glass of red?"

"Sounds like bliss."

They went to Carlo's, a little Italian in a side street off Green Park. They found a place for two at the back of the room, single candle in a glass holder burning in the middle of the table on a chequered tablecloth. A young man with red hair and a pasty complexion played classical guitar in a corner, although the delicate music fought a losing battle with the hum of conversation. They ordered food and two beers, Al telling Emily about his day attempting to solve a Diophantine equation, involving the summing of three cubes, using the university supercomputer. Normally, such mathematical complexity would entrance Emily. She loved problem solving, especially involving numbers. But while she listened dutifully, her mind wandered.

"And tomorrow I'm juggling on a unicycle in front of the whole class," said Al, recognising he did not have Emily's undivided attention.

"Err … what did you say?"

"Emily, you've hardly heard a word I've said tonight. What's the matter?"

"Sorry, Al. It's been a busy day. I'm worried about Bob. Can we go and check on him?"

"Now?"

"Yes. I'd hate to think he'd, well, you know, done something stupid like …" Her voice trailed off as another dark image invaded her brain, before she finished her sentence, "and we could have prevented it."

Al raised eyebrows but he knew there was no derailing Emily's train of thought. He recognised the signs. The troubled frown, the way her foot tapped an anxious beat under the table. Peace would return only when she attended to her concerns. Twenty minutes later they paid up and caught a cab to Clapham.

"He's probably on his second bottle of whisky by now, somewhere down town," said Al, as he rapped the knocker at Wilson's flat. He knocked again. No answer. A sash window slid open on the first floor and a student-type, mop of unruly brown hair, scruffy stubble, baggy sweater and vacant expression suggesting relaxation was under way, stuck his head out.

"Looking for Bob?"

"Yes," said Emily.

"Took off about half an hour ago."

"Took off?"

"Yeah. Saw them jump in a black car, a cab probably, and head towards town." He slid his right palm forward and upwards, as if simulating a plane taking off.

"Them?"

"Bob and another guy."

"What did the other man look like?"

The lad pulled a cigarette from beneath the window sill and took a long drag, savouring it a little too tenderly for ordinary tobacco. "Just a normal guy. Chunky. Two arms, two legs, four eyes."

"You mean he wore glasses," said Al.

"Yep, shades. I didn't get a good look at him."

The lad slid the window shut.

"Sorry, Al, that was a waste of time," said Emily.

"At least you know Bob's okay, walking and breathing, even if he's probably out for another night on the town."

"That's what I'm worried about."

The feeling of unease remained for the rest of the night, Emily's sleep disturbed by visions of a sinister figure in dark glasses, and Wilson repeatedly slurring, "I know things".

13

As a child it was never enough for Emily to spend a day recording car number plates in her pretty pink notebook. That evening she would sift through her jottings, carefully arranging them in alphabetical order. Even and precise, for easy identification. If she noted the same vehicle again she could add a tick by the side.

The thrill she experienced when she added a tick was a mystery to her parents, but to Emily it provided a sense of order. Precision and completeness made her world spin in rhythmic fashion.

Which was why next morning she proceeded to create a spreadsheet of all the airports in the cities where Tinman had been active recently. Warsaw. Madrid. London. Berlin. Rome. The distances involved and the short time between murders ruled out trains and cars. She looked up flights into those cities on the day of the relevant killings, noting the airline, flight number and passenger list. She'd done much the same when sifting targets for the face recognition technology, but this new search was more exhaustive. By lunchtime she had determined that only one airline flew into Warsaw, London and Berlin on the relevant days. Red Kite Airlines. A budget operator in the UK using small airports with tight turn-around times.

She was pleased with her work and about to continue her research and request video footage and face recognition technology from the relevant flights when Scafell swept by her work station.

"Hi, Emily, got a big job for you."

"But I'm checking the airlines."

"Never mind that. I think we may be on to Tinman, and how he's giving us the slip."

"How?"

"By flying private."

"Chartering his own plane?"

"Not exactly.

"How then?"

"Russian oligarchs."

"But most of them were sanctioned after the invasion of Ukraine. Most of their wealth was frozen, mansions, yachts confiscated and planes grounded. Most of them still can't operate in the UK or Europe."

Scafell pursed his lips and nodded, as if in partial agreement with Emily's argument, but then he smiled.

"That was the case with the big-hitters such as Roman Abramovich, Eugene Tenenbaum and David Davidovich, but in Europe there are hundreds of Russians who owe their wealth to the days of Putin and still have freedom of access. Many own private planes, any of which could provide transport for Tinman. I have a list of potential collaborators. It's long, but I've culled a few from my experience in Moscow. It's a job that needs someone with your precision."

Emily could feel her head shaking. This didn't feel right. She'd identified a rhythm in Tinman's movements. The killings a few days apart. Two of them seemingly in the UK, the rest dotted around Europe. An oligarch's plane flying into each venue would be too risky. Attract too much attention. To Emily's mind, Tinman may as well emblazon *Assassin Airways* along the fuselage.

That's what she was thinking. "That's like looking for the proverbial needle," is what she actually said.

"I'm not saying it'll be easy, Emily, but we know Tinman is receiving help and it makes sense that it should come from those who owe their wealth and status to the Kremlin."

"Okay," said Emily, with a heavy sigh. "I'll get on to it right away."

She negotiated the assistance of two young analysts, Sam and Andrea. The rest of the day saw them searching the logs of relevant small airports in the vicinity of the last five killings. An absence of video footage from many of them presented an obvious flaw, but they persevered. When a suspect flight with Russian connections was identified, it was flagged up to the main team and an extensive search undertaken. By the end of the day that amounted to three flights, none of which had travelled to more than one of the locations.

It meant Emily arrived back at the Archway flat tense with frustration. Scafell may be right. Tinman could be shielded by a loyal oligarch. Perhaps more than one. But in Emily's field of probability it didn't seem likely. From all she had seen and read, Tinman worked alone, doubtless using the connections of agents in the relevant countries to collect weapons and ammunition, but staying in sole control of his timetable.

Al picked up on her mood as she walked down the hallway, the bag thudding into the shoe rack an instant giveaway.

"Fancy a drink?" he said.

"Sure. A large one."

"What sort?"

"Whatever's easy."

"They're all easy."

"Stop being difficult."

There were times when Al resented being unable to ask about Emily's job. This was one of them. He bit his lip, stayed silent, and mixed two gin and tonics.

Emily walked over to the window. Light rain fell from a leaden sky. Next door's cat, a scruffy, long-haired creature with one eye half-closed like a battered boxer, sheltered under a rhododendron bush, watching the world go by. Watching and waiting. Emily's mind skipped back to Portland Place. Watching and waiting with Mason Jones. She felt a momentary spasm of foreboding as her photographic memory once more focused, the events now two weeks away but detail still sharp and disturbing. She was wrong about the shooter. It wasn't a woman. All the evidence pointed to Tinman. She had to concede that. If Scafell's oligarch theory proved correct, and Emily had to admit it was logical, then concentrating on budget airlines would amount to a colossal waste of time. Maybe she wasn't cut out for work in secret intelligence. It required feel and perception, as much as detail. Life was much simpler in the insurance call centre.

"Penny for them," said Al. He'd noticed the crease in her forehead, straining to contain her thoughts. The repetitive tapping of her right forefinger in the air, as if relaying a message in silent Morse code. They were windows on Emily's mental health and he detected the barometer's needle shifting from fair to stormy.

"What?" said Emily.

"You're miles away."

"I'm thinking, that's all."

"Don't tell me, I think I can guess."

"What does that mean?"

"It means perhaps you should take time off. More than just a few days. Time to get to grips with things, Emily. You've witnessed one of your colleagues and friends killed. In cold blood. I'm not surprised you're obsessed with it."

"Obsessed?"

"Well, it's understandable …"

"Obsessed?" Her voice rose and although her face remained impassive her eyes betrayed a smouldering anger.

"I'm only trying …"

"Don't, Al, don't try to help me. I don't need your help. I don't want it." The words escaped in little seething gasps, as if Emily would burst if pressure were not released.

Al's mouth dropped open. He looked bemused. Sure, Al had witnessed Emily's temper before. She had been less than impressed when she learned his real name was Alexei Andreyevich and not Al Andrews. Not because he had Latvian parents and a Lithuanian grandmother who grew up in Moscow. She was fine with that, found it intriguing. She wasn't happy that he had kept it from her in the first months of their relationship.

Yet they had been together almost two years, time in which Al's easy-going, caring nature had helped Emily grow from a girl with mathematical genius but confidence issues into a woman capable of impressing the high-fliers at HQ with her logic and perception. This was their first proper row.

She rammed her gin and tonic down on the coffee table, grabbed her coat and bag, slamming the front door behind her. The half-eyed cat scooted from under the bush as she bustled past.

14

Emily walked aimlessly for half an hour, then strode up Highgate Hill, her body bent, shoulders hunched against the rain. A blanket of grey cloud draped the city in the distance, concealing the tops of skyscrapers.

She needed time to think, to clear her mind of overwhelming thoughts. Out of habit, she headed for her parents' house, although realising she couldn't discuss her work with them. Half-way up the gradient, she changed her mind, turning right towards Alexandra Park, along a leafy road, full of red-brick Victorian houses, imposing chimneys, well-kept gardens with the promise of stories to tell.

At number 19, she pushed open the iron swing gate and her coat swished against a protruding rose bush, showering wet petals on the crazy paving. She knocked on the door. No answer. She knocked again but wished she hadn't, concluding this was not a good idea. As she turned to leave, she heard a bolt slide and a tall, angular man with silver hair and a kindly expression filled the doorway. He wore corduroy trousers, slippers and a thin cardigan with tortoiseshell buttons. An air of gentle authority about his bearing. He could have been a learned professor.

"My dear, what a nice surprise."

"I'm sorry, I probably shouldn't be here, Mr Stephens."

"Nonsense. Come in."

He took her coat and handbag, laid them on a table before ushering her down a hallway with ornate black-and-white floor tiles, into a lounge where a Turkish rug languished on a wooden floor. Emily's gaze fixed on an enormous bookcase, full of hefty bound volumes. She could smell polish and cigar smoke. A Ravel piano concerto played softly from wall-mounted speakers, adding to the ambient sense of peace and serenity.

Stephens turned off the music, offering her a winged chair and a cup of tea. She sat, declined the drink, but already felt calmer. When Stephens recruited her to the Service, part of the deal included that she could always seek his counsel and advice if she had misgivings.

There had been no need. Until now.

"Miss Stearn." Like McBride, he always called Emily by her surname, but from the lips of Stephens the address somehow sounded natural, warm and affectionate, rather than stiff and formal. "What can I do for you?"

"I don't know. I'm not sure I can do the job anymore. Everything's so difficult. Whatever I do seems wrong. I think the job may be too much for me, after all." Emily's eyes lowered.

Stephens said nothing. After years listening to agents pouring out their worries and worse, he was good at saying nothing. As section chief, now director, of the unit responsible for recruiting and servicing field officers, he'd seen it all. From personal lives ruined by the job's long hours and fraught nature, to those who had lost their sanity living a lie for the good of Queen and country. And lately, King and country. Most of the time they didn't need advice. All they required was an outlet to dump their fears and paranoias. If it helped get the job done, he was happy to be their waste bin. So he waited, usually until he was certain they had nothing more to spew out and ready to hear his thoughts. With Emily, he gauged it right, his silence prompting details rather than generics.

She told him about the Portland Place incident, although as a director with agents in the field he had been briefed already. She also revealed Savage's investigation and that Wilson was suspended.

Stephens picked up on her angst at the mention of Wilson and gauged the time right to probe further, prompting Emily to reveal the fight with the barman in Soho. She omitted her concerns about Wilson's disaffection with the department.

"I must agree it's somewhat concerning that an operative of his standing should be rolling around the grubby floors of Soho fighting with bar staff," said Stephens. "I know Bob Wilson. He was for some years a field officer under my control and for most of those a damned fine one. Liked a whisky then, it seems he hasn't lost his taste for it. But I never had occasion to question his loyalty.

I shouldn't worry about him. I never knew an operative who didn't lose spirit, becoming jaded at times. Mettle fatigue. That's what I call it."

He paused, delighting in his play on words, although dozens had heard it before and failed to appreciate his reworking of *mettle* and *metal*. Emily was no different, her thoughts a million miles from the vagaries of the English language.

"But he seems so sad and angry, as if he's lost his way," said Emily.

"Bob's not your concern. He's big enough, and certainly ugly enough, to look after himself. How are you getting on with the current investigation? I'm liaising with officers in the field."

Emily didn't feel it right to voice her concerns in detail, lacking the experience to question the department's direction of travel to a senior executive. Instead, she asked a general question.

"If you were sure you, or someone else, saw something, but the facts, the forensics and everything else pointed elsewhere, what would you do?"

"It depends."

"On what?"

"Are you asking for a friend?"

"Sort of."

Stephens considered for a moment. "The job of an analyst such as yourself depends on a variety of things. On facts, on trends, on knowing or anticipating how people behave, agents, assassins, politicians, the ordinary public, and predicting what may happen next. Is that fair?"

"Yes."

Stephens leaned over and plucked a cigar from an exquisite wooden box on the coffee table. He didn't light it, instead twirling it in his fingers as if deriving pleasure from its mere texture.

"I learned something early in my career in the Service," he said, pausing to switch the cigar to his other hand. He sniffed it gently. His eyes closed for a moment. "Do you want to hear?"

"Go on."

"Some people tend to cherry pick and twist facts to fit their existing beliefs. If we wish or hope something would be true, then we can persuade ourselves that it is true because that's what we want to believe. Down the years I've learned it takes far more facts and persuasive information to make you believe something you don't want to believe than something you do. They didn't have a name for it back then, but now they call it motivated reasoning."

"What are you saying?"

"I don't know all the facts of your scenario, nor do I need to. Sometimes the facts are irrefutable. But I'm old fashioned. I tell my agents what I've always told them. 'Go with your gut'. It's the only way in the field. Does that help?"

"Maybe, I don't know. But I do feel better."

"Excellent, that's what I like to hear. The old man's still got it." Stephens chuckled before drawing breath and assuming a more serious tone. "Don't doubt yourself so much. A field officer's first mistake is often his or her last. But you're an analyst. You're still learning, and can benefit from your mistakes. There's a reason you were chosen for the Service and a reason your bosses have upgraded your security clearance. Intelligence is about results. Nothing more, nothing less. That's what you're judged on. You have what it takes. I saw that, and so have others. Stick in there. Play the long game. Remember your Uncle Sebastian. It took more than 20 years for him to receive his first mission. He had doubts, lots of them. We all do. It's how you deal with those doubts that matters. In the fullness of time, your uncle helped change history for the better. And so can you."

"Thanks. I'm sorry to have bothered you." The subtle mention of her uncle in such revered tones offered Emily a place to park her concerns, which was doubtless Stephens's aim.

"No bother at all. How's that young man of yours?"

Emily smiled. "He's good, thanks for asking."

She went on to tell him about Al's maths course, their trip to the coast and the new historical fiction book her father, commissioning editor at an independent publisher, was excited about releasing. Stephens showed interest. Real or feigned, Emily wasn't sure, but either way she appreciated his warmth.

After 20 minutes, when conversation arrived at a natural pause, Stephens said, "I'll get your coat and bag."

Half an hour later, she returned to the flat. The half-eyed cat dominated the window sill, motionless and aloof, like a garden ornament. In her haste to leave, Emily had forgotten her keys. She rapped on the knocker. Al opened the door.

She threw her arms around him, hugging tight. "I'm sorry, Al. I'm an idiot."

"Me too, takes one to know one."

15

By profession, Savage was a lawyer who loved asking questions, which probably explained why Emily thought he tried to trip her up every time he opened his mouth.

He had requested she attend his office on the top floor. Busy researching the movements of Russian oligarchs with Sam and Andrea, she contemplated ignoring the summons. She did not take to Savage and could ill afford the time. Scafell advised against dodging the appointment. "Never upset the taxman and never antagonise a man spearheading an internal investigation," he said.

Savage seemed more amenable than the last time they met. He was by himself, no *secretary*, no *eyes and ears*. He also sat at his desk rather than pacing around his office or gazing out of the window, and his tone was less formal. All the while, however, he probed while giving nothing away about the state of the inquiry. How did she get on with McBride and Scafell? Did she enjoy her role as an analyst? Was she happy with the pay? Did she consider herself a loyal person? He asked about her relationship with Al, but without the negative chimes of two weeks earlier. He implored her to think again if she could remember anything new about the shooting of Mason Jones.

"So you don't want to change your story in any way?" he said.

"No. I'm happy the statement I gave was a true and accurate recollection of what happened."

"Even though you thought the shooter was a woman."

Emily recalled her conversation with Stephens and felt a surge of confidence. "Yes. I realise some of the facts suggest different and I am fully committed to the current investigation, but I can only go on what I saw and my gut feeling was that the shooter was female. I can't change my memory."

"Of course not." Savage scratched his neck and lowered his head to consult a file on his desk. He was a strange fellow, she thought. His head seemed too close to the desk for his eyes to focus, following the writing in a rhythmic motion, side to side like the crowd tracking the ball at a tennis match. He asked his next question without looking up.

"Can I ask, Emily, why you visited Bob Wilson's home in Clapham earlier this week?"

Emily's mouth dropped open. Her eyes darted back and forth as she struggled to comprehend. Where was this line of questioning leading? Her voice laden with bewilderment.

"You've been checking up on me. Did Bob tell you? Was it his neighbour? What do you suspect me of?"

Savage raised his head, slowly slumping back into his chair, placing his forefingers together under his chin as if contemplating. "Now, now, it's not a case of suspicion. It's a fact. You visited Bob Wilson with your boyfriend. For what reason?"

"He wasn't in. We never saw him."

"That's not what I asked. Why did you make the trip across town to visit your colleague?"

"I wanted to make sure he was okay. I knew he'd been suspended. I was worried about him."

"Are you close friends?"

"Not really."

"Did you go to compare stories about the shooting in Portland Place. Make sure you were both singing from the same hymn sheet?"

"No."

"Sure?"

"Definitely not."

"What about the altercation in Soho?"

Emily's mind skipped to her meeting with David Stephens. She had told him of Wilson's fight with the Soho barman. Surely Stephens wouldn't betray her confidence. He was her mentor. Her connection with Uncle Sebastian. They had a special bond. For a few moments a fog of confusion clouded her thoughts, an air of foreboding descended. When it lifted, suddenly she saw everything clearly again. Of course Stephens would tell them. His loyalty remained to the Service. His whole life had been devoted to keeping his country safe. and Wilson was a liability. Emily knew that. He had come close to compromising his identity and that of the Service during his whisky-addled altercation with the barman, receiving a painful boot between the legs as a result. Stephens could not let that information lie. Emily had been naïve to think she could protect Wilson.

"He had a bit too much to drink, that's all." Emily had computed the Service knew everything. Failing to cooperate would serve no purpose. The truth may be the only way to help Wilson. She told Savage how she and Al had stumbled upon him in the bar and taken him home in a cab. Savage insisted on full disclosure, down to the state of Wilson's flat and a verbatim account of the discussion with the spaced-out neighbour from upstairs. When Savage's questions at last were exhausted, Emily asked one of her own.

"What will happen to Bob now?"

"That's not your concern."

"But I feel responsible."

"Don't delude yourself, Emily. You're but a careless whisper in the career of someone such as Bob Wilson. He's helping us with further enquiries."

"You mean he's been arrested." She remembered the drug lad's gesture of Wilson being swept away in a car by a man in dark glasses.

"Put it this way. He's with the Service section that specialises in getting to the truth, the whole truth, and nothing but the truth."

Once a lawyer, always a lawyer, thought Emily, but there was still one question she needed to ask. "You think Bob's the leak, don't you?"

"That question, Emily, my dear, is so far above your pay grade it's covered in snowflakes. Thank you for your time. You may go."

Emily caught the lift to the third floor, her spirits descending along with the elevator as various permutations from her conversation with Savage churned in her brain. Had she read Wilson wrong? Was her memory of Portland Place a false memory? Could she trust David Stephens? The questions were piling high.

As she walked into the office she saw Scafell at her desk talking to Sam and Andrea, the conversation animated, Scafell leaning over her desk, scribbling notes on a pad.

"Let's give this top priority," she heard Scafell say. He looked up as she approached. "Ah, here she is. Some good news. We think we may have a lead."

"That's great," said Emily.

Scafell pointed to a name he had scrawled on her pad. Yevgeny Sukerov.

"Who's he?"

"Sukerov is dangerous. A big player with a small profile. The worst sort. Well-connected. I remember him from my time in Moscow. Had the ear of the Kremlin. Made his money like so many from the oil business, but never sought the ostentatious lifestyle that some oligarchs lead. Not into bling, but he was a frequent visitor to the Grand Kremlin Palace under Putin. That's testimony to his importance and why there's every chance he came into contact with Tinman. Somehow, he seems to have slipped under the radar."

Emily thought it strange she had not come across him in her research, but Scafell had an impeccable knowledge of Russia, its government and its influencers.

"Okay we'll get on to him straightaway. I presume he owns a private jet," said Emily.

Sam piped up. "Yep, I've taken all the details."

Before the day was out they had ascertained that Uzbekistan-born Sukerov owned two private jets. One of them, an Airbus A340, had flown to Dubai, along with hundreds of Russian-owned aircraft, to escape European Union and UK sanctions at the start of the invasion of Ukraine. It had not flown since. The other, a much smaller Bombardier Global Express jet, registration LX-EAD, remained out of the authorities' reach, having been transferred into the ownership of one of Sukerov's distant relations, thought to be a cousin from Latvia. The plane was now registered in Luxembourg, but Flightradar24 data showed it made frequent trips to Farnborough airport in the UK.

Emily and the team could hardly contain their excitement. Their most promising lead so far. A Farnborough base was perfect to reach out across Europe. Now all they needed was to pinpoint the Bombardier in the killing grounds of Warsaw, Madrid, Berlin, London and Rome on or around the relevant dates.

"You check Warsaw and Berlin, Emily. Me and Andrea will do London, Madrid and Rome," said Sam.

It took an hour or two for extensive checks before they met back at Emily's desk. The previous excitement had dissipated. Emily shook her head. No recording of the Bombardier flying to Warsaw or Berlin while the data concerning London was inconclusive. The plane had flown out of Farnborough the day after Mason Jones was killed in London. Tinman could have been aboard under an assumed name. But the Bombardier had flown to Geneva, where it remained for three days. Tinman could have travelled from there to Berlin by train to take out German defence chief Johannes Berendt, but that would have increased the risk of detection. There was also no evidence the plane had travelled to Madrid or Rome in recent times. Sukerov had been a decent suspect, but the pattern the Service sought required more than one probable hit, two hopefuls and two definite misses.

Emily took the findings to Scafell.

"Hmm, that's disappointing," he said. "But stick with Sukerov for a while. He's still a decent connection between Tinman, the Kremlin, the UK, and by association the rest of Europe. The plane could have turned off its transponder to evade detection."

"Not from a UK airfield, surely. That, in itself, would have aroused suspicion. There would still be a trace, the flight manifest for instance." Emily's logic was difficult to deflect.

"Good thought, Emily. Check it out thoroughly, let me know how you get on."

Emily believed the Sukerov inquiry was a fool's errand, a dead end, a wild goose chase. She thought of all those clichés and more, but kept her musings to herself. She was learning to play the long game.

16

A car awaited Admiral Michel de Bruyne outside the Kortenberg office block in Brussels. He hated that building.

Full of box windows with aluminium frames, stacked in rows like battery hen cages. A grey and soulless granite block. Built initially for an insurance company, it had come to epitomise so many of the European Union bodies it housed. If an architect wanted to build a monument to dullness and lack of imagination, then the Kortenberg fulfilled the brief.

De Bruyne was chief executive of the European Defence Agency, responsible for supervision and co-ordination of its many units. An essential but thankless task. Try encouraging committees from two countries to work together in harmony, let alone the mushrooming mish-mash of the European Union.

He had chaired another meeting where plenty of coffee and tea was taken but nothing agreed, other than the Danish pastries on offer were delicious. As he strode past the building's modest entrance with its huge stainless steel columns, the only features of note, his bodyguard held open the rear door of his official vehicle on the corner of Rue Le Titien.

"How long to the Atomium, Marc?" said De Bruyne as the car set off. His bodyguard in the front passenger seat, alongside the driver, consulted his watch.

"Roughly twenty-four minutes, depending on traffic, of course."

De Bruyne fumbled in his bag, dug out a mobile phone and punched in his wife's number.

"Hi darling, only me. On my way to the reception. On time at the moment, should be home in a couple of hours. Tell Phoebe not to worry, I won't be late." He smiled as his wife informed him he would be a dead man if he arrived late for his daughter's graduation party.

Little did he know how prescient that comment would prove as the nine massive steel balls of the Atomium hove into view.

"What a wonderful sight, Marc, don't you think? A tribute to science and a fitting symbol of how our little country is at the heart of everything Europe decides."

"Yes, Admiral. Each ball represents an atom, I believe."

"That's correct. An iron crystal to be precise. Except the ones you see are one hundred and sixty-eight billion times bigger than the real version."

De Bruyne had done his research. He was due to make a speech and open an exhibition at the Atomium Museum, where he intended to share his views on climate change. An advocate of nuclear power, the Admiral believed clean and renewable energy made perfect sense in a modern world hurtling towards oblivion if it continued spewing toxins from fossil fuels. The speech departed from his usual brief, but in his world everyone had a responsibility to join the fight to save mankind.

He flicked through his notes as the car approached the structure. The bodyguard viewed the milling crowd at the entrance, his eyebrows meeting in a worried frown. This was unexpected. Two hundred or more protesters blocked the road, many carrying banners displaying pithy messages. *The climate is changing. Why aren't we?* and *There is no Planet B!* De Bruyne nodded in approval.

The mood seemed lively, raucous, not yet ugly, but Marc took no chances. "Round the back," he barked at the driver. Marc had recced the structure the week before, noting a staff and catering entrance located at the rear. He directed the driver around the throng. The car parked up about 20 metres from the doorway, two rusting rubbish skips preventing it from edging closer.

"Okay, Admiral, stay put until I give the sign."

Exiting the car, the bodyguard jogged to the doorway. He knocked on the door, it opened and he stepped inside to ensure the immediate area was secure.

De Bruyne leafed through his speech notes one more time, oblivious to a scruffy man approaching, a white bandana helping tame a mass of grey curly hair. He held a sign proclaiming *Tell the Truth* in his right hand. The driver waved him away but he kept coming, mouthing the chant that filled the air. *No more coal, no more oil, keep your carbon in the soil.*

When he was almost upon the car the driver wound down the bulletproof window to remonstrate with him and the protester's left hand emerged from behind his back. The driver slumped in his seat, a single red-stained hole in his forehead, the sound of the gunshot swallowed by the sustained chants. The Admiral glimpsed the pistol, recognised the steady, determined look in the eyes of the professional assailant, instinctively raising his bag as a protective shield. Too late. Three more shots. He wouldn't make Phoebe's party.

17

Emily woke with a start. It happened quite often.

She'd researched the condition in a medical dictionary. Something to do with waking from a deep dream during which connections to motor neurons were inhibited to the point of paralysis, the body's way of preventing people jumping off cliffs thinking they can fly, or wandering downstairs still asleep.

In most people the paralysis wears off gradually before they awake, but if you wake suddenly, the muscles twitch. A myoclonic jerk. Emily thought *jerk* summed up the experience perfectly. She also read it was most often caused by stress. Emily and stress were like moths to a flame.

She lay there for a few minutes, body tense, allowing the uneasy feeling to evaporate, taking comfort from Al's steady breathing beside her. The clock on the bedside table read 5.25am, too early to rise in normal circumstances. But her mind was active, fighting to make sense of the workload in the day ahead.

She slid out of bed, taking care not to disturb Al, slipped on her dressing gown and padded stiff-legged through to the tiny second bedroom which they had converted into a study. Al had worked some magic with white flat-pack furniture, assembling a sweeping corner desk incorporating a bookcase and computer station. A black leather swivel chair on wheels completed the office ambience.

She pressed the button to fire up the computer and while she waited flicked her mobile phone to the news app. The prospect of a three-day train strike led the bulletin, but Emily's eye was drawn immediately to the foreign news item half way down the page.

Admiral shot dead at climate protest.

The headline stark, accompanying copy sketchy, but Emily's antennae twitched at the mention of a shooter. When the computer loaded, she researched Admiral De Bruyne, discovering he had become administrative head of the European Defence Agency two years ago. In effect, De Bruyne was chief co-ordinator of Europe's

78

defence policy. Better known, more high-profile, targets may have existed. De Bruyne was not a household name but if Tinman wanted to send a chilling message to test the resolve of those on anonymous committees across Europe, making decisions designed to freeze out Russia, then disposing of the admiral was a logical move.

Emily sidled across to the window where a rising sun daubed the London skyline in a rich red hue. She spied the half-eyed cat crossing the road, disappearing underneath the rear end of a parked 4x4. As she mused, she anticipated the orders when she arrived at HQ. More research on Sukerov. More laborious analysis of oligarchs, most of whom had been reduced to impotent has-beens over the past few years. In her estimation, Tinman was not the sort of professional to rely on such support. She viewed Tinman as a maverick. A man who carved his own furrow, relying on no one, involving as few people as possible. His lone gun approach represented his strength. In her opinion, that was the main reason the department struggled to find roads leading directly to him.

She sat at the desk and wrote the venues of the killings attributed to Tinman on her notepad. Warsaw, Madrid, Devon, London, Berlin, Rome, Brussels. All in little more than a month. That was impressive execution, she thought, immediately scolding herself for the distasteful play on words. Logic told her there must be a pattern, even allowing for someone as evasive as Tinman.

She turned to her computer. It boasted none of the state-of-the-art software and security features of the machines at work, but could search airline schedules. Tapping in Red Kite Airlines, she brought up the website. From her previous research she knew the low-budget airline flew to some of the venues. For her hunch to have legs it would have to fly to all of them.

Within half an hour she ascertained that it did. Another half hour discovered that while other budget airlines flew to some of the venues, Red Kite was the only one in the UK to fly to all of them. Her excitement surged at a heady gallop. She forced herself to rein it in. If Tinman flew to the venues, she knew he could also be using another low cost airline in another country. All would need checking, requiring manpower. Mixing and matching airlines presented another possibility. That may also appeal to Tinman's evasive character. Offer a moving target at all times.

Red Kite remained inconclusive. Emily accepted that, but it was the nearest she had found to a pattern. The tricky part came next. Convincing Scafell and McBride.

"You're up early. Bad sleep?" Al poked his nose around the door.

"No, slept fine. Just had another of those rude awakenings. Thought I may as well start the day."

"Got much done?"

"Think so. I have an idea. But it depends on what the bosses think."

"The secret with an idea is making the bosses think they thought of it first."

"How does that work?" Emily looked puzzled. Subterfuge in the workplace, any place, was alien to her, which was odd for someone who worked in intelligence, where lies, damned lies, double-dealing, disguise and manipulation were essential tools of the trade.

"You have to plant the idea in their head. Talk around it. Let the seed grow. Don't push your idea as a cutting edge breakthrough, but something familiar. People fear anything that's too different. And when you've done the spadework ..."

Emily interrupted, wearing a bewildered expression. "Plants, seeds, spades, sounds like gardening. What are you talking about?"

Al laughed. "Never mind. Don't think it's quite up your street, Emily. Better just come straight out with it."

An hour later Emily walked into HQ. As with the killing of General Mantelli, the office seemed charged with anticipation. The big screen flickered, containing an image of Admiral De Bruyne alongside bullet points of his defence role in the European Union. Underneath, a tickertape scrolled with live news updates. No sign of McBride or Scafell.

Sam and Andrea sat at their desks alongside Emily's. On the train into work, Emily had mused on Al's *gardening* conversation. She didn't comprehend the concept of workplace manipulation, but did understand bosses required hard evidence. She launched straight in, explaining her theory about Red Kite Airlines, imploring Sam and Andrea to help with what Al would have called the spadework.

"What about McBride?" said Sam.

"He's not here right now. Neither is Luke. It may only take an hour or so."

They agreed, Andrea reluctantly, as she was deep into oligarchs' research. An hour later they swapped information. Sam had checked foreign airlines individually and determined none flew into all the venues. Andrea had compiled a potential mix of foreign airlines that could have been used, but most could be eliminated because timetables didn't tally with the shootings. Emily had concentrated on Red Kite flights. One, in particular, caught her attention. A flight into Exeter airport on the day General Parker was killed. The airport was 10 miles from the general's home.

"That's interesting. How many passengers on the flight?" Sam was intrigued.

"Sixty-five. Mostly Brits returning from a beer conference in Munich."

"Even better. Sift out the Brits and the rest should be easy to trace."

"You're forgetting Tinman will be travelling under an assumed name with what appears a valid passport. He could be anyone on that plane. Brit, German, who knows what nationality he's forged?"

Andrea had listened in silence, uncertain on which side to fall. Suddenly, she jumped. "I think you're on to something, Emily. It adds up. Forms a pattern. Maybe the one we're looking for. When are you going to tell McBride?"

"No time like the present." Emily motioned to the far side of the room at a bunch of executives emerging from the lift. McBride, Scafell, Easton and three others filed into McBride's den. A solemn tread matched the stern expressions.

Emily smoothed her black skirt with both palms, grabbed her file of papers, and headed towards the glass-panelled office. She knocked and heard McBride's deep tone. "Not now."

She knocked again, this time more insistent. The door flew open. McBride.

"Didn't you hear? Now's not a good time." His voice was tense, expression severe.

"But I think I …"

"Miss Stearn."

McBride made to close the door. Something snapped inside Emily's head. A myoclonic jerk of the brain. It had happened two years before when an altercation with the supervisor in the call centre where she worked turned nasty. On that occasion, she'd put her foot down, thrown in some harsh words and sworn her way out of a job. This time she stuck her foot in the door, jamming it open.

"I think I've discovered a pattern."

A shot of purple coloured McBride's cheeks. This wasn't the timid Emily he had been urging to gain more confidence these past months. Here was a woman with a jutting jaw and a defiant manner. A woman with promise and a sharp analytical mind but who struggled to read the most basic behavioural signs. A recruit he decided needed the raw edges smoothing. With 'C' on his back, the foreign secretary screaming for his blood and an assassin seemingly killing at will, now wasn't the time. He kicked her foot away and slammed the door.

18

Emily dug her nails into her palms and steeled herself.

She sucked in a lungful of air, held it, closed her eyes, thought of her father, said a little prayer. Then she jumped.

The sensation of falling was strangely calming. Not nearly as terrifying as she had anticipated. Her heart rose in her chest, arms flapped involuntarily. A pleasing warm wave coursed through her veins, while her mind imagined gravity sucking her forcefully into another world, like the toilet flush of a jet aircraft.

When she hit, it wasn't painful. No more than a slap on the thigh.

Emily had never jumped from the 10 metre board at the leisure centre she used after work once a week, and she had nailed it. For a moment she felt disorientated as the rush of water on impact compromised her senses, but two strong leg thrusts powered her to the surface.

She sucked in air again and swam to the side, a heady feeling of triumph planting a wide smile.

"Good job. First time?" The lifeguard, a young lad with straggly blond hair and an engaging grin, pointed up at the board. He had watched Emily's tentative deliberations.

"First time, probably the last," said Emily, gasping as she clambered up the corner steps. She grabbed a towel and sat on one of the poolside chairs.

"Why? It looked fun."

"Long story," said Emily, burying her face in the towel as the lifeguard walked by.

It wasn't a joke. Emily understood her shortcomings. David Stephens had pointed them out when he offered her a job in secret intelligence. A lack of confidence. An inability to make instant decisions and a reluctance to overcome her fears. She had worked on them ever since with an obsessive zeal at times.

Fear of water was not the problem. Her father had brought her to this same pool on many occasions as a child. Heights, however, induced dread, to the point where the prospect of crossing a bridge with spectacular views generated a feeling of nausea.

Emily had worked up to her high board leap in incremental stages. Diving in from the side. Bouncing on the springboard. Sliding off the five metre board. She had read the theory. The manuals called it exposure therapy. Gradually and repeatedly entering feared situations until you feel less anxious. There was the rub. The problem wasn't the height. Rather, controlling the anxiety caused by the height. Managing anxiety was an essential characteristic in her new job.

She showered, dressed, threw her swim bag over her shoulder, deciding to walk to the flat, assessing the events of the day. Ever since McBride physically pushed her out of his office, she had seethed. The meeting had lasted most of the day. High-level decisions were required, Jack Easton's presence suggesting they included operational matters she would not expect to be privy to. Yet that was no reason for rudeness, especially as Emily's information, the discovery of her pattern, could be instrumental to their plans.

Scafell had sidled to her desk when the meeting broke up late afternoon to apologise for McBride's brusqueness. Emily nodded curtly. She'd decided to keep her Red Kite flight revelations between herself, Sam and Andrea, until they uncovered some hard evidence. They had isolated seven flights for scrutiny, involving more than 500 passengers, narrowed down to 283 when they excluded women and children. Further enquiries had determined 12 names appeared twice or more on the flight manifests. Probably businessmen flying regularly to various parts of Europe. All needed checking. Emily thought Tinman unlikely to use the same name twice, but he may have slipped up. She needed to trawl through any available video. Two passengers with different names on different flights may have carried the same bag, worn the same clothes, offered some clue as to Tinman's alias.

The task required the department's total manpower, not merely the attentions of Emily, plus Sam and Andrea in their spare time. As Emily walked home she sifted the permutations, resolving to speak to McBride the next day. Engrossed in her deliberations, she failed to spot the figure on the opposite footpath, in the shadow of overhanging trees, not until she was a few streets from the flat. By chance, a car performing a U-turn caught him in the sweep of headlights, illuminating the baseball cap pulled down to shield the top half of his face and the furtive half-glance as the lights caught, a sure sign of a stalker.

Stay calm. Don't panic. The rudiments of Emily's training kicked in, although her mind immediately cursed her lack of concentration. Be observant at all times. That was the central core of her first practical lesson in the Service's tradecraft more than 12 months ago. Never engage autopilot, as she had since leaving the leisure centre, allowing the outside world to pass by unheard and unseen. Easy to say, difficult in practice in an age awash with self-absorption.

Her heart and mind began to race. No bus or cab in sight. She stopped to gaze into the window of an estate agent, collecting her thoughts, feigning interest in pictures of a Thames-view penthouse with a hefty price tag. Dusk was falling, streetlights reflected in the window. The man stooped to tie a bootlace, careful not to reveal himself. Emily took a calming breath and strode on, remembering the office code in such circumstances. Mix things up. Don't go straight home. Instead of carrying on to Archway, she turned left, then first right and dodged right again into a road where she knew shops traded late. She could smell curry, sweet and spicy. Indian music blared from an upstairs window overwhelming the animated chatter of foreign voices and people enjoying themselves. Three or four shoppers browsed at a clothes stall, heads bobbing above racks full of vivid dresses. Emily swerved around them, thankful to embrace the fleeting safety of ordinary people going about every-day chores. Some gave her curious looks. She could stop and tell them. But what would she tell them?

After 50 yards she glanced behind. The man rounded the corner. He'd mimicked her detour and on her side of the road she detected another figure, another man, same dark clothing, this one wearing a flat cap, striding with athletic purpose in her direction.

The first hint of panic jolted her system. She contemplated darting into the next shop to ring the police. Instead, she steeled herself to act as normal as possible, gradually picking up pace, almost to the cusp of a jog, eating up the yards, her breathing heavy. The men responded and now she was past the shops, clear of people, out in the open, terraced houses either side with no hint of life. No obvious escape route. She sensed them closing in. Heard, or imagined, the scuffle of their steps, although her ears thundered with the rush of adrenalin.

She was 30 yards short of her street when she could hold the tension no longer. She dropped her swim bag, sprinting for her life. She turned the corner, at the same time glancing behind to determine how close they were, only to collide with a man walking in the opposite direction. They went flying, Emily slumping to her knees, grazing her elbow as she steadied herself on the pavement, while the man spun around, ending on his back with his feet in the gutter.

Emily gazed down, mouth open, shocked and bewildered. "Al, are you all right?"

"What's the big hurry? Who's chasing you?" Al clutched his ribs, a dazed expression on his face as he gasped for breath.

Emily looked around. No sign of men in caps.

19

They hobbled back to the flat, Emily babbling apologies, Al explaining he was on his way to the shop to buy a bottle of milk.

Emily helped clean up a gash on Al's knee, covered it with a sticking plaster and tried to pass off the collision as a freak coincidence.

"Emily, I saw the look in your eyes. You were terrified. What's happened? Why were you running and what, or who, were you running from?"

"I don't know."

"You don't know?" Al's tone was tender but there was a slight raise of the eyebrows.

"I thought a man, maybe two men, might be following me, one a big guy in dark clothes and a baseball cap."

"Did he threaten you?"

"No."

"Did he say anything?"

"No, he never got close enough."

"Did he …?"

"Stop asking questions, Al. He didn't do anything, apart from walk the same way as me. It wasn't my imagination, if that's what you're thinking."

"I wasn't."

"I did everything by the book. Everything I learned in training. The stops, the detours. I couldn't shake him off. He was still there."

"A professional then."

"Looked like it, but when we collided I looked around straight away and he was gone. No sign of him."

The doorbell rang. Al and Emily looked at each other, worry lines etched around their eyes. Al rolled down his trouser leg while Emily edged to the door. There was no spy hole, so Emily placed her ear to the wood panel. A muffled siren yelped in the distance, but she could hear the shuffling of heavy feet close by and the harsh rasp of someone clearing their throat. Could be the two men following her. They may be armed. Emily fought to stem a surge of alarm. Would they announce themselves by ringing the doorbell? Probably not, she reasoned.

"Who is it?" Emily's voice soft and diffident. No answer. She asked again, this time more strident.

"Bob Wilson."

Emily glanced at Al and mouthed "Bob?", her face scrunched in an oil painting of perplexity.

She eased the door open a few inches to ensure he was alone before inviting him in. Wilson's face was Merlot red, veins raised around his nose. His hair was unruly, sticking out at odd angles. He'd trimmed his beard to an uneven stubble, peppered with grey, giving his face a feral appearance. His coat was creased and stained, his gait shambling, but his eyes were clear, his hands steady and there was no sign of the desperation they had witnessed in the Soho bar. Crucially, the lingering smell in the hallway was of male deodorant rather than stale whisky.

"You look better than the last time we saw you." Emily's opening remark was not meant to imply criticism, but it came across that way.

"Huh." Wilson shrugged, a trace of embarrassment in his eyes. "That bad, was I?"

"I didn't mean …"

"I think she means you were a little tired and emotional. So tired we tucked you up and left you sleeping like a baby." Al rescued Emily.

"That's why I'm here," said Wilson. "To apologise and thank you for looking after me. God knows what may have happened …"

"We came to check on you the day after, but you were out." Emily filled a pause, trying to ease his discomfort.

"I shouldn't be here."

"It's not a problem, we're pleased to see you looking well."

"No, I mean I shouldn't be here. Intus warned me not to be in touch with any of my colleagues until the investigation was complete. I'm still suspended."

"Oh."

"Don't worry, I made sure I wasn't followed. If there's one thing I'm still good at, it's giving the department trackers the slip."

"Why are you suspended, what do they think you've done?"

"They won't tell me. I've spent three days locked up with Savage and his cronies, going through my whole life, a career devoted to their bloody Service, by the way. They wanted to know all about my time in Afghanistan and Iraq and Syria. I can hardly remember I've been to some of the places they brought up. I know what they're doing. They're trying to find a link, some faint possibility that I may have been in contact with anyone connected to the guy they think killed Mason."

"Have you?"

"No." Wilson looked hurt. "No, Emily, I haven't."

Emily remembered Stephens endorsing Wilson's credentials, maintaining his loyalty was not in doubt. She believed him.

"So they're still hunting for the leak?" said Emily. Al rose from his seat in front of a dining table and made to leave the room. The conversation had taken a detailed turn into delicate office business and he had no desire to find himself on the wrong end of an Official Secrets Act investigation.

"You don't have to go," said Emily.

"I think I do," said Al, disappearing into the back room.

Emily turned to Wilson.

"They're pretty sure there's a leak," said Wilson. "Not just because of how Mason died. From what they've intimated suspicion's been smouldering for some time. They're paranoid about it. Have been ever since Iraq and the dodgy dossier all those years back. Probably why they hauled me in. I'd nothing to do with dodgy intelligence coming out of Iraq, but I was in the country at the time and every agent around then seems to be tarred with the same brush.

"I can see why they're sensitive. Fleet Street's got it in for the Service. All the business about that Saudi prisoner being water-boarded 83 times by the CIA as well as being beaten, deprived of sleep and locked in a box. The Service didn't do that. It may have provided questions to be answered by him, I've no idea. It may have known he was being tortured. But our world is dark and murky. It's not perfect. Things happen. Things out of our control."

Emily wasn't following Wilson's train of thought. "Are you saying Mason's death may have something to do with Iraq or the CIA?"

"No, I'm saying someone, somewhere, must be leaking stuff to the press, to other agencies, to the Saudis, to the Russians. Not in a rush of secrets, but in a steady drip. Maybe over years. unconnected pieces of information that are stored and acted upon at a later date. Maybe Mason was a victim."

If Wilson was right, then the chances of the leak being plugged anytime soon were remote. He was talking about an agent embedded in the Service, so securely entrenched that suspicion was unthinkable. A director, a section chief, a technician, an ordinary evaluator, someone in the post room, maybe even a humble secretary with eyes on all manner of confidential papers, probably with an unblemished record, one with a reputation and a pension to lose.

"They could even be working for Intus," he said. "What better way for an informer to hide in plain sight than to investigate their own crime. Wielding the baton. Closing down the drums. Freezing out a violin here and there whenever the fancy takes them."

Emily dismissed Wilson's music analogy as tortuous and fanciful. He was a grizzly old operative with plenty of reasons, some legitimate, others imaginary, to feel hard done by. The life he'd chosen had systematically sucked the life out of him, replacing it with mistrust and fear, to the point where he had abandoned the importance of unimportant daily rituals. No longer did he routinely bid others good morning or go for a walk or listen to birdsong or read the newspaper. Or clean his flat. The divorce hadn't helped. He had tried to pay Mary more attention on the rare occasions they shared moments of intimacy, as well as buy into the routine events of married life. He knew the marriage was in trouble, but if truth be told, he had not tried hard enough, always hiding behind the requirement for secrecy, rather than confronting the fact that he and Mary had grown apart. Their conversation rarely contained matters of substance, instead dwelling on the mechanics of the household, such as who did the shopping and who put out the rubbish bins. Ten years ago he returned from a short posting in Tehran to find an empty flat and a stark note from Mary informing him that she could take the icy loneliness of their existence no longer. A parting reminder informed him bin collections were now fortnightly. The marriage was over.

But for all his hang-ups and personal problems, Emily believed Wilson was shrewd, especially when it came to office politics. To her, the main thrust of his argument rang true. Emily thought of Savage and his probing. Was he striving to uncover the truth? Or were his questions little thought grenades, primed to detonate in the mind, hours or days later? A subtle way of undermining the collective responsibility of the Service. She thought of McBride, too, and the way he had closed her down, physically ejecting her from his office, depriving top-ranked executives from hearing her theory.

"I'd better be going." Wilson made for the front door. He slipped the lock but turned, slow and deliberate, fixing her with eyes as hard as diamonds. "Be careful, Emily, don't trust anyone."

Then he was gone.

20

Stations fascinated Emily. A bit like the ocean. Forever changing, but always the same.

People hurrying in all directions to unknown destinations. Sharp-suited businessmen rubbing shoulders with ragged creatures hustling commuters for the price of a cup of tea. Tannoys blaring. Guards whistling. Trains rumbling. Gun-toting police on patrol.

At stations, noise and crowds seemed logical. She could sit back, observe the chaos, as though viewing an ant's nest of activity from on high. It was a shade after 9am. The morning rush had lost its manic fervour and two hours remained before she had to report at HQ. Hence the reason she accepted Leanne's text inviting her for a coffee and chat on the way to work. Since their picnic on Primrose Hill they had tried several times to meet up, an evening date proving elusive due to work commitments.

Emily arrived first, taking an outside table at a café opposite the champagne bar at St Pancras station. She ordered a cappuccino and watched a Eurostar train board and depart, counting businessmen and holidaymakers into the various carriages. She couldn't help it. Counting formed part of Emily's DNA. Always had done. Some people pop tranquilisers. For Emily, counting had become as automatic, and calming, as breathing. Her thoughts strayed. She wondered if Tinman had used this route, boarded this train, deciding that was unlikely.

She spied Leanne passing The Lovers Statue at the station's terrace entrance. The loose material of Leanne's bright red dress swished as she walked while the black strap of a shoulder bag crossed her body at a diagonal, as though she wore a seat belt. A welcoming smile played on her lips, Emily deducing that here was an attractive woman comfortable in her own skin.

They hugged at Leanne's insistence and to Emily's mild discomfort, Leanne at the same time gesturing to the waiter, ordering a skinny latte.

"What a splendid meeting place," said Leanne, glancing across at four businessmen quaffing flutes of champagne. "How the other half live. Bit early for me, though."

"And me. At this time of day, the only bubbles I have are in the bath."

"Nice one, Emily, I knew we'd have a lot in common the first time we met."

This was uncharted territory. Meeting women friends for coffee was not an everyday occurrence for Emily. The prospect of making small talk filled her with dread. She couldn't explore mathematics or science with Leanne, at least she didn't think so. They'd discussed West End musicals the last time they met on Primrose Hill, but Leanne and Scafell had driven that conversation.

"How's Luke?" Emily's stab at a chatty opener.

"You tell me. You probably see more of him these days than I do."

"True, work's pretty full-on at the moment."

"It always is." Leanne's eyebrows raised, lips tightening in a thin smile of resignation. "Must be a strange business to work in, surrounded by classified files piled high like cans of baked beans. Luke always says he has a job for life. The nation may run out of oil and gas, but we'll never run out of secrets."

"I'd never thought of it like that."

"No?"

"For me, it's all about problems to rectify, conundrums to resolve. I love sinking my teeth into something that seems unsolvable and coming up with the answer."

"You make it sound like a maths exam."

"That's how it feels sometimes. The beauty with maths is that there's an answer for everything, even though sometimes it takes months, years or even decades to find it. It's all about patience and perseverance, believing nothing is impossible." Emily experienced a warm glow, a sudden surge of contentment, Leanne's lively manner making conversation easy. The latte arrived. Leanne stirred in a spoonful of sugar. Emily realised she was enjoying this coffee morning.

They chatted about maths after all, as well as Emily's foray into engineering following her graduation, a career curtailed by a surfeit of theory and several years of boredom. She revealed the wasted year that followed in the insurance call centre and Leanne cackled at Emily's description of the stand-off with a supervisor that precipitated her departure.

"Oh Emily, I can't imagine you swearing."

"I don't, it was strictly a one-off, never to be repeated."

"Some people deserve an F-bomb now and then. It would be rude not to oblige."

They laughed, Leanne pointing out the four businessmen filling their glasses as another champagne cork popped.

"Have you got your teeth into something at the moment?" said Leanne.

"Pardon."

"You said you love sinking your teeth into something unsolvable."

"As a matter of fact, yes, I have, although it's a problem that requires an answer pretty soon. I don't like deadlines. They make me nervous."

"A race against time. Sounds exciting. Tell me more."

For the first time, Emily felt uncomfortable. She understood Leanne was only making conversation, but talking about work, even in unspecific terms, seemed unprofessional. Being married to Luke, Leanne should have known any mention of work agenda was off limits. A fact drummed into those with loved ones in the Service as the only way to ensure security and confidentiality. Maybe it was a test. Perhaps Leanne would report back to Scafell. Maybe Scafell had suggested the meeting. Emily's mind churned with possibilities. She sought refuge, changing the subject, asking about Leanne's teaching job.

"I'm not working at the moment. Having a break. I'll get back into it next term. It helps pay the bills but I could do without the hassle. Too much paperwork and organising, not enough teaching anymore. And I can get to the gym a little more frequently."

"I thought you worked out. You always look so fabulous and fit."

Leanne laughed. "You should be my agent."

They chatted for another 15 minutes, mostly about the station's Victorian architecture, wondering back to the days when locomotives trundled alongside the same platforms spitting plumes of steam into the cavernous space more than half a century ago.

The waiter arrived to clear their cups. Emily looked at her watch. "Perfect timing," she said. "Time for a cab to the office." They grabbed their bags and Emily followed Leanne's lead as they hugged lightly.

"I enjoyed our chat, Emily. Great location. We must make this a regular thing."

Emily wanted to say *I'd like that* but didn't, instead raising a hand, twiddling her fingers in a self-conscious wave. They parted and Emily passed through the front archway onto the cobbled road outside the Midland Hotel, where taxis hovered and a bell boy struggled to haul heavy luggage onto a trolley. Glancing over her shoulder, Emily searched for faces hidden behind caps. She spotted none.

***

When Emily reached the office it was quiet. The listeners sat in silence in their corner, headphones rammed into their ears, some with eyes closed in concentration. None of the executives were present. Emily assumed they must be attending another high-profile meeting, possibly in 'C''s office.

Sam and Andrea sat at their stations, noses in computers. When Emily dropped her bag on the desk Sam looked up, eyes bright and eager, like a spaniel anticipating meal time, an excited tone in his voice.

"We've checked and re-checked, Emily. Red Kite is the only airline that connects all the relevant locations. We've also tracked the twelve names that appear twice on the manifests and they all check out. All bona-fide businessmen, apart from one old guy who gives lectures on marine insurance for a living. He checks out too."

Emily looked puzzled. "So no sign of Tinman. Why do you sound excited?"

"Because we, me and Andrea, that is, have located video of all the passengers on the relevant flights. We've requested clearance to put them through face recognition technology. If Tinman was on those flights, then there must be a good chance of matching him up."

"What if he's used different disguises and passports?"

"It doesn't matter. The technology sifts out similarities, using biometrics to map facial features. It reads the geometry of the face. The distance between eyes, the distance from forehead to chin. Sixty-eight distinguishing characteristics. It all makes up your unique face print. Even a master of deception such as Tinman can't disguise everything."

"Is it fool-proof?"

"No, but not far off. The best identification algorithm, and that's what we're using, has an error rate of just nought point nought eight per cent. Negligible considering the amount of footage we have."

Andrea piped up. "That's good enough for me. If Tinman is using Red Kite, then we've got him."

A surge of elation shot through Emily's system, even though she fought to suppress it. Sam and Andrea's work sounded promising, but Tinman was a hardened professional. Emily could not envisage him making mistakes.

"We've got to tell McBride," said Sam. "He'll have to sign off on the recognition technology. The sooner the better. He'll want the whole team working on this."

"Okay, I'll ask to see him as soon as he comes in."

The prospect of facing McBride again did not appeal to Emily. She understood he was under pressure, his angst plain when he slammed the office door in her face, but she still bridled at the disrespect. Carrying on as if nothing had happened amid an awkward atmosphere was not one of her strong suits.

She needn't have worried. When she rapped on his office door an hour later his call to enter contained the welcoming trill of someone in a bright and positive mood.

"Ah, Miss Stearn, come in, sit down, tell me more about this pattern you've discovered." The contrast could not have been starker.

Emily placed a folder on McBride's desk in which she had assembled the relevant information on Tinman's potential movements. She slid out a few papers, offering them to McBride.

"I've put a file together, dates, flights, venues ..."

"Never mind that now, Miss Stearn. I'll read it later. Cut to the chase"

For a moment, Emily was taken aback. Her natural world worked to order. As in start at A and end at Z. To her, cutting to Z was plain wrong. But she did anyway.

"We know how Tinman's getting around."

"How?"

"Budget airline. Red Kite Airlines to be exact. Based in the UK and travelling to all the venues where Tinman is thought to have killed in the last two months, including Exeter where General Parker was shot."

"Are you sure?"

"Pretty sure."

"Pretty? Too vague. What's pretty as a percentage?"

Emily pondered for a moment, remembering what Sam had told her about the face technology, but factoring in her own caution about Tinman and mistakes.

"Ninety per cent."

McBride whistled through his teeth. He rocked his cheekbone with a forefinger for a few moments, a sure sign the news had tweaked his attention, before fixing Emily with eyes that danced with anticipation.

"What do you need?"

Emily set out the requirements. Analysts to check and recheck dates, log turn-around times, aircraft stop-overs and passenger manifests. The urgent need for face technology clearance and staff to compare results with videos from all venues.

"You've got it," said McBride.

Emily nodded, squirming slightly in her seat, euphoria blending with anxiety as the sudden burden for shaping the team's strategy weighed heavy on her shoulders.

21

Al forced himself to stay awake. Every time his eyes closed he slapped his face and took a swig of bottled water. Fizzy and warm, but it served its purpose.

He had run six miles with training friends from the football team that evening. They'd ended up in a pub, celebrating one of the group's birthday. The conversation flowed, as did the beer. Al had sunk more pints than normal, mainly because he'd received a phone call from Emily. "Don't wait up," she said. "It could be a late one."

Al wasn't drunk. Not to the point where the room spun anyway. An unpleasant experience on his 21st birthday when he had dropped his mobile phone in the river and insisted he could retrieve it himself, only to be rescued by the fire service, had seen him vow never to fall into such a state again. Ten birthdays later the pledge remained intact. But he was tired and the clock ticked towards midnight. Still, he had no intention of going to bed before Emily returned, especially after her troubled encounter with the men in caps.

He sat in the dark, listening for the diesel clatter of a taxi at the front door. Instead, he heard a sharper, grating noise at the back of the flat, rather like the metallic shift of a bin lid. London's urban foxes came to mind. It wasn't unusual to observe foxes searching back yards in the area, sniffing out pet food, pawing bins, gnawing at plastic bags casually discarded, full of half-eaten takeaways. Al had spotted a fox family only days before, sunning themselves on a flat garage roof a few houses down. He'd watched entranced as the cubs tormented the patient mother, constantly scratching her face, chewing her tail.

Rising cautiously from his chair, Al padded to the back patio doors. The night was black as pitch, no moon to cast a silvery half-light, the only illumination the soft reflected glow of streetlights at the front. Standing statue-like and fumbling with an outstretched hand to find the outside light switch, he detected a scraping sound, expecting to see a bushy tail and a fox's nonchalant stare. After a few seconds he pressed the switch, white light flooding the yard. Al froze.

A crouching figure, clad in black, spun towards the light, shielding eyes from the harsh glare. Al spotted the jerk of an arm and instinctively dropped to the floor, burying his face in the carpet, a tremor of fear making his heart thump. The sinister sights of a hand gun settled on his silhouette behind the glass, the intruder's arm rigid, steady, controlled. A professional.

Cold sweat trickled down Al's back. He braced himself for the crack of a gunshot but none came. When he summoned the courage to raise his head, the intruder was gone.

22

Emily knew something was wrong. She could not put her finger on it, but something didn't add up.

The operation room crackled with energy all day, packed with analysts, full of technicians, all poring over video footage, applying the latest hardware in the hunt for Tinman. McBride had thrown staff, money, technology, the full works, behind Emily's theory. He had nothing to lose, he calculated, only time. Interpol had come up with *hee haw*, McBride's derogatory description in colloquial Scottish, connecting Tinman to any of the recent killings. There were no clues, no fingerprints, no witnesses supplying any worthwhile evidence. The only concrete leads were the ballistics findings.

If Emily's Red Kite theory was correct, however, it placed Tinman in the vicinity of every killing. More than that, it would present a timeline, an itinerary to track, a window into his thought processes. It may even identify who and where he was likely to strike next.

"Are you sure this technology's fool-proof?" Emily's voice contained a frustrating lilt.

"Pretty much," said Sam. "I don't understand why we haven't had a positive ID yet."

McBride briefed the entire department on Emily's Red Kite theory. Every available operative joined the hunt, crucial software tracing each relevant passenger. In addition, Scafell assembled a team with eyes on the videos, manually scanning, searching for similarities between them.

For 10 hours the department functioned with collective drive. Everyone on the same page. A tingle of excitement permeated the air. Breaks ignored, takeaways ordered instead. No one wanted to leave the office, the team committed to the mission, noses in computers, like hounds on a blood trail.

As each hour passed and the sun went down with no Eureka moment the mood changed. Scans complete and every relevant flight checked, doubts began to seep through the office, faith in Emily's theory slowly evaporating. At a quarter to midnight McBride decided enough was enough. He stood on a chair in the middle of the operation room beckoning everyone to gather round. His tone wavered between appreciation and disappointment, but Emily detected only disappointment.

"Thanks for all your work today, ladies and gentlemen. It's been a long day, but it looks like we've struck out. Red Kite was a good theory, but it's time to go home. We'll recalibrate in the morning."

The throng dissolved into little groups, murmuring in resignation, collecting bags and coats, heading for the lift.

Sam and Andrea having departed, Emily sat alone at her desk mulling every aspect of the day's deliberations. Her mathematical mind demanded an answer to every equation. Stopping without a solution wasn't acceptable. She pored over dates and names, searching for something, anything, she may have missed. A hand on her shoulder returned her to reality. Scafell.

"Don't worry, Emily, these things happen."

"Not to me, they don't."

"To everyone, sometimes sooner, sometimes later." His tone was tender, expression caring. "All part of an analyst's job. The facts can lead you down a promising avenue and it turns into a cul-de-sac. Not the first time this has happened. It won't be the last. No harm done. We've eliminated possibilities, that's always useful. Get a good night's sleep and don't rush in the morning."

Emily felt a crushing weight of humiliation. It came in surges, deep and overwhelming. She didn't need platitudes or sleep, or even logical explanations. She wanted to scream. Scafell was trying to be kind, she knew that, but he wasn't helping. The entire department had spent a full day and most of the night working on what they all now believed to have no more substance than steam rising from a kettle. Emily's mistaken notion. A whim. She needed air.

"Thanks Luke. I've got to go."

She grabbed her bag, heading for the stairs to avoid knowing looks and the queue for the shuddering lift. When she reached reception the night security men were processing staff exiting the building, each person required to swipe their plastic pass through the scanner.

A woman in front fumbled with her pass, the lanyard having somehow tied itself in an awkward knot. The security guard, a middle-aged man with a round, jolly face and a booming voice that reminded Emily of a TV comedian, though she couldn't think of the name, leaned over to assist.

"You've got this in a right state."

The woman made an apologetic face. "Sorry, must have got tangled when I took off my cardigan."

After a couple of attempts, the guard eased the knot loose and the woman swiped the pass through the scanner.

"Don't lose it," said the guard. "Your whole life's on that pass."

The woman smiled her thanks, Emily swiped her own pass and strode into the night. Sucking in breezy river air that tasted of mud and weed, she hurried to hail a cab. A thought struck. She stopped for several seconds, eyes fixed on the illuminated dome of St Paul's in the distance. "That's it," she muttered, experiencing the same elation she'd felt on occasions when solving a particularly tricky differential equation. Everything suddenly became clear.

Twenty minutes later, the cab pulled up at Archway. Al stood in the doorway, a strange expression on his face, drifting between shock and concern. Emily didn't notice. She wanted to tell him everything. She wanted to rush into his arms and pour out the details of the longest day of her life. *Did I only meet Leanne at St Pancras this morning? Feels like weeks ago.* She wanted to tell him about her increasing desolation as it became obvious she had wasted everyone's time. Tinman was not a passenger on Red Kite Airlines, after all. She accepted that. She wanted to share her euphoria that despite the setbacks she had a new theory. And this time she was sure it would fly.

She knew none of that was possible. She couldn't share, say or reveal anything. That was the infuriating but essential nature of her business. But Al could, and as she reached the front door, he did.

"I've called the police. They're on their way. There was a man with a gun in the back yard."

23

They say when you've stared down the barrel of a gun your soul ponders death forever.

Al couldn't remember where he had read that pearl of wisdom, but now it made sense. The image of the arm tracking his shadow, expecting at any moment to see the flash as the bullet discharged, invaded his every thought. Would he see the flash? Depends. If hit in the leg, arm or chest then almost certainly he'd have seen the flash followed by the report, as light travels faster than sound. Although given the distance was 20 feet at most, if hit in the head he'd have been dead before computing either as the brain would still be processing the data when interrupted.

Macabre musings churned through his mind all night. Waking. Sleeping. Tossing. Turning.

The police had dispatched a so-called fast-response unit of four officers, carrying punchy-looking machine guns but who could hardly be described as fast considering they arrived half an hour after Al's call, enough time for the intruder to have hit the motorway and sped miles from the capital.

Al had supplied details of the intruder to a plain clothes policeman, amounting to little more than he or she was medium build, average height, dressed in black, wearing a balaclava and pointing a gun.

"Sorry, I didn't get a good look. He or she was startled by the light and I was freaked by the gun," said Al. "I hit the deck and was left staring at the carpet. I can describe that if you like."

The officer ignored Al's attempt at humour, scribbling in his notebook with the indifferent attitude of a man who had seen and heard the same or similar hundreds of times. Working in London for the past 10 years he probably had. He revealed there had been a spate of burglaries in the area over recent weeks and that the weapon was more than likely an imitation.

"It didn't look like a fake," said Al.

"How many times have you looked down the barrel of a real weapon, Sir?"

"Well, never."

"Precisely."

"What does that mean?"

"What colour was the gun?"

"Pardon."

"It's a simple question. What colour was it?"

"Black, I think. Why?"

"By law and to comply with manufacturers' codes of conduct, toy guns have to be brightly coloured. So red, orange, yellow, green, blue, pink, or purple would be acceptable, but black or brown would not."

"It definitely looked black."

"I'm sure it did. Criminals want you to associate the shape and action with images you have seen. Almost certainly from the TV. They paint fake guns and toy guns black. If it looks like the real deal, then your brain accepts it without questioning. Most criminals carry fakes to induce fear. Most times that's exactly what they do."

"I can vouch for that."

"It doesn't matter. Fake or real. Under the Firearms Act, 1968, Section 16A, it's an offence for a person to have possession of a firearm or imitation firearm with intent by means thereof to cause a person to believe that unlawful violence will be used against them or another. As far as I can see that covers proceedings tonight."

Al was impressed at the officer's eloquent, if pedantic, recall of the relevant act and considered mentioning who Emily worked for, but decided against it. The police rummaged around the yard, poking into a shed, checking locks. They stayed long enough to appear they were not leaving with indecent haste, but only just.

When they departed, Emily and Al held each other close for five minutes, warm and safe in their embrace, a sudden weariness, due to the lateness of the hour and the day's traumas, enveloping them. Time for sleep.

A shade after four Emily jolted awake. She sensed Al moving beside her.

To be sure, Emily whispered, "Al, are you awake?"

"Yeah." Al's drawl muffled by one of his pillows.

"How easy do you think it would be to clone someone's identity?"

"Depends." A yawn and a sigh.

"On what?"

"On how much of their life you wanted to clone. On whether they were dead or alive. Identity theft is rampant these days, especially in big cities such as London. People clone driving licences to evade parking and speeding fines. They steal passports and set up benefit frauds. That's why everyone should keep their details as safe and private as they can. Proving you didn't do something when all the relevant papers say you did must be a nightmare."

"You seem to know a lot about it."

"Not really. A teacher friend of mine got a speeding ticket through the post a couple of months ago. He hadn't driven for a month, never been to the town in question and never hired a top-of-the-range Mercedes, or any other car for that matter. But the ticket came in his name and he's still trying to convince the police he's nothing to do with it."

"Hmm. That's what I thought. Once a person's in the system, however fraudulent, the system begins to protect the intruder at the expense of the innocent."

Al yawned again, loudly, and turned over. "That's too deep for me at this time of night, Emily. And can we stop talking about intruders?"

"Sorry, you're right. Go back to sleep."

Emily lay awake wondering, questions flitting through her mind. Where was Tinman? Whose identity may he have cloned?

24

Emily knew she was close when she spied the Five Bells pub and medieval turreted church of St Mary's, the green in front resplendent with early summer colour.

She tapped the cab driver on the shoulder. "About 400 yards, take a left, it's right in front." The engines of a huge jet whined close by, the pungent aroma of aircraft fuel hung heavy in the air, the expanse of Heathrow airport spreading into the distance.

The headquarters of Red Kite Airlines nestled amid an industrial site on an anonymous road in the ancient village of Harmondsworth, to the north of Heathrow's runways. A convenient spot for an airline, except that Red Kite no longer flew out of Heathrow, a steep rise in the cost of landing and take-off slots forcing it to cheaper locations such as Bristol and Exeter. The owners had kept their HQ for administrative purposes, largely because the office they occupied rubbed shoulders with the plusher home of British Airways. The location appealed to Red Kite's ego. Made them feel more visible, their soaring bird-of-prey logo invariably receiving television exposure when the cameras turned up to report on the nearby refugee asylum centre or when activists protested against plans for an additional runway.

That morning, Emily had woken late and instead of heading to the office had phoned McBride, imploring him to allow her to continue investigations into the airline. She didn't want to explain her theory over the phone, McBride's sighs signalling he wasn't interested in hearing it. He had wasted enough time and manpower on Red Kite Airlines the day before and had no intention of repeating the exercise. He explained that Emily's request was not within the Service's remit, relenting only on condition Emily involved no other staff, apart from a secretary to arrange a meeting, and returned to the office that afternoon to report directly to him.

When she arrived at Red Kite's HQ, a receptionist filing a heap of invoices greeted her with a disinterested tone.

"Can I help?"

"I'm Emily Stearn. Here to see Mr Eriksson." Emily flopped her ID card on the counter.

The receptionist paid scant regard, but motioned for Emily to take a seat and muttered into her phone. Five minutes later a short, stocky man, dark suit a size too small emphasising his dumpiness, emerged from an adjoining office.

"Ah, Miss Stearn, I've been expecting you."

He led her through to a room with a large and impressive polished wood conference table, if anything a touch too grand for its mundane surroundings. They sat on opposite sides.

"I believe you have some questions about our staff practices. Can I ask what they are concerning?" said Eriksson.

"General enquiries, that's all. For instance, what checks are done on cabin staff?"

Eriksson's eyebrows met. Emily's interview style was direct, brusque even, not strong on empathy.

"Extensive background checks, as per the industry standard," said Eriksson.

"Such as."

"A basic criminal record check. That's a strict requirement to receive an airside pass. We also require an overseas certificate for all countries in which an employee lived continuously for six months in the last five years. We do electronic ID checks via information held by credit referencing agencies, the electoral roll and telephone databases. On top of that we insist on character references, education qualifications and employment checks for the past five years. We take security very seriously."

"I'm sure you do. But you don't routinely video staff boarding aircraft?"

"No. In common with most other airlines, each crew member would have an airside pass as a known crew member. Their pass is scanned and most airports allow them access via a crew airside door, away from the passengers. It makes sense, the best way of boarding staff efficiently, especially with tight turnarounds."

"Can I ask you about specific flights?"

"Such as?"

Emily fished in her handbag and pulled out a piece of A4 paper with a column of dates and corresponding Red Kite flight numbers.

"Would you be able to tell me the names of crew members working on these flights?" She slid the paper over to Eriksson's side of the table.

"What exactly are you investigating? If you're accusing one of our crew members of something, I think we have a right to know."

Emily thought for a moment. She didn't want this interview to stall, resulting in a stand-off escalated to her bosses. She was in enough trouble already. Divulging enough information to keep Eriksson on side seemed the logical move.

"No one's accusing anyone. The investigation is at an early stage but we're looking into the movements of a known terrorist. We think he may be using various airlines to travel around Europe. For completeness, we're checking the budget airlines like yourselves as well as the big boys. We don't know whether he's posing as a passenger or staff member, but I'm sure you realise we have to explore every possibility." Emily was rather pleased with her phrasing. Eriksson's shoulders relaxed.

"I understand," he said. He picked up the paper and made for the door. "Hang on here, it shouldn't take long."

Ten minutes later Eriksson returned. He walked around to Emily's side of the table, placing several sheets of paper in front of her. Leaning over her shoulder, he pointed to groups of names corresponding to flight numbers and dates, stretching back almost a year. Emily could smell strong male deodorant mixed with stale sweat and contemplated warning him he was invading her space. She didn't. Instead she asked an obvious question.

"Why do some flights have three cabin staff, others only two?"

"Good question. All down to Civil Aviation Authority rules. For a flight with fewer than fifty passengers only one flight attendant is required. Between fifty and one hundred it's two, between one hundred and one hundred and fifty it's three, and so on."

"Does it depend on seats or passengers?"

"Another good question."

Emily bristled, but tried not to let it show. She found Mr Eriksson's manner patronising.

"Our A319 aircraft, that's the biggest we fly, was configured with 156 seats, but we took out half a dozen. Saves one cabin crew member per flight and when you're operating under tight margins that's a crucial saving."

He leaned over a little further, his suit brushing Emily's dress, stale cigarette breath almost making her gag, as he pointed out another column.

"These are the flight crew. A pilot and co-pilot and occasionally an extra officer if it's a training flight, or if a pilot is hitching a ride back to base."

Emily picked up the sheets of paper. "Can I keep these?"

"I'd rather you didn't."

"Why?"

"Data protection and all that. After all, you're not the police, are you? Crown servants. You're subject to UK law."

Emily stiffened once more, but Eriksson was correct. He knew his rights.

"Of course. Can I have five minutes to study the papers, please."

"Five minutes, Miss Stearn. And I trust you won't photograph the information."

She shook her head, Eriksson left and Emily searched her handbag for a notebook and pen. The relevant dates were etched in her memory and she swiftly cross-referenced them with the flight information, copying the names. She had barely finished when Eriksson returned.

"All good?"

"Yes, thanks for your help."

"Red Kite at your service. Always happy to assist the spooks."

A creepy sensation slithered along Emily's shoulders, but she summoned a forced smile, shook his hand, and hurried out into the fresh air.

After walking to the green by the Five Bells, she sat on a wooden bench with a gold plaque commemorating an elderly plane-spotting couple of yesteryear and phoned for a taxi. While she waited, she scanned her jottings, already having decided she could discount flight staff. Nothing in Andrei Reblov's record suggested he had undergone flight training.

The list of cabin crew comprised mostly women. But one name alone featured on every date, on every relevant flight. A man's name, jumping out at Emily, a pulse of electricity sending hairs on her nape erect. She stared at it for a minute or more. Adam Lewandowski.

"That's Tinman," she muttered. "I'm sure of it."

25

The taxi arrived within 20 minutes. Emily slid into the back seat, a jauntiness about her movement emanating from renewed clarity of thought and the certainty Lewandowski was the wanted man. Time was crucial. Assassinations were running at one a week for the last couple of months. No sign of Tinman stopping. They had to find him before he reached his next target.

It's a matter of law that when something needs doing and needs doing right now, then everything that can go wrong, will go wrong. Murphy's Law. Sod's law. Take your pick. Emily cursed Murphy and Sod, and anyone else she may have missed who had lent their name to an infuriating law, as her taxi ground to a halt on the M4 travelling into London, a snaking line of traffic ahead.

She heard indistinct chatter on the taxi's radio. The driver tilted his head, paused, still and concentrating, in the pose of a man listening to some distant sound, before relaying the news.

"Accident. Lorry and a petrol tanker. Only just happened, which is why it wasn't on satnav." He pointed at a billowing cloud in the near-distance, rising like cigar haze into the slate-grey sky. "Could be here a while."

Somehow, Emily held her frustration in check. She wanted to scream from the top of the London skyscrapers that seemed so close but in reality were hours away. *Why does everything always happen to me?* Instead, she fished in her handbag for her phone, punching in Sam's number. He answered on the third ring.

"Sam, can you do something for me?"

"What are you up to now?" Emily detected weariness in Sam's voice, as if the mention of her name was synonymous with another crackpot idea. The thought worried her. She didn't need people to like her, but she wanted them to, even if it didn't always seem that way.

"We need to check into a guy who works for Red Kite Airlines."

"I thought that was all sorted yesterday. We've moved on. Me and Andrea are looking into ties with Russian Mafia bosses. Where are you?"

"Stuck in a traffic jam, but we need to move fast, Sam. Tinman's nothing to do with Mafia bosses. He's working alone."

Sam was a trainee. He'd joined the Service alongside Emily, learning the job together, offering moral support, enjoying each other's company. They had formed a bond of sorts, although Emily's preference to go it alone whenever possible was not the best adhesive when it came to friendships with work colleagues. Sam was sharp and eager, an analyst of rare potential, but not one to flout authority.

"Emily, are you sure you should still be investigating Red Kite?"

"Yes, I spoke to McBride this morning. He gave me the go-ahead. I'm reporting my findings to him later this afternoon." She omitted the bit about McBride ordering she didn't involve other members of staff.

"What do you need?" A resigned sigh from Sam.

"Check out Adam Lewandowski." Emily spelled out the surname, repeating the latter half to ensure Sam included the second W. "He's a Polish steward with Red Kite Airlines. He worked on all their flights that flew to the assassination locations. Be discreet, Sam. Red Kite are reluctant to give up too much information but, if I'm right, a guy with the same name probably worked as a steward in Poland so we can check from that end."

"What if McBride or Scafell ask what I'm doing?"

"Just stall them until I get there."

"How?"

"I don't know. You're in the Intelligence Service, Sam, you're supposed to be good at subterfuge."

"I'm not a spy. I'm an analyst."

"That's why I'm sure you'll think of something."

She ended the call. A fire engine sped by on the hard shoulder followed by a police car and ambulance, blue lights flashing.

Emily slumped back in her seat, closed her eyes and pondered the next move. She decided on a calculated gamble. Flipping her notebook to the page on which she'd scribbled the Red Kite flight

113

information, she punched the company's contact number on her phone.

"Mr Eriksson please. It's Emily Stearn. I spoke with him earlier. He's expecting my call." A pause.

"Putting you through now."

"Eriksson here."

"Sorry to bother you again, Mr Eriksson. It's Emily Stearn."

"Forget something?"

"Making sure I've no loose ends, that's all."

"Go ahead."

"The last flight on the list you kindly compiled for me. Flight number RK7095."

"What about it?"

"Can you tell me its next location, please?"

"That's easy, should be landing about now. Paris."

"Which airport?"

"Beauvais."

"Is that actually in Paris?"

"A short ride away."

"How short?"

"Around 50 miles, only an hour or so." Emily detected Eriksson bristling at her questions. Red Kite, along with other low budget airlines, fielded increasing criticism for setting up low cost bases miles outside city centres while still advertising the city as their destination. Unwary travellers found themselves paying for expensive taxis or being funnelled into the queue for the airline's bus transport, handing more cash to another Red Kite revenue stream they were not expecting. It was sharp, albeit legal, practice.

"Just one more thing." Emily had plenty more questions but didn't want to push her luck. "Is there a return flight or will the plane be staying over in France?"

"Back this evening. Should be a tight turnaround. Don't do stopovers if we can possibly avoid them. Can't afford the hotel costs. We're not in the business of paying staff to live it up at our expense in exotic locations."

Beauvais? Exotic? That's what Emily wanted to say. Instead, she restricted herself to, "Thank you Mr Eriksson, very kind of you. Bye."

As she watched the smoke plume darken and an air ambulance arrive, circling in search of a landing spot, Emily pondered another conundrum. Who was Tinman's next target?

A possible answer surfaced as the bored taxi driver drummed the fingers of one hand on the steering wheel while turning up the radio volume with the other.

"The Prime Minister, defence minister and several Army chiefs today flew to Paris for talks over the next two days with the French president and German chancellor. They are expected to discuss NATO security along Russian borders and, in particular, more aid for Ukraine." The newscaster switched to financial news but Emily began to shake, gulping air, a wave of panic threatening to overwhelm.

"Shit." The profanity spilled from Emily's lips.

The taxi driver, resigned to making the most of an extended lunch break, slouched to an almost prone position, two more fire engines speeding by on the hard shoulder.

"Shit squared, if you ask me."

26

When she finally reached the office three hours later she was in a foul mood. It wasn't helped by stepping into the first available lift and spotting Savage's condescending smirk.

"I was just talking about you, Emily. Could you pop in and see me again later? I have a few more questions, if you don't mind."

Emily clenched fists. "Very well, but I think I've told you all I know."

"All you think you know. They may not be one and the same."

Savage's smirk irritated Emily. Her brain hurt. She had spent the last few hours in a stationary taxi piecing together cataclysmic scenarios involving the fates of high-ranking government ministers, including the Prime Minister. She had little patience for Savage's riddles, but she chewed her lip.

"Tomorrow morning, okay?"

"That'll do fine."

She squeezed out of the lift before the doors fully opened and detected animated expressions on Sam and Andrea's faces at their desks. They were comparing three photographs. One of them the dark-haired, sullen, brooding image of a pasty-faced Andrei Reblov, the picture that had dominated the big screen for days. The others were of two softer, smiley men with blond hair, blue eyes and healthy sun-tanned complexions.

"Who's this?" Emily pointed to the second image.

"That," said Sam, pausing for effect, "is your man, the Polish guy you asked us to check out. Adam Lewandowski."

"Are you sure?"

"Sure."

"One hundred per cent."

"Nothing's one hundred per cent, Emily, you know that, but pretty sure."

Sam and Andrea explained their investigations had discovered Adam Lewandowski worked as a cabin steward for Polish budget airline, Smartwings, until eight months ago. He was single without close dependents and had quit suddenly to take a 12-month sabbatical travelling the world by himself.

Sam couldn't hide an excited tremor in his voice. "I asked them if they had a photo on file and they fired over this." He fluttered the image. "But it gets better. The same Adam Lewandowski, or someone purporting to be him, joined Red Kite four months ago."

Sam jabbed a forefinger towards the third image. "We've blown this image up from a recent promotional picture online featuring Red Kite's cabin crew."

Emily's eyes squinted. "Good work. They look identical."

"Not quite." Sam held up the images of the blond-haired men. "This one," he pushed his left hand forward, "is the real Adam Lewandowski working for Smartwings." He thrust his right hand this time. "This one is Tinman in disguise, in Red Kite uniform."

"Are you sure?"

"I refer you to my earlier answer. Not one hundred per cent, but as near as makes no difference. We've put the images through FRT (Face Recognition Technology). The Polish guy and Tinman have similar characteristics but aren't a match. Tinman and the Red Kite steward had the machine lighting up like Oxford Street."

He held up the images again. "You're looking at the same man."

"Have you told McBride?

Sam spluttered, shaking his head. "No way. It's your baby, Emily. Your idea. For what it's worth, I think you've cracked it."

"So how do we explain it?" Andrea spoke for the first time and Emily was ready with her answer.

"It's obvious. Tinman does nothing without meticulous planning. He's not killing high-ranking officers across Europe on a whim. It's all part of a plan hatched over many months. Probably in the inner reaches of the Kremlin. He must have identified Lewandowski as an easy match to impersonate, probably when some Kremlin agent discovered the Polish steward was quitting to travel. The Russians must have eliminated the real Lewandowski, allowing Tinman to assume his identity a couple of months later."

Andrea's nose wrinkled. "Surely Red Kite would have done an identity check. Taken up references from Smartwings. That sort of thing."

"Maybe they did and doubtless Smartwings gave a wonderful reference. Sounds like this Lewandowski was a good worker but a bit of a maverick. The airline probably thought he'd changed his mind about travel plans and wanted to get back into the industry. We shouldn't underestimate Tinman's ability or his shrewdness."

"I agree," said Sam. "The sooner you tell McBride the better."

Ten minutes later Emily knocked on McBride's door, stomach churning for two reasons. One, she remembered the time she'd knocked and been thrown out before she'd even stepped across the threshold. She was determined that would not happen again. Two, she wanted her theory to be proved right but knew that would mean Tinman was on the brink of his most spectacular assassination.

Scafell opened the door. "Not now, Emily, we're in the middle of something." His voice almost a whisper, tone grave.

Emily could see past him, identifying Jack Easton and McBride, but couldn't place another man and woman.

"I'm sorry, Luke, this won't wait."

Scafell made to shut the door but Emily was ready for him, stomping her foot in the gap, wedging it as she had done with McBride, but this time pushing with such force that the door flew open, thudding against Scafell's shoulder. Three strides and Emily was in the middle of the room, leaning over McBride's desk, suddenly afraid and vulnerable, sweating, face burning red, the room glaring at her.

"So help me, Miss Stearn, this had better be good." McBride growled.

At first, Emily said nothing. Her hands trembled as she slid three photos out of a blue file and placed them in a row on the desk. A deep breath settled her nerves.

"This is the unholy trinity we've been searching for. Three men in one. Take a good look. I believe these are the faces behind all the recent assassinations."

The group assessed the photos in silence, Emily holding back, allowing them to absorb the images. For the first time since she had joined the Service, Emily felt comfortable in the presence of the office hierarchy. Her mind had assimilated the information of the last few hours. She had inspected it from all angles with the diligence she afforded every equation. The same answer kept recurring. A good sign. This was her domain and as she began to explain her theory the stress of the last few days thawed like melting snow.

For half an hour or more Emily held centre stage, gaining in confidence as the room absorbed and accepted her logical delivery. Lots of nodding and appreciative grunts. When questions came she was ready and persuasive.

"How does a cabin crew member of a budget airline find the time to go around killing people? They work to tight timelines, sometimes barely an hour on the ground before jetting off again." Easton was following his special forces training. Looking for flaws. Digging for inconsistencies.

"You're right." Emily consulted her file, pulling out a sheet of paper containing dates, times and flight numbers. "But Sam and Andrea have researched Lewandowski's work schedule on the day of each assassination. Some of the flights arrived at their destination in the morning with a return journey later that afternoon, giving the crew almost six hours' free time. Easily enough for a well-prepared professional hitman to find and eliminate his target."

She pointed to one particular flight, RK7490 to Rome, underlining the date.

"This is the day, or I should say, night, that General Mantelli was murdered. Lewandowski's flight arrived in Rome from the UK around noon and should have taken off on the return journey late afternoon, but it was delayed until next morning due to a mechanical fault. The crew stayed over in a hotel on the outskirts of Rome. Lewandowski, aka Tinman, had time, opportunity and as a resourceful operative he took it."

McBride, Scafell and Easton swapped knowing glances. For the first time the other woman piped up. She spoke with an American drawl, although her tone carried the same sharpness as the pins tying back her auburn hair in a tight bun.

"This is all very impressive, Miss Stearn. But what we need to know is where Lewandowski, or Tinman, is now and what, or who, is his next target? We have reason to believe ..."

"Paris," blurted Emily.

"Pardon."

"Paris. In France."

"I know where Paris is. Are you sure?"

McBride jumped in. "I should have said, this is Monica Stratton from the CIA. We've been co-ordinating intelligence in light of a credible threat to the Prime Minister." Emily had never met anyone from the CIA. She nodded nervously.

"Are you sure about Paris?" Stratton repeated the question.

"Yes. Lewandowski's flight landed a couple of hours ago."

"When does it return?"

"This afternoon, I think."

A knock on the door. They all turned as Sam walked in.

"Sorry to interrupt, but I think you'll want to know this."

"What is it?" McBride barked.

"I've spoken to Red Kite Airlines and Adam Lewandowski requested a two-day stopover in Paris to visit relatives."

"Holy crap." The CIA lady put her hands to her forehead. "We were right. He's planning to take out the PM."

27

It was one of those balmy summer evenings that enhance Paris's reputation for enchantment.

In the distance, lights twinkled invitingly on the Eiffel Tower while the River Seine rolled by, lapping gently against the lichen-covered bank, reflections shimmering in a thousand directions. A man sat at a corner table on a rickety terrace, a half-carafe of red wine in front of him, alongside the bony remnants of a fish dish. He toyed with a cigarette, twirling it in his fingers but with no intention of lighting. The evening was still young, the restaurant not yet half full, the ambient air heavy with the sweet smell of candy floss floating from a nearby kiosk.

"Finished, Monsieur Adam?" said the waiter. The man didn't reply at first, instead taking a measured sip of wine. When he spoke his accent confounded accurate detection, a European hybrid laced with harsh guttural edges, but his French was fluent.

"Tell me, Antoine, why do they call it Pont du Garigliano?" He motioned towards the dark metal bridge to his right, where a massive barge silhouetted against a rising half-moon was navigating a tentative route through one of the arches.

"The bridge is named in memory of a victory by a famous French Army General." Pride bubbled in Antoine's tone. He had clearly told the story many times.

"Who?"

"Alphonse Pierre Juin. The general won a great triumph at the Battle of Garigliano in Italy in 1944, and he was later made Marshal of France. He was also one of NATO's top commanders."

"How interesting."

"Unfortunately, the bridge is also famous for a grisly reason."

"Tell me more." The man seemed genuinely intrigued.

"It's the highest bridge in the city. Eleven metres above the Seine. Quite a drop. In recent times, those trapped in a wretched frame of mind have found themselves drawn to it."

"You mean suicide?"

"Yes, Monsieur Adam. Suicide. In 2006, Boris Fraenkel, a famous Communist politician, took his life here. Many more did so before him and there have been several since." Antoine pointed out the spot where Fraenkel died at the far side of the bridge, the river swirling around the supports, ready to suck more hapless souls into its depths.

"How dreadful."

The waiter stacked plates, cutlery and a bread basket, using a napkin and knife to collect crumbs from the tablecloth. His work neat and meticulous.

"Would you care for dessert, Monsieur. A coffee maybe?"

"I'm afraid your story has curtailed my appetite, Antoine. I'll just finish my wine, thank you. It's quiet tonight. Will I see you tomorrow?"

"No, Monsieur."

"Day off?"

"Not exactly. I'm serving at the palace tomorrow." The waiter's eyes danced a conspiratorial jig. He leaned closer into the table so none of the other diners could hear, yet was careful not to brush any stray blobs of butter with his pristine white cuff.

"The palace?"

"Yes, the Palace of Versailles. A big dinner for presidents, prime ministers and other dignitaries. I'm one of the trusted staff enlisted when they need extra help."

"I'm not surprised, Antoine. You're one of the best. You must be very proud." The waiter stood tall, puffing out his chest a fraction as he accepted the compliment.

"You mustn't tell anyone." The waiter's hushed tone carried a trace of anxiety as if regretting his revelation.

The man shook his head before whispering, "Your secret's safe with me." He didn't mention that he already knew many of Antoine's innermost secrets. Where he lived alone in a Paris flat. That he was recently divorced and had undergone a kidney transplant two years ago. Most pertinent, that extensive security checks had cleared him as a reliable and honourable employee to serve occasionally at state occasions.

"What time do you get off work tonight?"

THE HIT LIST

"Around 11pm," said Antoine. "Been here since noon. I'll be going straight home to bed and sleep."

"Sweet dreams." The man rose, tipping his wineglass in an impromptu toast before draining the contents. He slung a rucksack over his back, slipped a 100 Euro note from his wallet and left it on his side plate, anchoring it with loose change.

"Thank you, Monsieur Adam. Very generous."

Three hours later, Antoine ambled along Victor Boulevard in the direction of Porte de Versailles. Normally, he cycled to and from work, occasionally took the tram, but the forecast was set fair and part of his recuperation from kidney problems required plenty of walking. He passed the Ministere des Armees, turning left into Rue de Hameau, where he rented a second floor flat. It was a quiet quarter, near the Expo dome, a huge hall in which rock stars occasionally performed, but away from the incessant bustle of central Paris. One of the capital's ubiquitous scooters raced by, the vroom of its engine cannoning sharp and grating against the tall buildings either side. Dropping into the wine bar across the way for a relaxing calvados crossed Antoine's mind. Most nights he would have succumbed to temptation, never more than one as his medication precluded too much alcohol, but he decided against it. The weariness of a protracted day weighed heavy and he required rest. Tomorrow would be a late one.

The sky was dark, clouds having wiped away the moon, the balmy evening taking on a clammy feel. He fumbled for his keys, struggling to find the lock before finally connecting, the huge wooden outer door of the apartment building creaking open.

Climbing stone stairs, he waved his arms to trigger the motion-activated lamp. Nothing. Bulb blown again. He stored a mental reminder to speak with the caretaker. Movements tentative, groping for the familiar bannister, he edged his way up the stairs, narrow slits of light escaping beneath the doors of neighbouring apartments casting sinister shadows. He could hear music, the faint strains of Vivaldi if he wasn't mistaken, accompanied by muffled peals of laughter.

Reaching number five, he bent over, caressing the door with his fingers in the manner of a safecracker, trying to locate the lock.

The key eventually slid, turned, and he staggered backwards, already choking. He tasted blood, lots of it, filling his throat, ears popping and ringing, eyes bulging as if to burst. A soft, gurgling sound emanated from his throat as the cheese-wire sliced through the carotid arteries. His legs kicked and jerked for a few seconds, but he felt no pain. Instead, a curious, hot, dizzy sensation as he slipped away down a dark tunnel on the road to oblivion.

The man caught him as he fell, supporting him with his right arm while his left hand juggled with the key. Tinman let himself in. First part of the job complete.

28

Jack Easton had the cut of a man who knew how to deal with most things. When Emily first met him in the operations room he hovered on the periphery of the action. A watching brief. There to make up the numbers, to keep special forces in the loop in the unlikely event they may be needed. He had stayed mostly silent, appearing, if anything, slightly embarrassed by his own presence.

Now he stood centre stage, resembling an experienced medic approaching the scene of a car accident. His jaw jutted, head nodded, taking in every angle, blue eyes narrowing as he assessed priorities. The camouflage hue of his battle dress uniform gave his demeanour an added sense of urgency and purpose.

Everything known about Tinman, pictures, contacts, preferred weapons, shone from the screen on McBride's wall. Scafell, McBride, the CIA lady and two other officers sat around the desk. Emily was also there. Easton had requested her presence on the basis she had researched Tinman's itinerary in minute detail over the past weeks, tracking him to Red Kite. More than anyone, she had a feel for his recent movements.

The revelation that Tinman may already be in reach of the Prime Minister concerned Easton. There was no time to waste, the need for speed and decisive action obvious, but in the soldier's world methodical planning remained paramount. Easton's credentials as a hunter were impeccable. Schooled in counter-terrorism, his regiment had chosen him among an elite force ordered to capture or eliminate 200 British jihadis, bound for acts of terrorism in the UK after the war in Iraq. Following the Manchester Arena bombing in 2017 he hid in plain sight on the streets of the UK's big cities for more than a year, disguised as a homeless person, hunting down would-be terrorists. The intelligence he gained led to the capture of a dozen individuals thought to be planning suicide attacks.

Easton had also spent more hours in the special forces' *killing room*, where live ammunition was used in close-quarters training, than any other soldier. His experience put the task at hand in sharp focus, yet he was taking nothing for granted. Eliminating young, impressionable, radicalised fanatics was one thing. Taking out a hardened, resourceful professional such as Tinman quite another. Even so, a tingle of excitement ran up Easton's spine. As head of G-Force, a highly secretive, mobile and acute arm of special forces, set up primarily to support intelligence operations, this was what all that training was for.

"Where's the most likely killing zone? That's what we have to predict." The tone was earnest as Easton laid out a detailed map of Paris on the desk. He plucked a pen from his top pocket and scrawled three circles, two in central Paris, one in the south. Drawing a line linking the three locations, creating a triangle, he jabbed his pen at the top circle.

"This is the Elysee Palace where the PM is meeting the French president for talks. Guarded by elite staff, armed to the teeth. The area is dense, escape routes uncertain, easily sealed, and bodyguards will surround the PM at all times. We can dispense with this location."

The CIA lady wore a perplexed frown. "Can't we cover all locations?"

"No." Easton dismissed the notion with a curt shake of his head, stretching over to point out the next circle.

"Why not?"

"Because we have less than 24 hours to react. Our mission isn't to protect the PM and his entourage. That's for others. Our aim is simple and focused. Find and eliminate Tinman. We'll need the French on board and there's no way they'd agree to flooding Paris with armed British special forces."

McBride intervened. "The Foreign Office is on the case. Clearance for a small elite force should be forthcoming within the hour."

"How small?" Scafell weighed in.

"Four officers, including me," said Easton.

"Is that enough?"

"If we locate the correct killing ground, then four is more than enough. Makes movement and communications simpler."

Easton pointed out the second location in the city's 7th arrondissement. "This is the Hotel de Matignon, the official residence of the French Prime Minister. It's where the PM and the Defence Secretary will be staying tonight and tomorrow. Again, it's in a densely populated area. The building is difficult to breach, easy to defend, especially when you consider the number of security personnel on duty."

Finally, he pointed to the most southerly circle. The Palace of Versailles. "A vast sprawling estate with acres of space and a multitude of entry points. This is the venue for the state dinner, a social occasion with many guests, although important speeches are also planned. This should be our target."

"But it's a fortified building like the rest," said Scafell.

"Not like the rest. For much of the year it's open to the public. People wander around the gardens, admire the fountains, marvel at the treasures and artwork. It's full of soft spots."

Emily had listened in silence. The strategic details of such a mission lay outside her domain, but she knew Tinman. She'd studied him to the point of obsession over the last two weeks and was beginning to understand his thought processes. Emily worked in probabilities. The more she learned the more she recognised Tinman bore the ruthless attitude of a professional gambler. Rejecting uncalculated risks, dealing only in certainties. Pitching up at a fortified building surrounded by guards was not how Tinman operated. His planning was subtler, more sophisticated. To date, his killings had benefited from an element of surprise, anticipating moments of weakness. General Parker at his summer home, Claudio Mantelli strolling unprotected in public view, Admiral de Bruyne poring over notes in the back of a car at an unguarded location. Even Mason Jones, distracted by a bogus accident, unarmed, out in the open.

Easton detected Emily computing the odds.

"What do you think?" He fixed her with his steady gaze, firing out the question.

"I'm not sure I should …" Emily's natural diffidence surfaced.

"You've studied him. What would he do? Where may he strike?"

Emily slowly stretched an arm, finger pointing to the Palace of Versailles.

"Why?"

"Not because of the building, although I agree it's vast and unfathomable, but because tomorrow night's dinner is a social event at which the PM is giving a speech. A speech most likely outlining support for Ukraine and all European countries threatened by Russia. There will be hundreds of guests, many staff and opportunities. Things don't always run to time at such events, plans become disorganised. Tinman is a master of cutting through the chaos, spotting the soft target, taking advantage of his surroundings."

"Exactly." Easton seemed surprised but energised by Emily's keen grasp of the situation.

Scafell piped up. "How do you intend to deploy your force, inside or outside the palace?"

"I can't and won't share operational details here, but it's safe to assume we'll be inside and out."

"But there'll also be the French police," replied Scafell. "And the president's bodyguards, the PM's personal bodyguards and no doubt half the GIGN."

"GIGN?" Emily looked bemused.

"The Gendarmerie Intervention Group." McBride pitched in helpfully. "They're a special French force trained to deal mainly with hostage situations but, with Tinman on the loose, I expect they'll have a presence in Paris over the next few days."

"That's my point," said Scafell, a derisory edge in his tone. "Tinman will know all that. Is he reckless enough to wade into an event that has every chance of turning into a trigger-happy shit-show? We have a saying. Too many spooks spoil the broth."

Easton pondered for a few moments. "You're right. When everyone carries a gun, confusion can lead to unforeseen consequences. Friendly fire's always possible. But maybe that's Tinman's opportunity. Perhaps he's planning to spread confusion and capitalise on it. Whatever he does, we'll be ready."

McBride raised his hands, palms outwards, drawing a line under the meeting. "Okay, think we've heard enough. Depending on

Foreign Office approval, Versailles sounds like a plan, Jack. We'll supply all the back-up we can. Satellites. CCTV monitoring. We'll liaise with the French and we have guys on the ground you can call on if needed."

McBride's voice lowered to its deepest register as he scanned the room. "And, of course, Section Seven applies. Written authorisation will be forthcoming."

Eyes met, but no one spoke. Everyone knew what Section 7 meant, even Emily, although it was the first time she had heard the phrase used operationally, permitting agents of the Service to break foreign laws overseas without fear of UK prosecution. Effectively, it constituted a licence to kill, and McBride's mention of it suggested 'C' had already gained approval for the mission from the Foreign Secretary.

Easton nodded his appreciation, grabbing his jacket. "I have the go-ahead from my end. We'll be on our way within the hour. You'll need the communication code to access our radio frequency."

"What is it?" said McBride.

Easton slipped McBride a piece of paper which read, *Red spy at night,* although neither of them shared the code with the rest of the room.

"Very droll," said McBride.

The meeting broke up, McBride and Scafell staying to run through logistics while Emily wandered back to her desk. She experienced a strange and confusing feeling of deflation. Neither on the inside, nor the outside. Shackled by secrecy from mentioning anything about the active hunt for Tinman, yet no longer part of the inner circle tracking the progress of that search.

Her job was done, although somehow it didn't seem that way.

29

Antoine sat motionless on a high-backed kitchen chair, face set in a vague rictus grin, eyes open, head still and upright.

Tinman had strapped the waiter's body to the chair with duct tape, placing a rod fashioned from a broom handle behind its back to keep it rigid. Then he had raided Antoine's fridge, drinking a couple of beers while waiting for nature to take its course. The first signs of rigor in the small facial muscles surfaced after around two hours, purple-blueish blotches appearing due to the collection of blood in skin vessels. Tinman checked every so often, but he was in no hurry. Rigor would steadily progress to the limbs over the next eight hours and he knew it was easier to work on a stiff corpse.

He busied himself searching Antoine's apartment, familiarising himself with the waiter's daily routine. Copies of L'Equipe overflowed the newspaper rack, a Paris St Germain baseball cap hung on a hook near the front door. Antoine obviously enjoyed sport.

The fruit basket brimmed with oranges and apricots, bananas ripened on a window sill. A heady aroma emanated from a sliced clove of garlic, while the kitchen cupboard revealed vegetarian options including packets of Quorn mince. A healthy person's kitchen, or at least that of someone determined to live more frugally for health reasons. In a desk draw in the tiny office Tinman found Antoine's medical records. Thick folders of them. Some going back decades. One plain white piece of paper on top revealed his date of birth, August 30th, 1980, as well as his health insurance details, recording his kidney transplant at Saint-Louis hospital in Paris two years ago. Another paper revealed he would need to take a combination of immunosuppressant drugs for the rest of his life, a prescription nearby containing scrawled requests for tacrolimus and cyclosporine.

Tinman absorbed the information, realising the slightest fact could prove vital. He reached under the folders, moving his fingers in a sweeping motion until they detected a plastic card. A carte vitale. A green plastic card bearing Antoine's photo, embedded with a chip containing his name, address, and social security details, denoting Antoine was eligible for free French health care.

It was useful and Tinman slipped it into his pocket, but he was hunting for a different plastic card. He moved on to the wall cupboard, swinging the doors open, so packed that a tennis ball rolled out and bounced across the wooden floor. Meaningless bric-a-brac filled the shelves, as if hiding something more important. A cunning trick, but not one to deceive Tinman. He lifted out the contents, taking care not to send anything else clattering. A small electronic steel safe nestled in the corner of the cupboard, bolted from the inside to the wall behind.

Ripping it from the wall crossed his mind, but that would involve a sledgehammer, several meaty blows and banging noises that would alert neighbours. Even then, it would take a steel cutter that he didn't have, to gain access to the contents. Tinman needed the combination. He returned to the office desk, sifting through the drawers. Despite warnings to the contrary, most people write down passwords, access codes and combinations, the churn of daily life too hectic and cluttered to retain abstract information. Either that, or they use the same code for multiple devices. The safe required four digits.

Tinman began with the obvious, Antoine's birth year gleaned from his medical records. He punched in #1980# and tried turning the lock. It didn't budge. The safe reset and this time he jabbed the day and month. #3008#. A long beep, the door jerked open. A quick glance was all it took for Tinman to discard a sheaf of bank statements, old cheque stubs and insurance letters. He rifled through the remaining contents, alighting on a plastic bag tucked under a small ipad.

The bag contained a leather wallet packed with an impressive array of bank cards and around 500 euros in large notes. Underneath the wallet, lying on top of an envelope, sat a lanyard, ribbon fashioned in blue, white and red bands. Attached to it dangled a white plastic card, containing a photograph, the name

Antoine Louis Dubois and the words, 'Authorised by the Ministere de L'Interieur'.

This was what he was searching for. He slipped a letter out of the envelope. Emblazoned on top was the official stamp of the Ministere de L'Interieur. The letter contained everything Tinman required. The date and time, 8pm, of the dinner at the Palace of Versailles, the number 15 Trianon gate where staff needed to report two hours before, the name of the manager in charge of catering, Monsieur Charles Moreau, and, most important, the security details. No jewellery, watches, rings, or metal objects were to be worn, mobile phones and bags not permitted. Pacemakers or metal medical pins needed to be declared beforehand. Staff were required to arrive in the uniforms provided, bring the letter with the official stamp, and sign in at the same time security scanned their passes. Metal detectors, body scanners, CCTV, and sniffer dogs, would be in operation.

Tinman smiled. How kind of the French authorities. They were making life easy for him. He cracked open another bottle of beer and slumped into the soft leather armchair. Within five minutes he was asleep, a deep slumber. Not of a man smug with arrogance, but of one confident he was smarter, better prepared, more meticulous, more focused and ruthlessly driven than any who may challenge him. It had always been that way with Andrei Reblov, ever since the car crash that wrenched his innocence and fuelled an anger inside which now dominated his dreams.

***

In the back of the car, little Andrei wipes the mist from the window with the palm of his hand. Like most young boys, Andrei loves the snow, especially when it falls thick and deep, smothering the land in a soft blanket of unsullied perfection. This is not such an occasion. The car's wipers are losing the battle against the worsening blizzard. Huge powdery snowflakes pepper the windscreen. Andrei's parents in the front are arguing again and the road home to Reutov, where his father Leonid is an expert scientist tasked with developing cruise missiles, is busy with all manner of vehicles. Andrei stares out of the window, the weather wild, mesmerising. A big, black car overtakes. Travelling too fast.

THE HIT LIST

As it passes, Andrei smiles and waves at the little girl in the back seat, younger than him but with wet rosebud lips and a face as sweet as honey. She waves back. The blizzard worsens and the rest of the journey becomes a blur. A maelstrom of headlights, blinding snow, a lorry's blaring horn, a woman screaming, the sensation of sliding, a sickening thud and the drip, drip of blood splattering on Andrei's twisted leg. The whiteness becomes blackness. Always blackness, anguish and regret, and a cold sense of futile loss, followed by a rage that he is certain can never be tamed.

***

Two hours later Tinman woke and checked on Antoine. The time was right and he went to work. He had chosen Antoine Dubois with his usual precision. The shape of the head, distance between the eyes and the contours of the features were not dissimilar from his own. Antoine's hair was darker and thinner, his eyes a different colour, but that would not prove a hardship.

Digging inside his rucksack, Tinman placed a tool kit on the kitchen top. Gelatine. Latex. Silicone. Chavant clay. Platsil gel. Plaster. Deadener. Medical grade adhesive and sculpting knives as well as sponges and cotton buds. Tinman preferred working with silicone whenever possible. Moulded pieces of durable silicone were almost as thin as skin, making it lifelike. The process of creating prosthetics that could fool colleagues and even family at close quarters was technically complex, but Tinman had mastered the technique over the years.

First he made a cast of his own face, resulting in a negative of his facial features. He filled the cast with plaster to produce a positive replica and began sculpting with sculpting clay. Antoine's forehead was broader, his nose larger. Tinman wielded his sculpting knife, taking minute measurements of Antoine's features, adding a bump to the cast of the nose, increasing the squareness of the chin, widening the forehead.

When he was satisfied he sprayed the mould with wax, poured in quick-curing silicone and left it to set. He returned to the leather armchair in the knowledge his prosthetic piece would be ready to colour and touch up with fine details when he woke up.

133

30

"Have you heard of Kim Philby?" Savage's question came from nowhere.

"Of course. Everyone has. He was Britain's most famous traitor. Well, after Guy Fawkes maybe." Emily's lips contained the faint hint of a sneer. The more she learned of Savage, the more she disliked him. He had the infuriating trait of a man who knew the answers to all the questions he asked, but asked them anyway.

"Oh, yes, Guy Fawkes. I'd forgotten about him. Devious, but not very clever. Wanted to blow up the King and the House of Lords." Savage cocked his thumb at the office window, pointing down the river in the direction of Westminster. "Philby wasn't so bloodthirsty, but by God he was dishonourable and potentially even more treacherous."

"More treacherous than killing the King?" Emily's eyes narrowed in a doubtful grimace.

"In my view, yes. Takes an industrial grade of betrayal to damage your country for as long as Philby did. The Soviets recruited him in 1934, and he started working for us in 1940, becoming a high-ranking officer, even serving as chief British liaison with American Intelligence? When suspected of spying, he resigned in 1951, but was publicly exonerated a few years later."

"Why?"

"Why what?"

"Why was he exonerated?"

"Good question. All boiled down to the fact that the department of spies wouldn't accept they could have been hoodwinked by a spy. Ironic, don't you think? No one wanted to admit that it had happened on their watch. Not very British. So Philby was paraded on television as an upstanding Cambridge graduate, a pillar of the community, his smug smile taking British Intelligence for fools. Not our finest hour."

"He defected to Moscow, didn't he?"

"Eventually. In nineteen-sixty-three to be exact, when he was finally unmasked as a Soviet agent after supposedly spying for us in Beirut. Nineteen-thirty-four to nineteen-sixty-three. That's a long time to be passing secrets to the enemy, a long time to be hoodwinking your friends and colleagues."

"Doesn't say much for British Intelligence." Emily wanted to snatch back the comment. She deemed it unseemly and overly judgmental, especially as her knowledge of espionage in the 1960s amounted to what she had gleaned from her Uncle Sebastian's diary and the odd James Bond film.

Savage nodded. "You're right, Emily. A sad chapter. A broken system. Blind faith. Call it what you will. The worst thing Philby did was make a mockery of the Service. That's why you have to put up with me and my questions."

"I'm not following." Emily blinked her lack of comprehension.

Savage wandered over to the picture window. A spirited breeze blew, wrenching at the flags on a passing tug boat. Making Emily nervous, he gazed in silence for several seconds as the early-morning sun cast a pale shimmer on the river, before returning to his seat.

"It won't happen on my watch." A determined tone in his voice. "When something smells fishy, in my experience there's usually a reason. It may be hiding behind the sweet stuff, but sooner or later your nose leads you to something, shall we say, not very savoury."

"I'm still not following."

"The shooting of Mason Jones. Can we go through that morning one more time?"

"But I've told you all I know."

"I'm sure you think that's the case, but since we last spoke new evidence has come to light."

"What new evidence?"

Savage rocked back on his chair, slid open the top drawer of his desk and took out a photograph. He planted it in front of Emily. The image was grainy, a high shot, capturing an overview of the junction at Portland Place. The image showed Emily, kneeling in the road, bent over Mason Jones who was pointing in the direction of the Post Office Tower. Emily peered at it for the best part of a minute searching for the relevance. Savage was infuriating, but he was also pernickety and meticulous. There must be something else. In the end, she asked the obvious question.

"Where did you get this photo? From the Chinese?"

"If only." Savage let the comment hang, before continuing. "We did explain the gravity of the situation to the Chinese, dodging around why we were really there. We're sure the Chinese know what was going on, but sometimes in this game it's in the interests of both sides to skirt around the truth. We're pretty certain the Chinese have clear footage, maybe even video footage of the incident. Their embassy has more cameras than a night at the Oscars, but they're hardly likely to release anything incriminating a Russian hitman on their doorstep at the exact moment they were serving lunch to a Russian delegation. We obtained this photo from the Polish embassy next door. It's taken from one of their rotating CCTV cameras, too far away for detail, a mere snatch of the action."

"I can't see anything relevant. It's exactly how I remember it."

Savage pointed to a fuzzy black-clad figure in the bottom left, half-way around the corner leading away from Portland Place.

"Hmm, not quite. We believe this is the shooter. Too indistinct to recognise. Too distorted to determine the gender, but that's not the point."

"What is?" Emily's brain was beginning to hurt.

"The point is the shooter appears to be escaping in exactly the opposite direction from where Mason Jones is pointing."

"But he said, 'She ran ...'" Emily's photographic memory kicked in, the upsetting details surging into her mind.

"Perhaps you were mistaken, after all."

A plug of bile hit the back of Emily's throat. She wasn't wrong. She couldn't be wrong. But the camera doesn't lie, not unless it has been rigged somehow, yet she could see no reason for the Poles, or Savage, or anyone, including the Chinese, to doctor the photo.

Her forefinger tapped under the desk. She fought a spasm of anxiety, while her mind filtered question after question. She pointed to the blurry image.

"Maybe it's the skateboarder."

"I wondered that, but your evidence was precise on both occasions we spoke. You were clear the skateboarder jumped up and sprinted away after the initial shot. He was first to escape which is why he's not in the frame. The shooter fled seconds later while you were clambering out of the van."

Emily's answer came in a whisper. "I don't know what to say."

"No one's accusing you of anything, Emily. You're still young and inexperienced, but you can see my dilemma."

"No."

Savage picked up a pen and began writing on his desk pad, doubtless a ploy to disconcert, driving home his point.

"If you were mistaken on the key issue of Mason Jones's last words and gesture, and by association the direction in which the shooter escaped, how can we give credence to any of your report? I should remind you that you were also convinced the shooter was a woman when all evidence now points to a Russian hitman well known to the Service."

Emily wanted to scream that it was her research and analysis that had discovered Tinman's alias, tracked him to Paris, where special forces were right now hunting him down. She knew she couldn't. It was classified information. But if Savage was right, what then? Emily had travelled a long way in her short time with the Service, making friends, trusting colleagues, feeling positive about her position in the world. But if she had botched her first major challenge, maybe she *was* in the wrong business. Her mind swirled. She felt as though she was stumbling towards a precipice. Tears fought to escape but she squeezed them back. Then, as if clutching a lifebelt, she remembered what Stephens had told her. *You have what it takes. Stick in there. Play the long game.* She heard his mellifluous voice in her head and a sudden implant of adrenalin provided fight and direction.

"I stand by everything I said in my evidence. It's my memory of what took place and I'm not taking any of it back." She snarled, eyes defiant.

"Very well, Emily. My report will go to your section chief. That's all for now."

Emily trudged out of Savage's office, legs stiff as iron girders, her heart heavy. No one was accusing her of anything, Savage had said. It didn't feel like that. It felt the exact opposite. With analysis on Tinman complete she had attended the meeting as a courtesy to Savage on her day off. Now all she wanted to do was go home to Al and cast the weight of the last few weeks from her mind.

As she checked through security, she caught the announcer's voice on one of the breakfast radio news channels.

"After a round of talks this morning on European defence and meetings with the French president and German chancellor this afternoon, the Prime Minister will attend a dinner at Versailles this evening where the keynote speech is expected to focus on ways to combat Russian aggression."

For a brief moment she paused, a chill descending, her whole body shaking with apprehension.

31

He woke early, ate a bowl of muesli, and settled down to work.

Tinman had learned down the years that when applying make-up as disguise it was always wise to set aside at least twice as much time as originally thought. Detail devoured the minutes, stretched the hours. There were so many intricacies to consider. The blending of colour, not fixed and solid, but mottled and lifelike. The application of flat moulds, fashioning a bump here or there, flattening out a feature, covering a scar or skin flaw.

First, he dealt with the hair. As Adam Lewandowski, Tinman had worn his hair longer and dyed it blond. Now he needed to revert to his natural dark brown colour, almost identical in shade to Antoine's.

He dug in his rucksack, locating a bottle of hair dye and filler. He knew from experience that he couldn't simply apply brown dye onto blond locks, not unless he wanted a green, muddy effect, that would have been a red flag to security staff. He applied the filler, letting it penetrate deep into the hair structures to create a base for the final dye. While he waited for the filler to dry, he worked on colouring the prosthesis. With Antoine staring back at him, eyes fixed and stern, in the attitude of an accusing barrister, he gauged the hue of the skin on his face and neck, a couple of shades darker than his own. A handsome corpse, Tinman thought. He noted the weal under the right eye, scar tissue from a childhood accident. A small brown birthmark on his cheekbone. All required insertion on the prosthesis, Tinman warming to his work with the pride and dexterity of a creative artist on the Left Bank.

When he finished he trimmed his dry hair to the right length, shaving carefully at the temples where Antoine's hair had begun to recede. Then he applied the brown dye. An hour and a half later when it was dry he began fixing the prosthesis in position with the medical-grade adhesive, smoothing the seams until they were unnoticeable.

When it was fixed he dug again in his rucksack, this time pulling out a long slim case full of contact lenses. Reaching for a mid-brown shade, he slid them in. He could hear the stirring tones of La Marseillese playing somewhere in a distant apartment and hummed the tune as he traipsed to the bedroom to grab a wall mirror. He returned, laid the mirror on the kitchen top, went around the back of Antoine's chair and, cheek to cheek with the waiter, peered into the mirror. His professional eye studied the two faces for half a minute before he nodded approval.

"That'll do nicely," he muttered, patting Antoine on the shoulder. "Sorry, comrade, but it had to be you. We're like brothers. You were by far the best option."

It was still much too early to make for the Pont du Garigliano RER station to catch the trundler to Versailles. But, like an actor before a performance, Tinman was anxious to slide into character. To feel the role. To assume the persona of a Parisienne waiter. He ambled back to the bedroom, opened the wardrobe and took out a uniform. He had discovered it hanging there the evening before after reading the letter with the official stamp. Now came the crucial test. He undressed and put on the white dress shirt with decorative black studs acting as buttons down the middle. A little too short in the sleeve, but not too short that it would prove troublesome. Next, he wriggled into the black trousers. Perfect length, although fastening the waist button required Tinman to suck in his stomach and pull tight. Antoine's health problems had seen him shed a few pounds. The black jacket provided would not be required while working but the shoulders fitted snugly and would suffice for the journey. Finally, the black tie. Tinman had many skills, most of them displaying impressive hand-to-eye coordination. He could hit a target the size of a full stop in a daily newspaper at 30 metres with a pistol. Fastening a bow tie proved more troublesome. To be fair, he didn't have much cause to practice. He stood in front of the wardrobe mirror for 20 minutes, tying and untying the bow until eventually he fixed on a shape, not perfect, but one he deemed acceptable.

He paced the apartment, visualising a room full of diners, imagining the hum of conversation, remembering his training. A waiter's job had much in common with that of an airline steward but when, months ago, Tinman had identified a professional waiter as his target, he had sought the advice of his friend and former university colleague, Dimitri Fedorov, who worked as maitre d' at the White Rabbit restaurant in Moscow's Smolenskaya Square. As well as learning how to skin a fish, he had brushed up on the correct protocol to lay tables, setting up linens, silverware, cutlery and glasses. He could also present a menu professionally, providing detailed information about portions, ingredients and potential food allergies, although he remembered Dimitri's advice, "All this is for nothing if you are not, in your heart, sociable and engaging." A strange combination, Tinman thought, when murder is also on the menu.

His operational mobile phone rang. A rare occurrence. There were only three people who knew the number. The Russian president, the head of FSB (the Russian security service) and Tinman's informant. The ID username came up as Koshka, the caller's codename.

Tinman crossed to the kitchen sink, turned on both taps and hissed into the receiver, "This is a bad time."

"You'll want to know this." Koshka spoke for close on a minute without interruption, after which Tinman put the phone down without a parting comment.

He pondered the call for several minutes before taking another look in the mirror and wandering over to the front door, seeking reassurance. The corridor was quiet, most of the neighbours at work in the middle of the day. Descending the stairway, he adopted the shuffling gait and the accommodating, kindly, almost serene expression, he'd studied in Antoine. He pulled open the heavy oak door, the bright light bringing tears to his eyes, clouding his contact lenses. An old lady, carrying two plastic bags, sticks of bread and other shopping threatening to spill, almost bumped into him.

"Antoine, thank you. Perfect timing. I couldn't find my keys. You off to work?"

"That's right. Work as usual." Tinman raised the pitch of his voice to Antoine's level.

"You're a saint. Have a good night."

"You too." Two thoughts crossed Tinman's mind. The first was pride, mixed with relief, that he looked the part for the biggest night of his career of terror.

The other? Even allowing for the brutal logic that propelled his warped world of justice and retribution, he wasn't, never had been, and never would be a saint.

32

Al didn't need any more clues to tell him something was wrong.

Emily had passed the half-eyed cat on the path without a glance. She never did that. Always stooped to give him a rub, letting him nuzzle up close, often with a few soothing words. Her conversation had been monosyllabic, not that unusual when work consumed her thoughts, but Al detected melancholy mixed with angst in her mood.

The clincher came when she turned down Al's offer of ground coffee and tiffin at the new coffee shop on the corner. Days off always included coffee and tiffin. They were Emily's umbilical cord with the real world, allowing her to relax. To listen to the gentle hum of innocent conversation, do a crossword together, escape the relentless pressure of work that drove her on, enriched her mind, but gnawed at her insecurities.

"What is it Emily?" Al's voice was soft, his tone caring.

"Nothing."

"Is it something at work?"

Emily stared through the patio windows at the bird feeder in the back yard where two blue tits bickered over the same square inch of seed, hopping, wings fluttering, scattering their meal onto the flagstones below. *Why can't we all share and share alike and live in peace?* She thought of Tinman, wondered where he was, what malevolent acts he had in mind this day. She thought of Savage, forever pecking over the incident in Portland Place. She understood he was only doing his job and accepted her account and the facts represented in the new photo didn't match. She trusted her memory, but the more she trawled through the events of the shooting the more uncertainties began to surface.

Al tried again. "Is it the day of the shooting?" He knew Emily couldn't and wouldn't talk about work, but Wilson had spilled the news that Emily witnessed the killing of Mason Jones. It was hardly a big stretch to deduce that her current mood may have something to do with that. No amount of training could shield a person, even one in the Intelligence Service, from the emotional trauma of witnessing a colleague gunned down. Al had worried about Emily these past weeks.

"Sort of, but not the way you think." Emily's voice faltered. Her whole life had seen her compartmentalise anxieties. Lock them away in a deep, dark place, hidden from scrutiny. Don't admit weakness. Never show emotion. A coping mechanism. "It's not the shooting itself. What's bothering me is not being able to understand the reason for it. Nothing makes sense. I'm sure I remember exactly what happened, but others see it differently."

She did not reveal details of Savage's investigation but told Al about the inconsistency in her account and the new picture that had come to light.

"Have you been back there since the shooting?"

"Portland Place?"

"Yes."

"No."

"I think we should. You have a great memory, Emily. I know that. But sometimes trauma can play tricks on the mind. Going back there may release something. May trigger a fresh thought. It may also give you some sort of closure. I think you need that. Don't, if you don't want to. I'm just saying what I would do."

A neighbour's dustbin lid banged and a couple of pigeons as well as the blue tits took to the sky. Emily thought for a few moments. "I think you're right, Al. Let's go."

An hour later they walked the short distance from Great Portland Street Tube station to the Chinese Embassy, Emily's stomach cramping as they approached the junction between Portland Place and Weymouth Street. They stopped by the bronze statue of Wladyslaw Sikorski, set on a plinth by a crossing on the central reservation, trees in full bloom lending the road a grand and pleasing ambience. Al read the plaque, commemorating the prime minister of the Polish government in exile during the Second World War, with interest. The statue was closer to the China building than the Polish embassy, which was 40 metres away, Polish and European Union flags fluttering above its entrance. Al scanned the rooftop for cameras. None were apparent but that meant nothing, modern surveillance technology was minimal and discreet.

They moved along until Emily became confident they were in the same spot the white van had parked, at an oblique angle of sight from the Chinese Embassy. She studied the road. It was nudging midday, the sun having broken through after a cloudy morning, raising the temperature. As she sniffed the air she detected a familiar warm smell of tarmac. Instantly, she was back sitting in the middle of the road, cradling Jones's head as his life ebbed. She'd read a magazine article in which eminent neuroscientists explained the close physical connection between smell and parts of the brain linked to memory and emotion. She'd been dubious, but the reality came as a jolt.

"There." She pointed to where Mason Jones had fallen. "Right there, I'm certain."

"How can you be sure?"

"The drain cover. See, there, Al." She pointed again. "I could see it as I held him, right in front of me, no more than two or three feet away. I don't know why I remember that, but I do."

"And which way did he point?"

"Towards the Post Office Tower. I remember catching sight of the top of it as I looked up to try to see the shooter."

"But the photo suggests he escaped that way?" Al pointed in the opposite direction, down Weymouth Street towards Marylebone.

"Yes."

"Why hasn't anyone investigating brought you back here before now?"

Al's question was obvious, simply put, but Emily had no answer. She had discussed the shooting with McBride and the team, with Savage on several occasions, as well as a routine interview with the Met Police, but not once had anyone suggested she revisit the scene. Maybe they wanted to spare her more trauma.

Traffic was light. Al waited for a lengthy gap in each direction before jogging into the road. He squatted on the drain cover, pointed his mobile phone down Weymouth Street and took a picture with the Post Office Tower in the frame. He returned at a jog.

"Anything come back to you?"

Emily shook her head. "Nothing new. But it was a good idea to come. I'm even more sure of what I saw."

Al fumbled with his phone, retrieving the picture he'd taken. He guided Emily along the pavement a few yards to benefit from the shade of the trees.

"That's it, almost perfect," said Emily, as she studied the photo. "I'm sure because that's all I could see of the Post Office Tower."

Al zoomed in and out of the street view, homing in on junctions and entrances to buildings. No idea what he was looking for, but exhausting every minute detail. Emily absorbed the scene too, but nothing new transpired, exasperation plain in her tone.

"Shouldn't we be looking at the other side of the junction. The side we now know the shooter escaped. This seems pointless."

"I'm just following the logic, Emily, the point being that Mason signalled in this direction. You're sure of that. I don't care if the shooter escaped some other way, Mason must have had a reason for doing what he did."

As always with Al, Emily couldn't fault the reasoning.

Five minutes later, Al stiffened. Emily sensed the formation of a theory and gazed at him expectantly.

"What is it?"

"I'm not sure. Maybe nothing."

He looked down at the photo, then up at the junction. He did so three times, zooming in on the foreground.

"Come on." He beckoned Emily.

They crossed the side road, turned towards the Post Office Tower, Al stopping after only a few yards in front of a street lamp, looking dead ahead as if searching for a clue on a treasure hunt.

"What is it?" Emily repeated the question.

"Remind me, Emily, what did Mason say when he pointed this way?"

"I've told you. 'She ran …' and then he …"

"I know, I'm sorry, I didn't want to bring that up again. It must be dreadful thinking about it, but I had a thought."

He pointed at the wall behind the lamp post in front of them. Easy to read, but high enough to deter casual graffiti, sat a billboard containing two advertisements. One promoted a summer exhibition at Earl's Court. The other, bigger, more colourful and prominent, advertised a concert at Wembley Arena. A familiar face with ginger hair smiled out of the ad.

"Ed Sheeran." The name hissed from Emily's lips. "What's he got to do with …?" And then it clicked. "Maybe Mason wasn't saying 'She ran …'. Maybe he was saying 'Sheeran'."

"That's exactly what I was thinking."

"But why? Why would your last words on God's Earth be the name of a pop star?" The sight of the billboard and the possibilities it presented flushed away Emily's angst and introspection. She was in the zone, mind sharp, searching for answers.

"It must be something relevant. Something vital. Maybe a clue," said Al.

"That makes sense."

"Was Mason a big Sheeran fan?"

"Don't know. He loved music. Pretty mainstream stuff from what I recall. Played in an orchestra back in Wales, too, I think."

"Not quite sure where this takes you, Emily. Perhaps float it by one of the bosses."

"Not likely. They already think I'm a fuck-up." Emily hardly ever used the F-bomb, preferring to abbreviate her profanities like text speak. That way they never appeared offensive, but she couldn't hold back, as if her bosses' opinion had been teetering on the edge of her tormented mind for weeks.

"I'm sure that's not true."

"Not all of them, but some do. I need to work out what this means before saying anything."

"Why don't you ask Mason's wife?

A thought struck Emily. A sad, inexcusable thought that made her shake with shame. It was almost three weeks since the shooting and not once had she contemplated visiting Imelda Jones to offer her condolences. The department had sent flowers and a sympathy card. McBride had met Imelda in her Camden home with a member of the Human Resources team, and a memorial was planned after the coroner released the body and allowed the funeral to go ahead. But Emily was the last person to talk to Jones.

The last person to cuddle and cradle him as he lay dying. The last living soul to feel his heart beating and blood pumping. Not once had she thought it may have provided some comfort for his wife to speak to her. To understand those final moments. To cherish the fact that he died in the embrace of someone who deemed him to be a good friend as well as a colleague.

Emily threw her arms around Al and hugged, so tight he felt his breath expel and ribs hurt. She buried her head in his chest and he sensed her convulse. No tears came, but dry sobs, racking her body, in turn bringing an emotional mist to Al's eyes.

"I'm going now, Al. I have to see her." She broke from the hug and Al detected determination, fresh purpose in the set of her jaw.

"Would it not be better to call first?"

"No, I don't think so."

"Do you want me to come?"

She shook her head. "No, thanks, Al, got to do this alone, I should have gone weeks ago." They walked back to the Tube station, Al heading home and Emily to Camden. On the way, Emily phoned Sam at the office to obtain Mason Jones's address.

***

Imelda Jones was a neat woman. Petite frame, fine features, freckled skin and mousy hair cut in a short bob. A tight mouth gave her a stern expression at rest, an unfortunate anatomical quirk, for when she smiled her face softened, an inner light promising fun and warmth. She hadn't smiled much lately, but when Emily introduced herself the light flickered.

"Mason's told me so much about you. Please ignore the mess." She ushered Emily into the small lounge which was not nearly as tidy as Imelda's appearance. Model cars and other children's toys littered the floor. A child's shoe lay on a coffee table, the remnants of a jam sandwich sat on a plastic plate on a settee while washing hung from a clothes drier. The room exuded a chaotic ambience. Emily wondered if two-year-olds always created such havoc.

"Archie's gone down for a nap. Gives me just enough time to clear up before it all starts again. Who'd be a mum?" Imelda tossed her head and flicked her eyes skywards before clearing a space on the settee for Emily to sit. "Anyway, how can I help?"

Emily didn't know where to start. She had expected a less generous welcome. Imelda had every right to feel suspicious. Details of her husband's death were still confused, the investigation ongoing. In normal circumstances police would have assigned a family liaison officer to keep her informed. The sensitive nature of the shooting and the potential compromising of national security meant that was not possible. Yet Imelda seemed accepting, as if being true to the life she shared with a member of the Secret Intelligence Service was what she knew and what he would expect.

"I was with him at the end." Emily blurted out the words, lowering her head, eyes fixed on the model of a petrol tanker on the carpet.

Imelda reached out and grasped her hand, squeezing tight. Emily was confused. She had anticipated hostility, not empathy and compassion.

"I'm sorry, it must have been awful," said Imelda. "But I'm glad you were there. It's comforting to know he was with someone who knew and cared for him."

"It was over very quickly. He didn't suffer. I wanted you to know that. That's why I had to come, Imelda. You know I can't go into any details but Mason was a great guy. I enjoyed talking to him. He doted on you and Archie."

A single tear escaped, rolling down Imelda's cheek, the mention of Archie triggering the realisation that he would never know or be capable of remembering his father. She snatched a tissue from a box on the coffee table, dabbed the tear away and sniffed. "Life has to go on. One day I'll tell Archie all about his dad."

"Did Mason like Ed Sheeran?" The question hung, odd, apologetic, somehow surreal and inappropriately mundane, in the void between them.

"Pardon."

"Ed Sheeran. Did Mason enjoy his music?"

"He liked all sorts of music." Emily's clunky delivery prompted Imelda's features to set in a suspicious frown. "Why do you want to know?"

"I'm not explaining myself very well, but one of the last things he said was *Sheeran*. I think it may be some sort of clue."

"A clue? A clue to what?"

"I'm sorry Imelda, I don't know, and if I did I couldn't say."

Imelda fixed Emily, damp eyes smouldering, the last phrase stabbing at her fragile psyche, years of wondering, waiting and worrying, bubbling to the surface in a snarl. "Can't say. Can't bloody say. You never can, you people. You're all wrapped up in a world of secrets you can't tell anyone, secrets that nobody gives a flying F about anyway. And whenever anyone asks, you never can say."

"I'm sorry, I didn't want to upset you."

"Are you married?" The question stark, creating a chilly void between them.

"No."

"Do you have a partner?"

"Yes."

"Do you think it's a good idea to have secrets in a relationship?"

"No."

"Welcome to my world. We were married ten years before Archie came along, most of them happy, but always there was something between us. Words unsaid. Actions never explained. A simmering tension. His bloody job." Imelda's tone was harsh, hands shaking, her demeanour transformed from the accepting widow she first appeared. She reached for a cup on the table, taking a slurp of water. Emily didn't interrupt, not because she recognised the importance of Imelda's impromptu outpouring of grief, rather because she struggled to handle sudden releases of emotion. Imelda continued. "I could tell when he was angry or frustrated. He tried not to let it show. Mason smiled a lot. Everyone thought he was a jolly chap. I'm not surprised you had lovely chats, but at home he wasn't always good at hiding his feelings. Sometimes, quite often lately, the feelings poured out. I'd get it in the neck, or he'd go quiet, all dark and moody, not talk for a week. Never an explanation. That was the hardest part. Because he couldn't explain it. He couldn't even talk about it. He wasn't allowed to. The Official Bloody Secrets Act. I was allowed to take all the flak, deal with his paranoias and obsessions, but never allowed to know why. The not-knowing wears you down."

Emily shuffled her feet, wondering if Imelda had finished. Yet, as suddenly as Imelda's thunder cloud appeared, it vanished.

"In there." Imelda composed herself and pointed to a large cupboard. "That's where he kept his music collection. All catalogued in alphabetical order. Mostly vinyl. He loved the hiss and the crackle."

"Can I take a look?"

"What for?"

"I don't know, something to do with Sheeran. It may prove helpful."

"He definitely had some of his albums. Not really my kind of music."

Imelda opened the cupboard and motioned for Emily to help herself while she went to check on Archie. It didn't take long for Emily to find Sheeran. Three albums in date order, each title conforming to Sheeran's mathematical theme. Plus. Multiply. Divide. She slid them out of the collection. Not knowing what she was looking for, she read everything, concentrating on the song tracks, hoping they may throw up something tangible. By the time she had pored over Plus and Multiply, Imelda had returned, her mood more relaxed.

"Can I get you a cup of tea?"

"No thanks, I'll be done shortly. Only one more to check." She held up Divide, with its stark division symbol on the front.

Imelda began clearing away toys. Emily slipped out the record, read all the tracks and scrutinised the sleeve. Nothing transpired. As she returned the record to its sleeve she felt resistance. Only slight, but enough to cause her to withdraw the disc and investigate. Slipping her fingers inside she felt paper stuck to the sleeve. She peeled off tape with her nails to reveal a slim white envelope. Sealed and resealed with transparent tape.

A message was typed in bold letters in the top left corner:

Secret and confidential. To be opened only by 'C'.

"Find anything?" Imelda had noticed Emily stiffen as she read the envelope.

"Not sure. It's a letter addressed to the Chief." She held up the envelope, pointing out the words at the top.

Imelda, teddy bear in one hand, mixer truck in the other, pondered for a few moments, as if wondering what her husband would have done. Finally, she concluded.

"You'd better do what it says."

33

The gates were constructed of gold and the chamber pots made of silver.

On the train to Versailles, Tinman read the palace guide included in Antoine's pack. The only essential information was the number of the gate to report to and the lay-out of the dining room and kitchens, details he had absorbed over the past few days. As a student of history, however, the contrasting reactions Versailles had provoked down the years intrigued him.

For some, the magnificent palace and its richly ornamental grounds were a glorious symbol of the absolute monarch, in particular Louis XIV who ruled France for 72 years. For others, the lavish building provided tangible proof of the waste and corruption that fuelled the flames of the French Revolution in 1789.

Tinman mused over the guide's picture of the impressive façade for several minutes, inevitably comparing the building to the Kremlin's grandeur, concluding that oligarchs and dictators were required to manage opulence and majesty for the good of the people. An official duty requiring dedication, even if those struggling for the next crust of bread did not always appreciate the nuances of the role.

He walked the short distance from the station to Versailles and, as he was in good time, paused to absorb the palace's beauty. Strolling around the perimeter, he viewed from different angles in the manner of a tourist, marvelling at the raised flower beds, the Swiss lake, the walkways, the fountains and paths decorated with statues and vases, bordered by hedges and shrubberies. For several minutes he appreciated the intricate gilding above the golden gates and atop the ornate boundary railings. The attention to minute detail appealed to his punctilious nature.

Yet all the while he was searching for signs of security, his sharp vision spotting three snipers on the roof, clad in black, one of them training a weapon on a distant object, the other two stretching legs, waiting for dignitaries to arrive.

Gendarmes were posted at potential entry points, some handling German Shepherd dogs, other police dotted strategically around the grounds. More than two hours remained before the scheduled dinner, but the palace already resembled a fortress.

Tinman ambled along to Gate 15 where four gendarmes scrutinised all comers. He joined a line of staff queuing to enter, all taking turns to pass through a metal detector. It resembled the familiar airline security, although without requirement to shed shoes or remove jackets. His heart pounded. Even Tinman, accustomed to danger and subterfuge, was not immune to the chemical process that betrays anxiety in most ordinary people. But he was adept at controlling it. He breathed deep and even, wearing a neutral expression. Once through the initial security, he followed directions to one of three entry points where a policeman, watched by three colleagues, ran a hand-held detector over his body. Another policeman performed a manual search before an official collected the letter of appointment, swiping his pass through another machine.

Tinman twitched as Antoine's face flashed up on a big screen. The danger point. Would his prosthetic artistry pass a professional's scrutiny? A policeman scanned the picture, glancing at Tinman three times for comparison before tying a 'Security checked' plastic bracelet to his wrist, then pinning a badge proclaiming 'Antoine Dubois – Waiter' to his shirt, and waving him through.

A young stewardess, dressed in the black uniform of a permanent member of the Versailles staff, waited beyond security to escort him to his place of work. Tinman chatted easily with her about palace architecture and the finery of the gardens as she led him to the Hall of Mirrors, the venue for the state dinner. They did not enter the famous hall, instead diverting down a parallel path leading to an ante-chamber where the event's waiters were gathering. The room was half full, a hum of conversation echoing around the walls as waiters who had met before at similar events reacquainted. Tinman hugged a wall, reading his guide, hoping no one recognised Antoine, but confident in his disguise if they did. Fifteen minutes later Monsieur Moreau, the catering boss, addressed the throng, which Tinman estimated numbered around 50.

Moreau had the fastidious demeanour of a consummate organiser. He went through the protocols, stressing the requirement for utmost discretion, congratulating everyone for their sartorial elegance, prompting a murmur of appreciation. White gloves, he said, must be worn at all times in the dining hall and would be provided from a sideboard at the back of the room.

Tinman was among half a dozen waiters allocated glassware duty, their task to ensure the crystal was presented unblemished, polished, sitting in its exact location. A wooden measure aided that purpose to the nearest millimetre. He was engrossed in his work when the head waiter asked him to visit the kitchen to collect condiments. He sensed an opportunity.

Following the instructions in his guide, Tinman tracked along the corridor towards the kitchen, located so far away from the main hall that delivering hot food presented a challenge. He noted a sign for Gate 10 and committed the route to memory. When he arrived at the kitchen, the room appeared close to bedlam. An array of chefs worked at different stations, each supervising staff, preparing vegetables, washing salad, basting huge sides of beef and lamb. Already, pans were bubbling on stoves, steam was rising, as were tempers, a young lad feeling the lash of the head chef's tongue.

"Espèce d'idiot! Come here, boy, this isn't good enough." The head chef held up a ragged slice of beef. "We can't serve this to the president. It looks like a dish rag." The lad left his station where he had been cutting meat, eyes cowed. Other kitchen staff tried to look busy but secretly stared from lowered eyes as the head chef threw the boy's work in the bin and reassigned him to more menial duties. Tinman had spied the discarded meat knife, lying on the kitchen top, blade bloody and greasy. Glancing to check he wasn't being watched, he plucked a napkin from a cupboard to his right before deftly swiping up the knife, wiping it clean, then slipping it inside his sleeve.

155

He collected the condiments' tray and was returning along the corridor when a voice barked from behind.

"Stop! You there. Stop!"

The knife slid slickly into the palm of Tinman's hand.

34

Whenever Emily, or Al, had a decision to ponder they always seemed to end up at Cheap as Chips in Camden, a café cum coffee shop more cultured than its name suggested. A haunt of poets and songwriters, popular with students, bare brick walls advertising the area's art and music events.

Emily bought a skinny latte, found a table in a quiet corner and stirred in a lump of sugar. The white envelope, unopened in her handbag, consumed her thoughts. What may it contain? Did it hold any secrets to the shooting in Portland Place?

The fact that it was hidden and addressed for 'C''s attention only, suggested it was sensitive. Mason Jones wouldn't have known 'C', probably never been in his company. Why wasn't the letter addressed to McBride, Jones's section chief, or one of the directors? That would have been the logical chain of command. Emily's mind fizzed with possibilities. Did Jones have doubts about the department? She knew he was critical of how the Service had evolved in recent years. He'd voiced his fears in the van in Portland Place. Too much watching and waiting, too much emphasis on transparency, not enough covert action. A Service too often inert in the face of Russian aggression. He had been coy about the extent of his frustrations, but they dripped out nonetheless. Maybe the letter voiced those concerns. Perhaps he was waiting for the right time to hand in the letter. Such criticism would have changed his life forever, perhaps seen him lose his job. But would it have crossed his mind to reveal the clue to a letter about the Service's direction of travel moments after staring down the barrel of a gun? As his blood formed a puddle on a London street? Surely not. The Sheeran clue in his dying words had to point to something bigger than mere office politics.

Emily sipped her coffee, wrestling with doubts. What if the letter was critical of 'C'? She had done good work tracking Tinman, but the department believed she was wrong in her recall and analysis of the Portland Place shooting.

She needed advice. And then she remembered. Cheap as Chips was located two streets away from where Scafell and Leanne lived. Leanne had pointed out their house on the visit to Primrose Hill, although Emily had seen little more than a mish-mash of different coloured roofs. But they had swapped addresses on meeting at St Pancras station. It was mid-afternoon. Scafell was scheduled for night duty, wouldn't be in until seven at the earliest to support Easton and his team with surveillance and communications logistics in Paris. He would know what to do. How best to approach 'C' with the letter.

She felt more positive, a weight lifting as she drained her cup to the gritty dregs. Five minutes later she knocked on Scafell's door.

Leanne's welcome was even warmer than she anticipated. She almost sang Emily's name, elongating the three syllables in musical fashion, enveloping her in a hug normally reserved for old and devoted friends, before leading her through to the kitchen diner.

"What a surprise. How lovely to see you, are you here to see me or Luke? Say me."

Emily laughed. "Both of you, of course, but I do have a couple of work questions for Luke."

"I knew it, never mind, we can have a catch-up too."

Leanne called upstairs and Scafell came pounding down, his heavy tread shaking the stairs, vibrations reverberating around the walls. It was a small, two bedroomed, semi-detached house. Emily remembered Leanne describing it as a cottage but that stretched reality. It appeared functional rather than quaint, although the tiny back yard full of pots and hanging baskets resplendent with colourful blooms offered the scent and ambience of a cottage garden. A narrow alleyway led to the main road and Emily could hear the drone of passing traffic a little too close for comfort. But it was home, in a convenient location, Leanne's pride evident in the smell of polish and pristine arrangement of ornaments and artwork.

"Welcome to Scafell Manor. To what do we owe the pleasure," said Scafell.

Leanne immediately scolded him. "Can't a friend drop in for a catch-up?"

"Of course, but you know me, I cut to the chase."

"I need a spot of advice." Emily's tone was plaintive. She looked uncomfortable for a moment or two, her eyes flicking between Leanne and Scafell. "Erm …"

Scafell laughed. He turned to Leanne. "I think she means, as they say in America, can we have the room, darling?"

Leanne chuckled, scooping her laptop from the table before wandering through to the lounge, closing the door softly behind her.

Scafell motioned Emily to sit opposite him at the breakfast bar. "Hope it's nothing too serious. What can I do for you?"

"I think it might be serious. I'm not sure."

"Fire away."

Emily proceeded to tell Scafell about revisiting Portland Place, her doubts over the details of the shooting, Al's theory about the Ed Sheeran advertisement, finishing with her trip to see Imelda Jones. She thought she detected amusement in the way his eyebrows lifted once or twice, while a hint of a smirk played on his lips.

"Don't you think it's time to let it drop, Emily? Accept you may have been mistaken. After all, Tinman is long gone from Portland Place. Tonight he may pitch up in Paris, we may get lucky and you'll have played your part."

"I know that, but this isn't about Tinman."

"What's it about?"

"I found something at Mason's."

"What?"

"A letter."

"You're losing me. A letter about what."

"I don't know, but it was addressed to 'C', marked secret and confidential. Only to be opened by 'C'. I found it in one of Mason's record sleeves … an Ed Sheeran album."

Scafell rubbed his chin. "It could be Mason playing cloak and dagger. You know he wasn't happy with the department. Saw ghosts and demons in every dark corner. Thought 'C' was too soft and the Service going to hell in a hand cart. What did his wife say?"

"She said take it straight to 'C'. What do you think?"

"Not sure that's a good idea."

"Why not?"

"The mood Mason was in lately, who knows what or who he may have pointed the finger at. He could have taken against any one of us. Accusations are easy to make, much more difficult to disprove. Mason was paranoid and delusional."

"That's a bit harsh." Emily struggled to equate the man she conversed with about the beauty of music, the warming glow of family and the wonder of little Archie these past three months with the unstable individual Scafell depicted.

"Harsh, but true. Can I see the letter?"

Emily shook her head, not ready to reveal her discovery until her fog of confusion cleared. She needed time to absorb Scafell's revelations. This meeting wasn't going the way she planned.

"I don't have it with me." She accompanied the lie with a protective clutch of her hand bag. As she did, her phone rang. Sam, from the office, lit up on the caller display. She mouthed that she needed to answer, Scafell nodded and Emily stepped out of the open patio door into the back yard.

"What is it, Sam?"

"Something's kicking off here. Not sure what exactly. We've been booted out of the operations room. Only those with highest security clearance allowed to stay. And 'C''s been on the floor most of the day. Any ideas?"

Emily did not know exactly what was happening, but she could guess. Easton's G-Force squad must be in position in Versailles. European leaders would be arriving. The net was closing in on Tinman. McBride's team, despite CIA assistance, would be feeling the pressure. It's one thing knowing and seeing your enemy, quite another predicting where and how an unseen enemy may strike.

Another lie tripped off Emily's tongue. "Not got a clue."

"Think it's something to do with Tinman?"

"No idea, Sam. There's so much going on with Russia and Ukraine. It could be any manner of things. Let me know if you hear something definite."

"I think you'll hear before me. I never get to hear anything juicy until all the shooting's over."

"Bye." Emily clicked off, but Sam's reference to *shooting* chimed in her mind. If her calculations were correct, Jack Easton and his team were in danger. So were the Prime Minister and the defence secretary. This was no time to act coy about a mysterious letter, regardless of strict instructions on the front. No matter to whom it was addressed. Action was paramount. She dug in her handbag, fished out Mason's letter and ripped it open, unaware Scafell was studying her through the glass.

Her mouth dropped, her knees trembled, a deep sense of foreboding chilling her bones as she read the first line:

There's a traitor in the department.

35

"I thought it was you."

The warmth of Pierre Laurent's greeting alone saved him from a meat knife in the gut as he laid a hand on Tinman's shoulder.

"How long has it been, Antoine? Twenty years? Maybe more."

Tinman turned slowly, careful to conceal the knife under the tray. Laurent wore a chef's apron and wiped greasy hands on a cloth hanging from a cord around his ample girth. His ruddy face glistened with sweat from the heat of the kitchen.

"At least twenty." Tinman adopted Antoine's pitch, mirroring Laurent's smile.

"Still at the Garigliano?"

"Still there. Still waiting on tables. Still poor."

Laurent guffawed. "How's Nicole?"

Tinman shrugged and his tight expression told Laurent that Antoine and his wife were no longer together.

"Sorry to hear that. You look different, Antoine."

"Twenty years is a long time."

"No, it's not that, it's …"

"I've not been well." Tinman blurted the information as if distressed, clutching at fragments of Antoine's history he'd committed to memory. His eyes lowered, expression sad and vulnerable. "Kidney transplant. Touch and go for a while. I'm still on strong medication and it affects the skin. But I'm still working, so I can't complain."

"Sorry, I didn't know, I …"

A call echoed down the corridor. Kitchen staff with a query. Laurent, who learned his trade as a young, trainee sous chef at the restaurant overlooking the Pont du Garigliano, turned, mumbled something incoherent and shuffled off, mouthing to Tinman that they should meet up sometime.

Tinman breathed easier, confidence bolstered by the meeting, although an inquisitive glint in the chef's eyes left him gnawing doubts. He proceeded down the long corridor, but instead of returning to the dining hall, turned right, following the sign for Gate 10. Like a rat digging multiple exits to its tunnel, Tinman scouted potential escape routes. Glass panelling afforded views of the manicured gardens, crowds of large-headed pink and blue hydrangeas forming an eye-pleasing backdrop against the verdant green lawns.

Four men engrossed in a huddle by Gate 10 caught his attention, two wearing battle fatigues, the others in black suits and ties. These were not your average team of bodyguards, not even for the most powerful politicians. The weapons gave them away. As with all elite soldiers Tinman was steeped in international weaponry and the C8 Carbines carried by the men in fatigues was a signature he knew as well as his own. The primary assault rifle of British special forces. One of the other men checked his handgun, a compact Sig Sauer Browning pistol. Again a favourite of special forces.

Tinman studied them, careful to hang back away from the glass in the knowledge that the reflection would help shield his presence. The group's leader was obvious. Tinman could sense his authority from the way he stood, tall and composed, the others leaning in to catch his every word, attentive and eager to please. After a minute or so the group broke up, one of the uniformed men staying to guard the gate while the others walked towards the front of the palace. Tinman watched them disappear behind a huge hydrangea bush before reappearing for an instant, the leader apparently gazing directly at him, a distinctive black mole on his cheek. Just as Koshka, his informant, had described him.

It was the first time Tinman had seen Jack Easton. Instinct told him that before the night was done, their eyes would meet again.

36

Emily's mind fizzed and burned. At least that's what it felt like. Unconnected thoughts jarring. She could barely believe what she was reading.

Mason Jones's prose was written in a tidy hand in black ballpoint, simple and dispassionate, no more than three or four sentences, but the enormity of the words brought a lump to her throat and a heaviness to her heart.

Jones had suspected a leak in the department for more than 12 months. He was the section's expert on technology, poring over computer programmes and investigating ways of making internal communications more efficient. He had found online reports describing assassinations in foreign countries altered, some erased. One of them an assessment of the imminent risk to British high-ranking generals with overseas connections, detailing their movements. One of the named officers was General Parker, shot dead in his Devon home. Only two people in the department had clearance to alter those reports. McBride and Scafell. Only one of them had the technical capability to delete content to evade detection. Jones's closing line left no room for doubt.

Scafell is the traitor.

Emily shut her eyes, desperate to focus on the implications of what she had read. If Jones was right, the obvious reason for Scafell to withhold a report on the danger to General Parker was to allow his assailant easy access. Scafell would also have had access to files on General Mantelli and probably all the other assassination victims. No wonder Jones wanted 'C' to open the letter.

She felt a sudden chill, afraid and vulnerable. She fumbled the letter into its envelope and headed for the wooden back gate allowing access to the alleyway leading to the main road. The gate creaked open, prompting a wave of relief. She could hear children playing and the reversing beeps of a supermarket van delivering groceries, the soundtrack of ordinary life and a safer world, but before she could slip away a violent kick yanked the gate handle from her grasp, dragging her back into a darker existence.

Spinning around, she saw Scafell, jaw firm, eyes fixed, but no panic. Almost as if he was prepared, having expected this day to come.

He snatched the envelope from her hand. "Now, what do we have here? I think we should go inside, don't you?" The grating tone reminded Emily of cold steel resounding on a stone floor. An accompanying jab in her back encouraged her to return to the kitchen. She tried to dodge past him, the open gate inviting, but he was too quick for her, grabbing her arm, twisting it roughly behind her back until she yelped. No contest. Scafell was eight inches taller and several stones heavier. Gone was the amiable boss from the office. The detached determination about his manner frightened her most as he bundled her into the kitchen.

"Is it true?" A tremor in Emily's voice betrayed her fear.

Scafell pushed her onto the settee as he scanned the letter, thin lips tightening.

"Never trusted Jones. Nosy bastard. Wouldn't let things lie." His voice harsh and loud as if he wanted others to hear.

"So it is true?"

Scafell didn't answer. Instead, he strode over to the patio door, turned the key, sealing the obvious escape route.

Emily's attention switched to the other side of the room, the lounge door edging open. The slight but athletic frame of Leanne filled the doorway, sing-song welcome banished, hard eyes gazing down at Emily. She had been listening. In her left hand she pointed a pistol, black and sinister, the long barrel indicating an attached silencer. At last Emily understood. The terrifying hush that followed was almost a relief. For weeks she had wrestled with the memory of the Portland Place shooting. McBride, Savage, the entire department, it seemed, had discounted her report, dismissing her detailed recollection, believing what they wanted to believe. She remembered her chat with David Stephens. Motivated reasoning, he called it, when people cherry pick and twist facts to fit their existing beliefs. That's what had happened. They had dismissed the truth, the testimony of someone closest to the action, a woman who had detected another female, in favour of the Tinman theory. Yet here was vindication standing not six feet away. The same stance, same angle, same quiet confidence and left-handed orientation, the same gender. Emily's photographic memory was accurate. The still frames that lingered in her mind from three weeks ago were identical.

"It was you, Leanne. You killed Mason."

Emily blurted out the accusation. No denial came. Leanne looked at Scafell, and Emily detected an almost imperceptible nod between them, as if a manual covered this specific situation. Perhaps it did. Emily now believed Scafell was a traitor. She was certain Leanne had killed Mason Jones and she knew why. The motive was obvious. Jones suspected Scafell of betraying the Service and was about to convey those concerns to 'C'.

She remembered the day of the shooting and the sight of Scafell twirling the hammer above his head after leaving the van. She thought it odd at the time but assumed he was stretching cramped limbs. Now the move sparked more sinister thoughts. Perhaps a signal to the driver of the speeding car and to Leanne. A sign conveying news that only Jones and Emily remained in the van.

The sequence of events rattled through Emily's brain. What she didn't know was who Scafell was working for. She didn't have to wait long. The answer she'd suspected arrived with the annoying mundanity of a generic ring tone. Scafell pulled a phone from his pocket, motioning for Leanne to keep Emily covered. He stepped outside the room but as he passed Emily, she detected the faint but jarring tones of a Slavic accent.

"Privet, Tovarishch." The use of "Privet" told her the caller knew Scafell well. She had studied Russian for the past two years and knew the difference between "Hi, Comrade" and more formal welcomes. She strained to listen, but although she heard Scafell slide into fluent Russian the delivery was too fast, too idiomatic, for her to decipher.

When Scafell returned there was an urgency to his movements, as if the call had generated a sudden call to action.

"So it's the Russians. You're passing secrets to the Russians." Emily's tone was laced with derision.

"Don't be so dramatic. I worked in Moscow for years. I've lots of Russian friends. Everyone knows that."

"How could you kill Mason? He was a colleague. A friend. You worked together."

He shrugged, his look dismissive.

"I suppose you'd call it collateral damage." Emily's tone increasingly sneering. "The Russians know all about that, don't they? What does collateral damage even mean? To me, it means the massacre of civilians in Bucha and Mariupol and Kherson. It means genocide and war crimes across Ukraine, raping women and killing innocent people for fun."

Scafell shook his head. For the first time since Emily had known him she detected a cold, chilling anger. When he spat his reply, the words were bold and ugly, discolouring the space between them, although Emily watched Leanne fairly glow with pride as he spoke.

"Death, rape, war crimes. You think Russia has a monopoly on such horror. Have you not heard of the sinking of the Belgrano? Or the illegal war in Iraq? Or the killing and torture of civilians and children in Afghanistan? Or the abuse of prisoners in Guantanamo Bay? There are two sides to every story, Emily. And let's not forget, Ukraine was entirely created by Russia. Russia saved it from oppression. It's part of Russia's identity."

He could have been Vladimir Putin spouting revisionist history on the steps of the Kremlin, insisting Ukraine, its people, language and culture did not exist. "But never mind history, let's concentrate on the here and now."

Emily fixed Leanne with a pleading gaze. The woman she met at St Pancras Station was warm, friendly and empathetic. They swapped numbers, planned a visit to the theatre. Emily did not make friends easily, especially women, but on that day she sensed a connection, a kindred spirit.

Now all she could see was the truth of the espionage world, a combat zone scrapped over without mercy by men and women who lie and cheat, making no concession to humanity.

"Coat off, hands behind your back." Leanne spat out the order, tying Emily's hands with Gorilla tape, before rifling through her handbag, locating her phone and sliding out the sim card.

"Okay. The car's parked at the end of the alleyway. I'll drive, you keep her quiet." Leanne's words were clipped, precise, and Emily realised this was not a husband-wife relationship. More an officer rapping out orders to her subordinate.

Leanne left the room to grab a coat and Emily was surprised at how calm she felt.

"How long have you been together?"

"What?"

"You and Leanne. How long have you lived together and what sort of relationship thrives on cold-blooded murder?"

Scafell ignored the accusation, knowing Leanne was still in earshot. "Leanka is my partner. Her father worked for the KGB, but we met in Moscow, share the same philosophies in life, and we've been together ever since."

"The Service would never allow that. They must have checked her background."

"Of course, you're right. For many years, Leanka has been useful to the Service, if you get my drift."

"A double agent?"

He didn't answer but Emily knew double agents, even deep into the 21st Century, remained the bone marrow of espionage. Not as numerous as during the Cold War, but still the ultimate prize on both sides. All this time Leanne must have been passing secrets to Moscow, Emily reasoned, while also supplying the odd item of false information to the Service via Scafell.

"Where are we going?" said Emily.

Scafell diverted his eyes, busying himself collecting bits and pieces from a drawer. His silence worried Emily. Not once had he bothered denying his betrayal, while in her desperation to know the truth Emily had denied the danger she faced. But now her stomach churned, a wave of anxiety catching her breathing as panic replaced interest.

When Leanne returned she unlocked the patio door to check the alleyway was clear. "All set?"

Scafell nodded, grabbed Emily by the arm and yanked her from the settee. Draping her coat around her shoulders to hide tied hands, he put his arm around her in the comfortable embrace of a courting couple.

"Not a sound." A glint of Leanne's pistol accompanied the warning, and she motioned with a roll of her eyes to Emily's bag. "Don't forget the bag, Luke, don't want to leave any loose ends."

The car parked at the end of the alleyway was an old BMW 3 series in dull, unremarkable grey, the sort no one notices. As they emerged from the alley Scafell tightened his grip around Emily's shoulders, opening the back door, guiding her inside. Leanne would have preferred to have bundled her into the boot, but they couldn't risk a nosy bystander clocking the move, noting the registration and calling the police. Scafell slid in beside Emily, while Leanne took the wheel.

"Where are we going?" Emily repeated her question.

"Somewhere quiet. Somewhere you won't be a problem."

Thoughts dragged through the mud of Emily's brain, each one requiring a physical effort to process, threatening to overwhelm her senses, but she persisted and when at last she regained control it all became terrifyingly clear.

Of course. Scafell knew the innermost details of the events in Paris. He knew the movements of the Prime Minister and defence secretary, was privy to all manner of timings, codes and security. Oh God, he even quizzed Jack Easton on the plans of British special forces.

The words, *Privet Tovarishch,* came to Emily's mind.

She swivelled towards Scafell and her voice managed little more than a whisper.

"It was him, wasn't it?"

"Him?"

"Tinman. It was Tinman you were talking to on the phone."

Scafell turned away, watching the traffic, apparently untouched and unconcerned.

That was the moment Emily decided she knew for certain. The moment she realised she was no more than an irritant in Scafell's world of lies and deceit. Rather like a wasp buzzing around a

169

dining table. The sort she believed he would stamp on without mercy.

37

Jack Easton took stock. A small battalion of gendarmes surrounded the perimeter of the palace. Snipers continued to scan the grounds from vantage points on the roof, although their worth would recede as dusk fell. An assortment of personal bodyguards arrived with each dignitary, while his own special forces team had taken up position. Easton was wired up and in communication with them.

"All okay, Cam?" Easton checked in with Cameron Mitchell, the soldier detailed to guard Gate 10, although he wasn't standing like a sentry. A gendarme performed that role. Mitchell had created an impromptu nest in the nearby hydrangeas, 40 yards from the building, careful not to damage the foliage, as well as avoid the roof snipers' field of vision. Shadowy figures triggering bursts of friendly fire was the last thing anyone wanted. Mitchell had found a spot affording a panoramic view of the gate's approach. Now he lay, breathing quiet and even, carbine trained on the wide sweep, effectively sealing off any back-door entry or escape. His night-vision apparatus unpacked and ready by his side.

"All quiet. Not even the scrape of a midge's foot."

Easton chuckled. He'd chosen his team carefully, all men he would trust with his life, having seen action alongside them in Iraq and Afghanistan. Mitchell was a crack shot, accustomed to skirmishes in darkness when considered decisions and a calm demeanour were paramount. Jake Jordan took a similar vantage point at the front of the palace.

"Any sign yet, JJ?"

"Not yet, Jack, due any minute. Blue lights approaching. Probably the PM."

Easton was inside the Hall of Mirrors with Macca. That's what everyone called George McManus. Not because of his Celtic surname, more because his fresh face and high arched eyebrows bore a likeness to Paul McCartney in his Beatles years. Easton and Macca both wore black suits and ties, weapons holstered out of

171

sight, apart from a slight bump. While the plan scheduled Macca to stand in a corner at the head of the room, within a few strides of the Prime Minister, Easton preferred to take an overview at the other end where workmen had erected a temporary stage, complete with curtain hiding audio equipment. It afforded Easton a secret and elevated sweep of the entire hall.

If truth be told, Easton was doubtful of seeing action. Liaising with French authorities, he had scrutinised security in minute detail and could envisage no way an imposter might strike his victim and escape. There was always the possibility of a suicide bomber or shooter. They were much more difficult to stop, but Easton deemed smuggling a weapon through such weight of security virtually impossible.

Not that he was complacent. He held a grudging admiration for Tinman, the sort all professional soldiers bestow on individuals whose work combines meticulous preparation with ruthless execution. No such individual could be underestimated. As an assassin, Tinman had proved one of the best, or worst, depending on your point of view.

"Not long now," said Easton, as he and Macca completed one last sweep of the room that once housed the two chambers of the French National Assembly in the days when Versailles acted as the official capital of France.

"Bet this place has seen some history, Jack." Macca arched his back and bent his neck to study the crystal chandeliers, light dancing and glimmering in the mirrors, a long bejewelled one reflecting the length of the room in all its majesty.

"I know it's where the Treaty of Versailles was signed between the Allies and Germany after the first world war. That's good enough for me."

His earpiece crackled. A whispered voice. "The PM has landed."

172

38

Al was worried. Several hours had elapsed since he'd left Emily at the Tube station.

He had wanted to accompany her to Imelda Jones's house but knew he couldn't. It was work. No way he could interfere. But the memory of her dry sobs, reverberating against his chest, haunted him. Emily inhabited a troubled place. That was obvious. Torn between thinking she could have done something to save her stricken friend and guilt at not visiting his wife and child to offer her condolences.

She should have been home long ago. He had rung her phone half a dozen times, the call diverting straight to voicemail. Perhaps out of signal in a Tube tunnel. Maybe the battery had died. Al had exhausted the simple explanations, unsettling feelings of foreboding and helplessness rippling at the pit of his stomach.

Because of the infuriating secrecy where she worked he didn't have a number to ring, nor did he know who to contact. There were times he cursed the Service. For an Intelligence unit, it didn't always seem very intelligent. Like a bunch of kids running around playing cowboys and Indians, some of whom ended up dead. Not that the public would ever know, because they were not trusted to know. If they knew, the Service might have to kill them too.

Al harboured such exasperating thoughts as he stared out of the flat window in Archway watching the half-eyed cat stalking a leaf dancing on the breeze.

He knew David Stephens lived within walking distance and he liked him, having met him two years ago in Cambridge with Emily when they picked up her late Uncle Sebastian's belongings. Stephens was a director of repute and standing. He would know who to contact. Al flicked through Emily's address book but, predictably, there was no number, no address.

Then he remembered. Wilson. He knew where he lived. He'd visited his basement flat twice, once tucking him up in bed after saving his inebriated neck in the Soho bar brawl. Wilson owed him.

Al grabbed his coat and five minutes later boarded a Tube train heading for Clapham Common. Wilson answered the door on the third knock, opening it no more than a foot. His face glowed red, demeanour sour, as if he'd spent the afternoon polishing off a dodgy bottle of Merlot.

"Yes?" A bleary expression greeted Al.

"I'm Al, Emily's partner. Remember, we met a few weeks ago in Soho."

"No."

"The night you got drunk, had a scrap with a barman."

"That's not narrowing it down."

Al smiled. "Look, I'm worried about Emily. She's not answering her phone. She went to see Mason Jones's wife and should have been back hours ago."

"So what, she's a big girl, the golden girl, some say, she can look after herself. You're not one of those sad guys who need their partner checking in every half hour, are you?" Wilson's tone was dismissive.

The derisive slur at the end of Wilson's sentence prompted Al to consider leaving. He didn't. Instead, he swallowed hard, his voice urgent. "I wouldn't have come here if I wasn't genuinely concerned."

"Why did she go there?"

Al was uncertain how much to divulge. He had no intention of revealing the potential clue in Portland Place, but needed to gain Wilson's trust. Fast.

"She still thinks there's more to Mason's death than meets the eye."

Wilson opened the door, beckoning Al inside.

"Bloody spies. Emily's in the wrong business. Spies aren't Mr Nice Guy next door. They're a squalid lot. Ego-trippers, drunkards, traitors. Bloody idiots who run around thinking they're saving the world but would shoot their grandmother for a clue to the tiniest secret."

Wilson was animated, his voice increasingly garbled. Al judged him on the capable side of drunkenness, but it was a close-run thing.

"I wondered if you knew who to call, or if you could call someone who may be able to help."

"I'm suspended."

"Oh."

Wilson didn't receive many visitors. Al was sensible, polite, sober, someone living and breathing he could sound off to rather than the usual wall. He wasn't letting the chance slip.

"Yeah, they call it the Intelligence Service, but most of the people are pretty stupid. Can't make up their minds whether I'm straight-talking or Anthony Blunt."

Al looked perplexed.

"Blunt?"

"Of course, you're too young. A Soviet spy, made surveyor of the Queen's pictures, given a knighthood and granted full immunity. You couldn't make it up, you really couldn't. And they have the audacity to suspend me on suspicion when all I've done is work for them for thirty years. Sir Stupid Bob, that's me. Been shot at, tortured, lost relationships and lived in squalor. And for what? Less than the average accountant earns in a year ..."

Wilson would have ranted on, but Al was anxious.

"Please, could you ring someone. Let them know Emily's gone missing."

Wilson stumbled over to his phone. "Stephens is the man. He's the one you need. No point talking to McBride or Scafell. They think I'm a washed-up has-been."

He punched in the number. After four rings, Stephens answered.

Considering his state of inebriation, Wilson explained the situation rather well, Al thought. After several questions, Stephens asked to speak to Al. Wilson passed over the receiver.

"Nice to speak with you again, Mr Andrews. It's been a while, but I've been following Emily's career. I spoke with her not long ago. You think she may be at Mason Jones's house?"

"That's where she was headed, but she's not answering her phone. That's not like her. I've got a bad feeling."

"I shouldn't worry. I'm sure there's a simple explanation. I'll make a few calls. We have ways of finding people, even ones who don't want to be found. I'm sure Emily will turn up."

The honeyed tone of Stephens's voice felt soothing and reassuring. Al had no idea what he had in mind or who he may contact, but he trusted him. "Thank you. I appreciate your help. Can you ask her to ring me when you find her?"

"Most certainly."

Al hung up. He turned to find Wilson filling two glasses after pulling the cork on another bottle of red.

"You'll have a livener before you go, won't you?" It was the last thing Al wanted. He yearned to hurry back to Archway to await Emily's arrival. He needed to keep a clear head. The more he thought, the more her behaviour appeared out of character. She had never failed to answer her phone for so long, always at least sending text or WhatsApp messages. His concern was growing more desperate as each hour passed. But Wilson's voice trailed sad and expectant, tone on the verge of beseeching. Al couldn't bring himself to refuse.

"Of course. Just one, though. Nice of you to offer."

39

Emily stared at the road counting lamp posts. Fine rain fell from a glowering sky, a light mist forming on the car windows. The Gorilla tape cut into her wrists, her arms numb behind her back, body weight effectively crushing the circulation. Fear wrapped its fingers, tight and suffocating, around her dry throat.

The car headed out of London. She'd spotted a sign for the A12 but traffic was heavy and progress slow. She tried to engage Scafell and Leanne in conversation but they ignored her, as if they had shut down. As if they had switched from a life of pretence in which they befriended her to a new stage, prescribed and pre-ordained for this eventuality, where conversation proved superfluous and guns and bullets were the only language that held currency. She attempted to alert a driver who drew up alongside at traffic lights by pulling anxious faces and mouthing HELP! but he averted his eyes self-consciously as if not wanting to become embroiled in some domestic squabble. Scafell spotted the move and dug her ribs so hard that her eyes watered.

And so she counted to control her panic. The process had brought her comfort ever since childhood when she had filled notebooks with the number plates of cars passing her parents' house. The pastime that convinced her mother she must be on some medical spectrum actually made Emily feel special. She knew she wasn't like other girls at school. All her life she accepted she was an outlier. Saddled with tension and stress, unable to cry or show displays of tender emotion, but also bestowed with gifts of logic and reasoning others could only envy. Never before, however, had she experienced this level of anxiety.

Even as she counted, her mind wandered, the scale of her predicament plain. With Mason Jones dead, as far as she was aware she was the only person who knew the truth about Scafell and his partner, other than their paymasters. The only person with solid evidence that they were traitors. She had been stupid. She conceded that. If only she'd taken Jones's envelope straight to 'C', involved no one else, accepted whatever consequences came her way. If only she'd taken Al with her to see Imelda Jones. He knew about the shooting. He uncovered the clue on the billboard when it had eluded investigators. Al thought like a detective, logical and considered. He'd have known the shrewdest course of action. Instead, she'd gone alone, wrapped in her own isolated world of guilt and skewed sense of responsibility. And it had led her to this. A silent car journey to an unknown destination with only one possible outcome. Scafell and Leanne had too much at stake to let her live. She knew that, the thought pounding her brain with such painful ferocity that she imagined she may be having a stroke.

She thought of Al, knowing he would be worried she hadn't checked in with him. He would have called her phone, of that she was sure, but Leanne had removed the sim card. If only she'd left a message before turning up at Scafell's place. The recriminations kept churning, Emily digging sharp nails into her palms to force her to think of something, anything. Yet nothing came. Except the rain. Lashing down with increasing venom, so that Leanne had to employ the car's window wipers on the rapid option, sliding back and forth, drumming a beat that echoed Emily's racing heart.

The weather slowed the car's progress and it seemed an age, although probably no more than an hour, before Leanne pulled the car off the main drag and took a minor road, signposted Epping Forest Visitor Centre, High Beech. They passed the visitor centre, a small brick building with a sharply pitched entrance hunched at an awkward angle against the downpour, like an old man shuffling up a slope. It was deserted due to the late hour but they pushed on further up the steady incline, Leanne eventually pulling into Claypit Hill car park. A set of chunky wooden bollards separated it from the road, but it was little more than a gravelled clearing, bumpy and uneven, half a dozen big puddles having formed. The BMW splashed through them and Leanne parked under the trees, low-lying branches masking the car from the road. The isolated spot was not chosen at random. Emily was sure of that. There had been no discussion of the route or destination on the way, the trip clearly part of a pre-conceived plan.

"Right, out." Scafell barked the order, Emily wriggling across the back seat before he helped pull her to her feet. Underfoot, the car park was already muddy. Clingy, cloying mud, and with rain unrelenting it crossed Emily's mind that any physical evidence of their presence, tyre tracks or footprints, would be washed away within minutes. A wave of hopelessness, bordering on despair, rose in her chest.

"You don't have to do this, Luke. You're not an evil person. I know you're not. You could get away. Just leave me here and go. I've got no phone. No one knows I'm here. You could be miles away. I'm sure you have an exfiltration plan." Her voice urgent rather than pleading. Scafell seemed impressed.

"I have to hand it to you, Emily. Logical and persuasive under pressure. That's the key in this game. A bit like tennis I've always thought. The player who plays the percentages, keeps a level head, usually wins. You would have made a splendid operative, but I'm afraid we don't get to choose the timing of exfiltration. We need to walk."

Instead of taking the left fork to Waltham Abbey and the Jewish Cemetery, where there was a risk of encountering hardy walkers and joggers, they diverted off the path, ducking under low-hanging branches into the woods. Raindrops ran down Emily's neck, her hair wet and bedraggled, jeans and trainers sodden, but she bit her lip hard, tasting copper, forcing back growing waves of panic as they trekked further into the forest, her hopes fading along with the light.

Leanne had come prepared in walking boots and a black waterproof anorak. She led the way, direct and sure-footed. Emily had not visited this part of the forest before but the general terrain was familiar. As a child she played in the forest many times with her parents, often on warm summer days with a picnic hamper, climbing, flying kites, making daisy chains. She'd done a school geography thesis on the area and knew all about the thousands of ancient trees that formed one of London's best-loved outdoor sites, but Emily being Emily, her research extended to darker, more macabre facts. Try, as she did, she could not prevent them surfacing. They arrowed into her mind, their poisonous tips piercing her resolve.

She remembered reading about the dozen murder victims discovered in the forest, including the Babes in the Woods, two children buried in a shallow grave, apparently cuddling each other in a final desperate embrace. And she recalled the case that gave her nightmares for a week, the woman found dead in a car with a crossbow bolt having pierced both sides of her skull.

The occasional dog-walker's path they followed petered out, but Leanne pushed on, through undergrowth and brambles, leading them 250 yards to a spot where the forest grew thickest, swollen ivy branches everywhere, intertwining like the sinews of a strong old man.

The rain seemed to ease, or maybe it was the extensive forest canopy providing extra protection. Leanne rounded a fallen tree, rot and fungi having gnawed hollow a huge beech trunk, probably over more than half a century. In years past, someone, possibly a forest ranger, had arranged poles and branches across it at an angle to form a temporary enclosed shelter, whether for humans or animals unclear.

Leanne motioned for Emily to enter the shelter. Emily swivelled, fixing on Scafell, her grimace imploring. His response was icy, pushing her shoulders so she stumbled a couple of paces.

"What about Tinman, or Adam Lewandowski, or whatever he calls himself now? Is he going to kill the Prime Minister tonight?" The question was directed at Scafell, but Leanne answered,

"What does it matter to you?"

"It's madness. He'll never get away with it. Paris is surrounded by security. There's no way anyone could smuggle a gun into Versailles. Not tonight."

"Who said anything about a gun?"

"What do you mean?" All Tinman's high-profile killings were shootings. Efficient and clinical, the hallmark of a virtuoso assassin. Emily assumed Paris would be no exception.

"The gun's not always our favourite method, isn't that right, Luke?"

Scafell looked puzzled, but he nodded, and Emily's brain sifted Russia's preferred dark materials, immediately alighting on the cases of Litvinenko and Navalny and Sergei and Yulia Skripal, all high-profile subjects of successful or attempted assassinations in recent times. All victims of the Kremlin's obsession with poison. And a thought struck Emily, so despicable and hateful that it made her shiver. Maybe Tinman's ambitions did not begin and end with the Prime Minister. Maybe his Versailles mission involved all the major European leaders. Exacting revenge as they broke bread and sipped wine at the same table would send the ultimate signal.

The thought jolted her senses and she detected the harsh Slavic essence of Leanne's native accent for the first time. The mention of Tinman had loosened Leanne's tongue, engaged her suppressed ego.

"Do you know where your Secret Intelligence Service falls down, Emily?"

"Sounds like you're going to tell me."

"Arrogance. My God, there's no nation on Earth as arrogant as Britain. You think the world still revolves around your skirts. You supply weapons and ammunition to Russia's enemies, but refuse to see what those enemies do to Russia. It has been the same ever since I was a little girl in Uglich."

"Uglich?"

Leanne's tone raised an octave, the passion for her birth nation gushing to the surface. "No, I wouldn't expect you to know my home town. British people are self-absorbed. They aren't inquisitive. Uglich is a beautiful town with a citadel, a museum, a church of St Dmitry on the Blood with frescoes on the wall commemorating the son of Ivan the Terrible."

"And that's a good thing?"

A sneer crossed Leanne's features. "I expected better of you, Emily."

"Right back at you."

"You know, Emily, we thought you had a future. We saw something in you on Primrose Hill that we could work with. Something different. You're not like the others with minds closed, towing the same old line because that's what they've always done.

To use a cliché, you think outside the box. A bright mind. Clarity of thought. That's something we value. We could still work something out."

"I'd never work with you. You killed my friend Mason. I felt his heart stop beating. His blood ran through my fingers." Venom laced Emily's words and she shivered, not with cold, although her hands and feet were numb, but with anger. A spontaneous rage of such smouldering fury that it overwhelmed every other emotion, including her fear.

It also had the effect of hardening Leanne's resolve. Fire glinted in her eyes, the sweet smile of St Pancras replaced by a violent and pragmatic nature. She motioned with her pistol for Emily to move back against the dead tree trunk. As she did so, water dripping down her neck, the smell of rotting vegetation assaulting her nose, Emily turned to Scafell and mouthed, "Tell Al, I love him," before closing her eyes in final acceptance.

40

Cameron Mitchell trained his gun sights on the entrance to Gate 10.

All quiet apart from the odd crackle in his ear. The French president was presenting a pre-dinner speech in a palace ante-room where guests and high-ranking politicians had assembled. Every so often a deep murmur of assent accompanied by an enthusiastic ripple of applause greeted the president as he confirmed France's continuing support for Ukraine, while also gently poking fun at the British prime minister.

"France and Great Britain are like Great Britain and the United States," said the president. "We have a special relationship. Except while Britain and America are separated by a common language, Britain and France are separated by an uncommon language as well as questions on fishing rights and asylum seekers and Brexit disagreements and, well, maybe we should leave it there." The French crowd loved it, the Prime Minister offered a coy smile although doubtless seething inside.

Jack Easton and Macca were in attendance, Easton supplying updates over the tiny microphone hidden under his black tie.

This was always the soldier's most vulnerable time. Logic told Mitchell the action and potential victims were elsewhere, probably far from his position at Gate 10, most likely in the ante-room oozing power and influence, but his training insisted he stay extra vigilant at such a moment. His side ached and legs twitched, little muscle spasms sending shooting pains down his calves. The grass was damp but the earth hard. He reached for his bottle of water, taking a couple of small slurps. The signs of dehydration were obvious, but he had chosen his position well and had no wish for comfort breaks to become a distraction.

A moving figure drew his attention and immediately he focused on a waiter approaching the gendarme at the gate from inside the palace. The ensuing conversation appeared friendly, the waiter, dressed in the obligatory black trousers and white studded shirt with black tie, apparently pleading with the gendarme to let him outside to smoke a cigarette despite this being against the protocol.

After a minute or so the gendarme pushed open the door and the waiter emerged, digging a cigarette packet from his pocket, lighting up and blowing an extended plume of smoke into the night sky.

The radio crackled. "You're missing out Cam. The president's talking about the writings of the Lumieres, Rousseau and Voltaire, equality and liberty. Very interesting." There was genuine appreciation in Jack Easton's tone.

"I'll take your word for it." Mitchell did not sound convinced. As he spoke he spotted the waiter shuffle slowly away from the gate, enjoying a couple of drags, disappearing from view behind a large hydrangea. Mitchell tracked back to the gendarme. Still guarding the gate, machine gun at the ready.

"Are there any waiters with you, Jack?" A trace of concern in Mitchell's tone.

"No. Must be taking a break during the speeches before the dinner gets underway. Probably in the kitchens. Why?"

"Probably nothing, just spotted one over here having a cigarette. Bit of a trek from the kitchen, but no problem."

"Okay, we'll be off air for a while as the Prime Minister's next up and we're closing in."

"Roger that."

The radio hissed and Mitchell contemplated turning down the sound. He didn't, estimating the action would begin soon. Half a minute went by. No sign of the waiter. A seed of suspicion formed in Mitchell's mind, although it had neither space nor time to grow.

He never saw Tinman. Never heard him approach.

His lateral vision detected a momentary swiping movement from the side, but too late to react before the meat knife embedded deep in his neck, the long curved blade slicing through the internal carotid artery supplying blood to the brain. Instant oblivion. Tinman rocked the knife sideways to ensure the kill before carefully sliding the plastic carrier bag holding the knife down the shaft and across the wound to avoid any blood splatter. He ripped the wire from Mitchell's ear to cut the hiss, observed the gendarme

184

for a few seconds to ensure all was well, then sauntered back along an arcing route to the gate, not the slightest stain on his pristine white shirt.

The gendarme held open the door, practising a friendly nod, unaware that his flexibility with the strict rules had helped the rat in Tinman burrow a potential escape route.

FRANK MALLEY

41

The whir of helicopter blades, low and thunderous, set Emily's teeth chattering. She opened her eyes as Leanne lowered her weapon and threw Scafell a puzzled expression.

Swooping out of the blackening night, the machine sent birds squawking and fluttering, search beam sweeping in vain through the mist and rain to penetrate the forest umbrella. A litter of leaves swirled in the downdraft. Circling police helicopters were a common sight in and around London, but rarely did they fly in this wretched visibility. Too dangerous.

Leanne's shout was tossed and torn on the buffeting air. "What the hell's going on?"

"No idea," said Scafell. "Can't be anything to do with us."

"Sure?"

Scafell looked at Emily. "Know anything about this, did you tell anyone you were coming to see us?"

Emily shook her head. It was the truth. She had told Al about visiting Imelda Jones but the decision to call at Scafell's was random, hatched in a moment of contemplation in the Camden coffee shop. As far as she was concerned, and to her unmitigated dismay, no one on God's Earth knew where she may be.

They stood rooted for several minutes, barely able to think until the helicopter moved off, still whirring faintly as it crabbed into the distance but no longer juddering every nerve as it tracked another section of the forest.

"Could be looking for a missing child or maybe there's been a smash on the A12," Scafell said. He rolled his eyes at Leanne, motioning to the shelter exit. As she edged into the forest to join him, she pointed her weapon at Emily in a warning gesture.

Once they had left, Emily seized her chance, feeling around. Too dark to make out detail, her tied hands quickly determined whoever erected the shelter had taken pride in their work. Even though some of the poles were rotten they were thick and lashed together with strong rope. No use. She would need free hands and an axe to hack her way out. Crossing to the opposite side of the shelter, she listened in vain to make out what Scafell and Leanne were discussing, detecting only whispered tones becoming increasingly animated.

Scafell was assembling a case to free Emily. He studied law at university and before joining the Service contemplated a career as a criminal barrister. His argument held logic. Emily no longer possessed Mason Jones's letter, nor did Jones's wife have any knowledge of the contents. There was no physical evidence to link Leanne with Portland Place. The whole sorry affair amounted to Emily's word against theirs.

"Not everyone in the Service is her biggest fan," said Scafell, warming to his theme. "They think she led them on a wild goose chase after the shooting of Jones. Some of them wanted her off the front line then, away from all operational duties. The powers-that-be don't forget or forgive easily. My bet is that if she goes to 'C' or any of the directors with this they'll have her drummed out. The Service protects its own. Always has done. We know that."

"You've thought it all through, haven't you?"

Scafell laid hands on Leanne's shoulders, his tone even more pleading. "The Service has always been reluctant to admit it has been compromised. I'm a long-serving, valued asset. She's a trainee with no track record. Just a decent kid really. They'll dismiss her as a fantasist."

Leanne's jaw jutted. "Yeah, but what happens when the investigation begins. You know it will. When the Service involves its field officers. When the Moscow agents are asked to nosy around looking into you and me, just to make sure. Asking questions. Digging up all manner of things. Somehow, I don't think the Kremlin are going to wear that. Not in the current climate. The best we could hope for is being recalled and hidden away in some desk job with no prospects, no privileges. Out in the cold. Humiliated. Do you really want that?"

"No, but if she disappears, there'll also be questions. Lots of them, knocking on our door, and heaven knows where that might take us. Maybe that helicopter is searching for us. She may be lying about not telling anyone she came to see us." Scafell's tone increasingly beseeching.

"We can handle that."

"But …"

"No! Enough, Luke. I'm sorry. It has to be done. It's never pretty when it gets to this. It's damned ugly. I know you don't like it, but better one soul sacrificed, so many can prosper. You know the drill. You know that's how we work. Look upon it as an operational convenience." Leanne sliced her right hand in the air, drawing a line under the conversation.

Emily could not hear the details but she sensed a grumble of angst and prevarication, hoping beyond hope that Scafell was brokering a deal for her freedom. A sliver of expectation momentarily raised her spirit. But then Leanne and Scafell trudged back into the shelter and the grave look on Scafell's face extinguished all hope.

Leanne did not hesitate. She brushed past Scafell, took two strides, and raised her pistol at arm's length, aiming at Emily's heart. Instinctively, Emily's shoulders hunched, her muscles jerked rigid. A warm trickle of fear ran down her thigh. Leanne paused to steady herself, gentle eyes transformed into icy pools of determination, the callous nature of her training clicking in. Slow and steady, she squeezed the trigger. Two muffled shots rang out. Emily, mouth open, a tortured mix of horror and bewilderment on her face, slumped to her knees, and a dark and miserable night rained blood.

42

From his vantage point behind the curtains on the makeshift stage Jack Easton spied the dining hall.

He could see Macca standing by a wall 10 feet behind and to the right of the Prime Minister, running his eye over proceedings. Other black-tie-wearing security men, mostly from the French security forces, were stationed around the hall. Any attacker had little chance of success and even less of escape. That gave Easton comfort. Tinman was no suicide bomber. Nothing kamikaze characterised his killings to date. He had planned them all with ruthless efficiency, not only in their execution but also with regard to his escape.

In Easton's estimation, Tinman was not a slave to ideology. He didn't kill because he believed in the dominance of Russia and the reign of its autocratic rulers. He didn't kill for revenge, although that was the avowed aim of the ruling politburo. Tinman killed, Easton was convinced, because assassination of the high and mighty in the world's military hierarchy provided the most rigorous examination of his reflexes, reasoning, intelligence and evasion techniques. Like a video gamer battling for number one status.

That was why any assassination attempt on the Prime Minister was likely to happen on the journey between Versailles and his hotel where hiding places and escape routes were plentiful.

Yet Easton knew there was no room for what he regarded as man's great weakness. Complacency. *If you aim low, you'll miss.* The favourite saying of his late soldier father came to mind and he smiled at the memory.

His hand edged automatically to his pistol, holstered under his jacket, to check it was still there, although he had done the same 20 times or more since the diners had taken their seats. The hard, smooth grip, tailored to his meaty hand, offered him comfort.

"All okay, Cam?" He whispered into his hidden microphone. No answer.

"Come in, Cam. No time to go dark." He tried once more. Again, no reply.

"Bugger." Easton muttered under his breath. He checked in with JJ at the front gate, receiving an immediate response, and with Macca, who nodded almost imperceptibly, realising he was in plain view.

A disconcerting gripe carved an acidic route at the pit of Easton's stomach. There may have been an innocent explanation. Cam had complained about hissy radio traffic already that evening. Security forces flooded the area, some using similar frequencies, but Cam's silence caused the hairs on the back of Easton's neck to rise. He sensed danger. He could almost smell Tinman.

Easton contemplated disappearing down the long corridor to check on Cam but at that moment a burst of action decorated the hall in vivid colour, a line of waiters scurrying through doors on all sides carrying silver platters packed with ice and laden with seafood. In his effort to keep his head high, wearing a beaming smile, one of the waiters failed to notice a woman's handbag protruding from beneath her chair. As he passed, the bag's strap lassoed his foot sending him tumbling. He tried to save the platter as he fell, succeeding only in pitching forward, spewing its contents over the floor, the steel tray clattering along the polished wood surface.

Easton drew his pistol, immediately alert and tense, realising distraction was a classic tactic in any assassin's armoury. Macca moved a pace closer to the Prime Minister. The headwaiter took over, ordering a group of wine waiters close by, including Tinman, to help clear the mess. Sinking to their knees they scooped up slimy squid, fleshy crab, giant lobsters complete with claws as well as scores of mussels that had escaped their dish and skittered across the tiles.

A few minutes later the panic was over, order restored. Easton holstered his pistol. The rest of the meal proceeded without incident.

43

It took many seconds for Emily to realise the blood was not hers.

On her knees, clothes sodden, nerves shredded, hands numb, ears ringing, she blinked at the muddy ground. She felt no pain but realised gunshot victims often don't feel pain if the bullet is small and fails to explode into flesh-tearing shrapnel.

She waited for white light, the warm feeling of her soul lifting, a hand beckoning, all those out-of-body experiences that custom and tradition had seared into her mind, but nothing came. Instead, she shook in muffled confusion, mind having succumbed to a neutral place where nothing mattered, not even the existential reality of whether she was dead or alive.

Then she saw Leanne. Lying at an odd angle in the mud to her right, eyes wide and vacant, mouth open, a curious expression on her face as if she'd encountered something as unexpected as it was devastating. A river of blood poured down one side of her face, dripping into a puddle of muddy rainwater and Emily couldn't work out where the grotesque hole in the side of Leanne's head had come from.

Emily looked up. She could see Scafell's lips moving, but no sound penetrated the irritating hiss around her bruised eardrums. The light from a small torch in Scafell's left hand cast silhouettes around the shelter, reminding her of cold but atmospheric times celebrating Halloween in the family shed. In his right hand she spied a gun, a pistol with a stubby barrel. Still smoking.

Scafell dropped to his knees in the mud, facing Emily, pulling her close to him, at the same time reaching behind her back to untie her hands. She could smell his musky deodorant mixed with hot sweat from the yomp through the forest. The warmth of his body felt comforting and she was grateful for it. She pushed her face into his chest as if hiding from the horror she had witnessed and he responded by pulling her coat around her shoulders. Rocking back and forth they comforted each other, neither seeming to know quite what had happened or whether anything would ever be the same again.

After what seemed like hours, but was no more than a couple of minutes, Emily spoke, her voice tremulous and frail.

"Why? Why?" She kept repeating the question as the ringing dissipated, her hearing slowly returning to normal to reveal the drone of a helicopter and the distant wail of a siren. Strobing blue lights, still some way off, pierced the wall of trees around them.

"Why, Luke? Why?"

"I'm not evil, Emily. Like you said, I'm not evil. But this could take some explaining. I couldn't let her shoot you, even if it meant breaking cover." He looked down at Leanne and a sadness seemed to engulf him.

"Breaking cover?"

"It's not what it seems. Nothing's what it seems. Not in this business. I hate this business. I'm tired of it. Tired of all the lying, all the deceit. Tired of innocent people getting caught up in stupid boys' games. But I can't tell you everything. Not yet."

Emily stopped shaking. She pushed away from Scafell and stood, unsteady at first but breathing deep, quickly recovering her balance and strength. She stared at the mess that remained of Leanne's face.

"But I thought you loved her."

"I do, or at least I did, but when she described killing you as an *operational convenience* I knew that couldn't be justified. No matter what."

"But she killed Mason."

Scafell held up his palms in a gesture of innocence. "I knew nothing about that. She must have believed she was protecting me. I thought it was Tinman, honest I did."

"I don't understand."

"You will."

They turned to hear the sound of men slashing their way through undergrowth accompanied by bright lights heading in their direction. Scafell made no attempt to run, dropping his gun in the mud next to Leanne. Half a dozen policemen, all in black, wearing flak jackets and bearing machine guns, broke their way into the shelter and ordered Scafell and Emily back against the beech tree.

They waited around 30 seconds until a tall, elegant man with silver-grey hair appeared. He wore a brown Barbour jacket, matching boots, and an air of easy authority. He could have been an aristocratic farmer on a shooting weekend.

"My dear Emily. I trust you are unhurt." The mellifluous tones of David Stephens washed over Emily's stinging ears like soothing balm. She nodded.

Stephens absorbed the gruesome scene without expression, a man clearly accustomed to sights and sounds that would turn an ordinary person's stomach. When he spoke, he fixed Scafell with an understanding but assured look. "I think you will be required to go with these officers. There is much to explain. I'll inform your section and send along the appropriate support."

"Of course."

Scafell disappeared into the forest flanked by four police officers. By now more teams were arriving. Police set up an exclusion zone, wrapping blue-and-white tape around trees, although the chances of anyone straying into the isolated area on such a foul night were nil. Men in white boiler suits appeared. Emily presumed they were forensic officers, although they bore no obvious identification. Half a dozen paramedics arrived, two of them fussing around Emily although she insisted she was unhurt. Stephens insisted they check her out. They walked her back to the Claypit car park, now packed with vehicles, stripped her of wet clothes, threw a blanket around her, checked her vital signs and gave her a hot drink.

Ten minutes later she stopped shivering, her brain again clear and focused. When Stephens arrived to check on her she blurted one of many questions.

"How did you know I was here?"

Stephens explained that Al, worried at being unable to contact her, had reached out to Wilson, who in turn had phoned him.

"But how did you know to come here, to the depths of a forest in filthy weather?"

"Ah, well …" Stephens pulled his jacket a little tighter, his lips pouted and he looked a shade uncomfortable. "Do you remember coming to see me a few weeks ago?"

"Of course."

"Your visit concerned me and I pondered it for many hours. I knew you had the sharp mind and the logical talent for this strange world of ours, but sometimes that's not enough. You need resilience too. Hard core cussedness. The sort that can shrug off events such as today that would break the average person. When we spoke, you were doubting yourself. You were tormented and, by implication, vulnerable. That can go one of two ways. You either succumb to it and leave the Service, or you overcome your doubts. You were working on sensitive stuff, Emily, with access to files jeopardising national security. We had to know which way your mood would fall."

"Oh my God, you've been following me."

Suddenly, everything became clear. The shadowy figures who induced fear as she walked home in Archway. The black-clad character Al had disturbed pointing a gun in their back yard. They weren't foreign agents or even local hoodlums. They were all working for Stephens. Spying on her. Or charged with keeping her safe, depending on your point of view.

"Looking after you is the way I see it." Stephens's soft, measured delivery could make any action, however malevolent or intrusive, seem perfectly reasonable.

"But I was almost killed. Why didn't you come sooner? Two seconds later I would have …"

She didn't finish the sentence, the image of Leanne's gun propelling a spasm of terror up her spine.

"I'll come clean." Stephens squirmed uncomfortably on the tailgate of the ambulance as a paramedic towelled Emily's wet hair. "When you came to my place, as I took your coat, I slipped a tiny tracker into the lining of your handbag. An insurance policy from which we could both benefit."

"You bugged me?"

"Yes, I suppose you could call it that. Just for a month or so. Not because we had doubts about you, but because you had doubts about us. You're young, inexperienced and you were working on the most sensitive operation. We needed to make sure you could handle the pressure. I'm not ashamed of what I did. You're not the first operative to be subjected to checks and balances, and you won't be the last."

"So why didn't you come sooner?"

"Two men from my section observed you visiting Imelda Jones and going on to meet Luke. They reported you leaving Luke's house with his partner in the family car. As far as they were concerned you were with a high-ranking officer from the Service and no longer in need of protection. So they stood down, although the tracker kept working."

Emily's mind fast-tracked back to Scafell's house and the exchange between Leanne and Luke to make sure they didn't leave the handbag behind.

"Did he know?"

"What?"

"Did Luke know I was being tracked?"

"Not to my knowledge. We got involved when Bob Wilson alerted us. The tracker led us to the car park and though it took longer than we thought to arrow in on your specific destination we got there in the end."

"Too late."

"What do you mean?"

"If I was relying on you lot, I'd be the one lying in that shelter with my brains blown out instead of Leanne. You got there after the shooting stopped, remember." Stephens let the insubordinate tone drift on the gusting breeze. Fine rain again fell and an uneasy silence sat awkwardly between them.

"What happens now?" The adrenalin of the last few hours had instilled a sharp pugnacity in Emily. She had cheated death, no thanks to the Service. She deserved an explanation.

"Luke will be interviewed and there'll be an investigation. Obviously, that will include you, especially with this Tinman business still going on."

"Oh God." Emily sat up rigid. "We've got to warn them about Tinman."

"Warn who?" Due to her ordeal, Stephens had made allowances for Emily's behaviour, but he was beginning to wonder if she was indulging an element of melodrama.

"Jack and his team. In Paris."

As director in control of foreign agents, Stephens had been briefed on the Paris mission, a couple of his men providing intelligence back-up on the security configuration at the Palace of Versailles. The overriding feeling conveyed to McBride was that a lone assassin, even a gunman as adept as Tinman, would find it impossible to breach the location.

"Don't worry, Emily," said Stephens. "Not even Tinman could smuggle a gun into Versailles."

"It's not a fucking gun." The profanity screamed from Emily's lips, wild and unexpected, like a wayward firework. "Ask Luke. He knows. It's not a gun. Leanne as good as told us."

A puzzled expression sat awkwardly on Stephens's face. Emily's earnest delivery wasn't melodrama. He could see that now. She wasn't milking the drama of a surreal and terrifying night, instead assembling the jigsaw of events of the last few weeks. She was convinced she'd found the final piece.

"What time is it?"

Stephens glanced at his watch. "Eight-thirty."

"That makes it nine-thirty in Paris. I've got to speak to Jack. Right now. Is there any way we can contact him?"

"Yes, but ..."

"No buts. We need to make it happen. Now. Jack and the Prime Minister's lives depend on it."

Stephens sucked in a deep breath. "Emily, this had better be good, and you had better be right."

44

The line was hissy and indistinct, but Emily detected irritation in Easton's tone, even though his voice was little more than a whisper.

"This isn't a good time."

"Apparently, it can't wait." Stephens sat alongside Emily in a Service communications truck, the same one used to track Emily to Epping Forest, now parked on the grass verge a few yards in front of the Claypit car park. They both wore large headphones and after Stephens had cleared it with McBride, the communications techie had entered the code, *Red spy at night,* and patched them into the frequency Easton and his team were using. Emily, wet clothes discarded, had slipped on a spare pair of green paramedic fatigues provided by the ambulance crew. Her mind pulsed with urgency borne of desperation.

"Jack, it's Emily, from the office. You may remember I discovered the alias Tinman was using, Adam Lewandowski."

"Okay Emily, go ahead. What is it?"

"Tinman isn't planning to shoot anyone."

"What?"

"He's not even got a gun, I don't think."

"How do you know this?"

"It's too complicated, Jack. Just believe me. You need to trust me."

"Is he here, in Paris?"

"Yes, I think so. He's probably in the same room as you now, or at least somewhere close by."

The hiss on the line cleared, Emily and Stephens hearing the clink of cutlery and background hum of chummy conversation. They could even make out musical French accents at Easton's side of the room.

"If he's not got a gun, then what's he planning?"

"If I'm right, Tinman's target is not only the Prime Minister. He could be out to kill all the main European leaders."

"A bomb?" Easton's reply raised a pitch, the incredulity plain.

"Where are the main European leaders seated?"

"At the top table. The PM, French president, German chancellor and Italian president, all with their partners."

The top table was configured at the far end of the room from Easton's vantage point, one long table branching off at the middle, stretching the full length of the hall with guests either side. The conversations between politicians and partners appeared genial. Macca stood at his post by the top table and Easton thought he registered a quizzical expression as he listened in to the radio chatter.

"All seems fine at the moment," said Easton. "Are you sure of this? I can't see Tinman getting a bomb past security. It's not his style."

"It's not a bomb, Jack. It's poison. Tinman's going to poison the Prime Minister. I'm sure of it. Maybe even poison the whole lot of them."

Stephens's expression switched from quizzical to concerned. He turned to Emily and for a brief moment wondered if her logic had been destabilised by the events of a terrifying night. He seemed about to suggest Emily reconsider, but then remembered his own advice to her. *Go with your gut instinct.* Before he could speak, Easton intervened. Emily had impressed him on several occasions. Sticking her foot in McBride's door. Pursuing Tinman with relentless zeal down avenues others would never have dared. He valued such independent thought. In truth, he saw much of his young self in Emily. Sharp. Logical. Bold. Fearless. A strong character who didn't conform to norms, but trod her own considered path regardless of the consequences.

"It makes sense, perfect sense. He's used poison before, or at least we think he did with Navalny. And we all know the Russians favour a drop of poison." Easton whispered as he watched waiters scurrying in all directions, some carrying salvers, or collecting dishes, some serving wine, others fussing over tables where diners had special requests. Each individual interaction was precise but the overall movement appeared chaotic, especially with copious mirrors magnifying the kinetic ambience of the room to an observer tenfold. It occurred to Easton that this was the ideal scenario for an assassin to elude detection.

Emily's mind had engaged overdrive. "It has to be a waiter. Tinman must be in disguise as a waiter. What are they wearing, Jack?"

"White dress shirts, black trousers, bow ties. Same as the guests, but with white gloves and no jackets."

"What better way to hide in plain sight? It's the only plan that makes sense. A man in a dress suit and black tie causes heads to turn. But if the whole room is full of men in dress suits and black ties no one stands out. They all become virtually invisible. As well as that, the waiters will probably leave at the same time, providing another crucial smokescreen. Tinman would blend in perfectly. He's the master of disguise, Jack. That's how he'd think. Safety in identically-dressed numbers."

Easton was silent for a while, mulling Emily's scenario, his attention fixed on the scores of white shirts, black trousers and bow ties bustling around the room, a gnawing twinge of foreboding in the pit of his stomach at Cam's radio silence. Eventually he piped up. "Macca, you getting all this?" A nod from the far wall. Easton consulted a pad containing the dinner's running order. In 10 minutes, the French president was scheduled to deliver a short speech expressing NATO unity, after which a toast would be offered in solidarity with Ukraine. The toast. Of course, that must be the killing point, surmised Easton. It made perfect sense. The only time all the dignitaries were guaranteed to drink at the same time. With liquid from the same bottle. That would adhere to Tinman's relentless pursuit of efficiency.

"Okay, Macca. Concentrate on the waiter or waiters serving the toast to the top table," said Easton. "They should be pouring bubbly shortly. No one will drink until after the speech. I'll talk you through it and I'll patch in the French to give back-up. I'll identify the waiter. Wait for my command and then take him out." It was a calculated gamble. What if someone took a sip before the toast was declared? It could happen. Frequent diners are not unaccustomed to testing the vintage. It was a risk Easton was prepared to take. His primary mission wasn't protection, but to locate and nullify Tinman.

"How will we know it's Tinman?" Stephens interjected.

"We'll know soon enough when we take his gloves off. Tinman's the one with the missing thumb."

45

Tinman slipped out of the dining hall, strode swiftly down the corridor and disappeared into the toilets reserved for staff. Gendarmes stood on duty at both ends of the corridor but their demeanour betrayed little concern. Starter and main course complete, many staff had passed by, a general lull replacing the overall bedlam.

There were four stalls in the toilet. The near one was occupied. Tinman swung open the other doors to check they were empty before taking the furthest from the entrance. He shut the door, sat down and untied his right shoelace.

Turning the shoe over, he fished in his pocket, pulling out a plastic paper clip. Using the rounded end as the head of a screwdriver he located a groove in the middle of the heel, twisting to reveal a secret, foam-lined compartment. Sat snugly in the middle, like a tiepin in a presentation case, lay a small cardboard box. Tinman extracted the box delicately, opening it to reveal a tiny glass vial filled with liquid. He had worked with poison before, novichok and polonium being Russia's standard killing agents. Not that poison was his favourite weapon. He preferred the speed and certainty of the gun and the knife. Spilling blood conformed to his assassin's code, requiring precision, nerve and courage. It conferred honour. Poison was imprecise, relying on the whim, movement and metabolism of the victim. The outcome rarely certain, depending on dosage, rate of ingestion, and speed of treatment. Poison could take between two minutes and 18 hours to induce the required effect. In its favour, it could be administered secretly, giving the perpetrator time and distance to make his escape as nerve agent symptoms were often mistaken for natural afflictions. To Tinman that only confirmed his opinion. A craven weapon.

But this was no time for ideological niceties. How else could he smuggle a lethal weapon close to so many European leaders? He replaced his shoe, slipped the box into his pocket, flushed the toilet as others had entered the room, and as he was leaving checked his appearance in the wall mirror.

That's strange, he thought. A row of bright red lumps raised on his neck, resembling a heat or sweat rash. He also felt warm and a little nauseous. The kitchen was stifling, the dining room full of hot food and bodies. It could be the dress shirt rubbing, but then he recognised the rash and knew immediately. The slimy squid he had helped clear away. Must have transferred remnants via his gloves and sparked his allergy. Crucially, the prosthetics were still in place. More urgent matters to attend to. He pulled up his collar and swiftly returned to the dining room.

He had prepared the ground for the next part of the plan within minutes of arrival that afternoon, informing the headwaiter of his expertise in handling the protocols of serving champagne. The man, an aloof sort with a Roman nose adept at looking down on subordinates, expected him to demonstrate his skills, which Tinman duly did, executing his cork-pulling, pouring and serving with the panache of a circus juggler, drawing nods and approving glances from the rest of the staff. It meant Tinman clinched the prestigious role of organising the toast for the section of the room closest to the top table.

On the headwaiter's signal, Tinman sprang into action, removing a long row of bottles of Louis Roederer Cristal Brut from the mobile chiller, popping corks, the sound eliciting a spontaneous clap and murmur of appreciation from guests. He prepared the bottles for distribution on a wine trolley, another wag of the headwaiter's white-gloved finger alerting him to release them to the waiters chosen to pour, all of whom knew precisely the section required to serve. Tinman handed out the bottles, saving the last for himself and the top table. As the waiters left the trolley, he busily folded napkins and cleared assorted debris, making it the easiest of tasks to slip the vial from his pocket, release it from its box and gently dribble the contents into the remaining bottle, taking care not to splash the slightest drop. No need to mix or stir. He knew well enough the aerosol released by escaping bubbles alone could prove deadly.

THE HIT LIST

The irony did not elude him. Here he was about to serve up a mixture of death and destruction in a bottle the western world coveted as a symbol of triumph and achievement. Champagne and novichok. He smiled. A potent cocktail his bosses back in Moscow would appreciate.

Grabbing the bottle, he sauntered towards the Italian president seated at the end of the top table. It was then he spotted the nod. The merest movement of Macca's head attracted Tinman's antennae. He tracked the direction of Macca's eyes, narrow and focused, fixed on a point at the far end of the room. The stage. The curtains. Something didn't feel right.

He knew the dining hall crawled with security. Of course he did. He had clocked half a dozen special forces personnel at the start of the dinner. Taken them to be French, mostly because they had an air of nonchalance, a swagger in their walk, a haughtiness about their manner. The French could disguise the way they dressed, even the way they talked, but not the manner of their shrugs. UK special forces were more understated, exuding precision, inclined to dourness. They prided themselves on staying incognito, dressed as they were in guest apparel, but Tinman was a trained observer. He'd spotted the micro receiver in Macca's ear and the bulge under his jacket hiding his weapon. But now he was up close he realised where he had seen him before. Talking to Jack Easton earlier that evening in the four-man huddle by Gate10. Easton must be behind the curtain. That was the obvious conclusion. A spotter. Marshalling his troops. Taking an overview. In Tinman's world that meant Easton and his men were on to something. The nod, eyes knowing and determined, disturbed him. To the mind of a trained killer, it was a gesture of anticipation as much as assent. There was only one logical move. Time for Plan B.

46

The French president intrigued Easton. They were around the same age, both in their early forties. As Easton watched him from the snick in the curtain, he marvelled at how lightly the vital affairs of state sat on his shoulders.

It helped that nature had played a kind hand. Fine features, high cheekbones, tight, unblemished skin, a full head of blondish hair, not a hint of grey. But it was the easy manner, calm and focused, that impressed Easton most. He would expect nothing less from a man who studied philosophy, was an accomplished pianist, excelled as an investment banker and married his high-school teacher, 24 years his senior, against the wishes of his parents. Great statesmen are rather like great soldiers, Easton mused, as he watched the president dispatch an aide's urgent whisper in his ear with a smile and a nod on one hand while sharing a joke with the Prime Minister on the other. Great leaders don't lack fear, rather they control fear. Taking decisions, big and small, in their stride, untouched and unfettered by emotion.

The aide's whisper had informed the president of Easton's request for French back-up in light of a clear, present and imminent danger. No point in inducing panic. Leave security to the experts. The show must go on. That's what Easton read into the president's nod.

Waiters had already charged most of the guests' glasses ready for the toast. A couple of minutes before the president was due to rise to his feet, the dignitaries, all in animated conversation, took scant notice of the waiter approaching the top table.

Like the others, he carried an opened bottle of champagne in white-gloved hands. Easton strained to steal a better view. The man looked older than Tinman, a weariness about his gait that didn't fit, but the general build matched.

"Turn round, you bastard." Easton whispered through gritted teeth. He was looking for a cross-like Tinman scar on the man's left cheek but that side of his face was in shadow as he bowed to pour the wine.

The serving proceeded with meticulous protocol to suit the occasion. From the diner's right-hand side, gold label facing out so guests could see the vintage, not touching or resting the bottle against the rim of the glass, pouring slowly to avoid splashes. The bottle in the waiter's left hand.

"That's him. Go, go, go." The left hand proved the giveaway. An infusion of heat sending Easton's pulse soaring.

He threw the curtains open, leapt from the stage, gun in hand, sprinting towards the top table. Macca reacted even quicker, much nearer and strides ahead of Easton when he flung himself at the waiter, spread-eagling him over the top table with a thumping rugby tackle, sending plates, glasses, food and wine flying. Several wives screamed, piercing shrieks that cannoned off the ornate vaulted ceiling. Chairs scraped, diners gasped, three French special forces officers arriving to help pin the waiter down, one with a burly forearm around his neck.

"Don't move, nobody move. Personne ne bouge." Easton screamed in English and French, training his pistol on the waiter. Luckily, the champagne bottle had spun sideways on impact, the liquid spilling out and streaming across the wooden floor, away from the diners. Two waiters made as if to mop up the mess, but Easton spun around, fixing them in his sights. "N'y touche pas. C'est du poison. It's poison, don't touch." They recoiled, fear on their faces.

Within seconds, bodyguards in protective huddles bundled presidents and the Prime Minister to the exit without regard for dignity or decorum.

Easton was eager to know for sure. He'd expected more of a fight, the cowed behaviour of the captured waiter troubled him.

"Turn him over, let's get a good look."

As Macca spun him around, the waiter shook with fright, letting out a series of yelps, pain raking his body from shattered ribs. This was not the demeanour of an assassin.

"Take his right glove off." Easton barked the command.

Macca ripped it off to reveal what Easton feared. A perfectly normal thumb.

47

"What the holy crap's going on, Emily?"

Easton seethed into his microphone. It was a tone Emily had not heard before. The desperate growl of a man with his reputation rapidly gurgling down the plughole. The French had allowed Easton to call the action, mostly because he had convinced them Tinman was about to enact his most grievous assassinations on their soil. The president, always with an eye on the next election, saw it as an opportunity. The chance to take credit for capturing one of the world's most wanted criminals on his watch. Easton had explained his strategy and French special forces agreed that a small focused team, backed by fool-proof intelligence, was the only way to flush out a man with Tinman's guile. From where Easton was standing that intelligence now looked more fool-hardy than fool-proof.

Emily had no time to think. A heavy weight crushed her chest, breathing laboured, her mind dizzy. In the last few hours she'd discovered a colleague was a traitor. She'd been abducted, tied up, yomped through a forest, had a gun held to her head, made peace with her maker and been reprieved. She barely understood why or how. Now she was wrong about Tinman, or so it seemed. But she couldn't be wrong. She'd tracked him to Paris. Why else would he have come? Questions arrowed into her brain. Two years ago such pressure would have drained Emily's resources. Her body and mind would have shut down to wallow in a pool of self-absorption. It was a close-run thing, but Easton's desperate tone re-energised her.

"Tinman's there, Jack, I'm sure of it."

"Where, Emily, where? The French are about to put my balls in a guillotine. So will the PM, if we don't find him …" His voice trailed off as guests milled in chaotic fashion around the Hall of Mirrors. Women in fancy gowns wore shocked expressions, men pleaded with gendarmes for news on what had brought the occasion to such a violent conclusion. A rumour circulated that a terrorist was loose in the palace after stabbing the French president.

Emily glanced at Stephens and saw a strange, troubled look on his face. She detected concern combined with a hint of fear, mixed with disappointment that his trust in her had been misplaced.

"Stay on the line." Easton's order crackled in their ears. The soldier in him had made its decision. Only one course of action required. The palace required locking down. Under the circumstances, considering the Service's intelligence appeared to be flawed, that was a tough ask.

It took all Easton's considerable powers to persuade the French commander of the nation's Special Operations Command on site to listen to him. Colonel Valentin Aubert had many qualities. He was tall, strong, demanding, courageous, and fiercely supportive of the men under his command. He owned a generous heart and according to the ladies, was impossibly handsome with slicked dark hair and deep blue eyes, but, as with many French officers, he lacked humility and distrusted the British.

"La course d'un imbécile." Colonel Aubert kept repeating the phrase, which Easton roughly translated as 'a fool's errand' as he strongly advised him to detain the guests in the Hall of Mirrors until all had been checked and verified. Easton also insisted police should hold the 50 waiters in the ante-chamber.

"La course d'un imbécile." Aubert shook his head. Easton's heart sank and the evening's events would have concluded there and then if Macca had not approached.

"A word, Sir."

"Go on."

Macca bent over and whispered in Easton's ear. "We've just found Cam by Gate 10 with a knife stuck in his neck."

48

Tinman was trapped. All exits from the Hall of Mirrors and ante-chamber were sealed. Colonel Aubert had responded to Cam's fate with speed and decisiveness, gendarmes and special forces flooding the palace's main arteries.

The guests were ordered to retake their places at the long dining table. With no explanations forthcoming, other than a security alert was in progress, questioning chatter and an air of irritation replaced the initial shock. A deputy in the National Assembly, head held high and shoulders stiff to compensate for his small stature, marched up to Aubert demanding answers in an entitled manner, only for two soldiers to escort him back to the table, a forceful nudge in his back planting him in his seat.

The mood in the ante-chamber also grew tense. Gendarmes had herded the waiters into the smaller hall and were watching over them like sheepdogs guarding a flock.

Tinman positioned himself in the middle of the group, where he could view all sides but his own countenance would be lost in a sea of faces. His neck burned and he pressed a gloved finger under his collar, scratching the red lumps, relieving the itch. He stroked his chin, mulling the events of the last few minutes. His plan had gone awry, but as he watched Easton and Aubert enter the ante-chamber deep in animated conversation, he knew he was right. They were on to him. He had read the room right. Macca's nod proved the clincher. That's why he had returned to the trolley and opted for Plan B, inviting Jean Daniel to take his place serving the top table. He'd asked with charm and grace, in the knowledge that Jean, who had helped him lay the long table earlier, spilling many of his personal details, was roughly the same build and crucially also left-handed.

"Jean, you have served so many of these occasions. Many more than I. You deserve the honour. Please, go ahead. Serve the president and his guests. A story to tell your grandchildren." Tinman added his warmest smile. An offer and privilege Jean could not refuse. His heart swelled, body stiffening with pride as he accepted the champagne and approached the table, thus lending the mission an extra layer of insurance.

Tinman's plan was to slip out of the Hall of Mirrors, head for Gate 10 and into the night under cover of the commotion certain to follow shortly after the top table had drunk the toast. It would have worked if Easton had not reacted so swiftly, Jean's explosive apprehension having triggered the immediate lock-down of all exits.

The detention of guests and waiters also told Tinman that Easton's team knew Jean was not their man. Or at least not the only wanted man. Not that Tinman was unduly alarmed. His preparation had been vigilant, disguise masterful and ID papers unimpeachable. All he need do was wait it out as Antoine Dubois.

Easton, with Aubert's approval, set up a verification system, requiring each waiter to pass through a cordon of gendarmes before arriving at a desk at the ante-chamber exit where officers scrutinised ID papers and two soldiers subjected them to a body search. The final crucial check demanded each waiter strip off their gloves and show their right hand.

Easton planted Macca at the back of the room to keep an eye on the throng while he stood 10 feet or so behind the desk, peering into the eyes and then at the hand of each waiter as they passed. He readjusted the microphone under his tie. There was no longer need for concealment. He had given a sketchy report on the run to McBride at HQ, picked up by Stephens and Emily in the tracker van.

"Emily, can you hear me?"

A puzzled frown settled on Emily's face as she glanced at Stephens. "Yes, I'm still here. What can I do?"

"You've studied Tinman more than anyone. Give me something to look for."

"The missing thumb?" It was phrased as a question, but also the obvious answer.

"Yeah, we've got that covered, but what else? Tinman's a genius at disguise."

"You can't disguise a missing thumb."

"Don't put anything past Tinman."

"The scar on his cheek. In the shape of a cross."

"Copy that. But too easy to conceal."

While they were talking Stephens had instructed the techie to bring up the most recent picture of Tinman on a monitor in front of them. Emily didn't need it. All Tinman's relevant details were preserved in her photographic memory. Already her mind was sifting through a vast assortment of pictures, facts and personal details, down to the minute measurements calculated by the face technology.

"I'll describe each man as he passes," said Easton, cursing his omission to add body cams to the mission. "If anything rings a bell, shout up."

The process was speedy but also meticulous. Each waiter trudged through in turn, some eliminated swiftly by height and age, Easton's running commentary concentrating on distinguishing features, but also on the men's gait and demeanour.

Tinman watched the process towards the back of the group. While the other waiters focused on the gendarmes checking each individual's ID papers, Tinman's eyes rarely left Easton. The Russian's professional awareness told him Easton was in command, taking the overview, assembling the whole jigsaw puzzle while those around him saw only the pieces. When each man's check was complete the gendarmes glanced at Easton for a nod of permission to release.

It took almost an hour for the line of waiters to dwindle by half, nothing Easton described resonating with Emily. Tinman was two from the front when one of the gendarmes barked an order at a waiter who spat back his response, his mood wearied by the wait. The name on the waiter's passport did not tally exactly with the information held by security. The man was in his forties, roughly Tinman's build and Easton's antennae twitched, although his description did not alert Emily. One of the soldiers ripped off the man's glove and Easton strode forward to observe. No missing thumb. Probably an illegal immigrant with false papers, Easton surmised. His shoulders relaxed.

"Okay, take him for checking." One of the gendarmes escorted the irate waiter from the room, leaving one policeman only at the desk.

Five minutes later it was Tinman's turn. He sensed the lone gendarme was no longer quite as precise or fastidious with his checks as he flicked past his photo muttering his name, "Antoine Dubois", with a casual glance at his face. Tinman's heart beat a touch faster. Not even a seasoned assassin, with all his training and experience of managing jeopardy, could totally control the ways of nature. Easton, however, remained calm, vigilant, eyes settling on the man's physique, ticking boxes in his mind. Emily sensed increased animation in his description.

"What is it, Jack? Is there something unusual?"

"Dunno, just a bit strange. Guy called Antoine Dubois. Right height and physique. Hair receding a shade. A red, purplish rash on his neck. Quite distinctive. How does that check out?"

"No bells ringing, Jack, I don't think." Nothing lit up Emily's memory, although, as she glanced at the picture on the screen to make sure, an indistinct thought nagged.

Tinman, at the gendarme's insistence, took off his right glove and Easton eased forward, anticipation heightened, hand feeling for his gun.

49

A perfectly normal hand, four fingers and thumb, all complete. The gendarme looked at Easton, who nodded. A grudging nod.

Tinman sauntered away, the hint of a smirk forming on his lips. His mission incomplete, but there would be another time, another day, when the likes of Easton and the French ran out of luck. He was also secretly proud that his new prosthetic thumb had stood up to such close scrutiny. Tinman lived with the stumpy remnant of that shattered thumb for years after saving Putin from his would-be assassin. It became a trophy of sorts. A daily, if ugly, reminder of the consequences of his chosen trade, driving him on to compensate in other areas for his affliction.

Twelve months ago, however, an expert in prosthetics from Moscow University had contacted him through Kremlin sources to reveal new technology in the prosthetics field was now capable of providing not only an artificial thumb which moved, bent and opposed as a natural one, but could also be grafted onto the wrinkled stump with such precision that only an expert would detect the join. It looked and, to another's touch, felt like a real thumb, even had a unique print, although it didn't grasp or shoot with the accuracy of his old one. There were no nerves or sensory perception, but Tinman had undergone the secret operation in the certainty that it formed a perfect disguise. The files of the FBI, CIA, MI6, Interpol, even the FSB in Moscow, documented his most identifiable characteristic as a missing thumb. The operation had rendered him anonymous. He had never put that to the test. Until now.

The nagging tap gradually increased in Emily's head until it was almost a drum beat, striving to connect various pieces of information. "I wonder." She mused to herself, but Stephens heard. Something was troubling her.

"What is it?"

"I don't know, maybe nothing."

"Now's the time to let it all out, Emily. Don't leave any thought, any theory, on the table."

Emily moved the microphone nearer to her lips. "Jack, what was on the menu tonight?"

"Pardon?" Jack's reply laden with incredulity.

"Was there any seafood?"

"For Christ sake, Emily. How in God's name can that be relevant?" Easton rarely lost his temper. Never get angry. That was the first rule of a special forces officer. Anger is the enemy of reason, a dangerous indulgence if unaccompanied by forethought. But there was a scathing rasp in his tone, one which did not escape Stephens's attention.

"I'm serious, Jack. It could be important."

"Yes, Emily. There was a seafood starter, although much of it ended up on the floor. One of the waiters stumbled, dropped a tray and it took half a dozen staff to clear it up. They were on their hands and knees for five minutes, scooping up all sorts of shellfish."

Emily began shaking, this time not with cold or in fright, but at the extraordinary possibility that lurked deep in Easton's information.

"Jack, Tinman has an allergy to shellfish. It's in his history. I remember noting it down at McBride's briefing weeks ago. It brings him out in reddish bumps like hives. Induces nausea. If he had helped to clean up the spillage it would be on his hands, on his gloves. He could have transferred it to his face and neck. Jack, that red rash could …"

She realised Easton was no longer listening. He was half-way down the corridor, sprinting towards Gate 10. Something had troubled him about Antoine Dubois. He couldn't explain it, but he'd experienced those feelings before. He remembered the young man in Luton during an undercover mission to hunt down a gang of radical extremists. He'd watched the man board the train to London with a rucksack on his back, along with a score of other passengers. Nothing untoward, apart from a nonchalance about his manner and a strange look in his eyes. Easton had jumped aboard, arrested the man at St Pancras, discovering a machete and a small pistol in his bag. He was bound for the Houses of Parliament to wreak bloody havoc at the seat of democracy. Easton wondered later what had alerted him, concluding that the strange look was zeal. Those unprepared to compromise could alter their dress, their looks, their words, but disguising the glint of their purpose proved almost impossible. Easton's father, a military man himself who saw action in Northern Ireland and at the battle of Goose Green in the Falklands, had explained as much to him many years ago. "The eyes, Jack, are the gateway to the soul. If there's a flicker of doubt in a man's trustworthiness, look hard enough and you'll detect it in his eyes."

As he ran, Easton reached for his gun. There was a dog-leg in the corridor and he expected to see Dubois, or Tinman, if that truly was his identity, as he turned, the approach to Gate 10 stretching out long and narrow. No sign of him. Surely he couldn't have escaped so quickly. Easton shouted to the gendarme on the gate but he looked bemused. When he reached the gate the policeman confirmed no one had passed in the last five minutes.

"Bugger!" Easton turned, sprinting back along the corridor, checking the staff toilets, gasping into his microphone. "Macca, JJ, he's heading for the front courtyard. It's Tinman in waiter's gear. Look for a man with a bright red rash on his neck."

"Copy that." Macca and JJ replied.

The corridors inside the Palace of Versailles are longer than touchlines on a football field, while the building is renowned for its labyrinth-like configuration. An empty gripe gnawed in Easton's stomach as he realised a man of Tinman's resourcefulness could even now be melting into the complex interior of one of the world's most lavish buildings. When he reached the entrance his spirits sank even lower. Guests were emerging from the Hall of Mirrors. He spotted Colonel Aubert 20 yards away. Striding over, he demanded the guests be held longer, explaining Tinman may still be in the palace.

"Absolutely not. The guests have been held long enough already."

"I've got a soldier with a knife in his neck. The killer is still ..."

215

Aubert interrupted, hands raised, mouth fixed in a contemptuous leer. "We have the palace surrounded. If the Russian's here, the French will take care of him. But let us not fool ourselves. A rat can smell danger. He's probably many kilometres away already."

Easton strode back to Macca and JJ. All around, guests, more than 250 of them in black suits, ties and white dress shirts, were milling about with their partners, some clambering into cars, others waiting for transport, all discussing the dramatic conclusion to an eventful evening.

Easton hated the prospect of failure, but the release of guests at that moment had presented Tinman with the perfect smokescreen.

"How the hell are we supposed to find him now?" said Easton. "Look at this lot. Like penguins on parade."

50

The stroll from the Palace of Versailles to Rive Gauche station is little more than 600 metres. No more than four or five minutes.

As Easton jogged along the Avenue de Sceaux he made even better time, passing a few guests who had not organised their own transport. They were easy to spot. The ladies wore fancy gowns, many with dazzling jewellery around their necks, the men in black dinner suits and ties.

The station was Emily's idea. Logic told her only organised, pre-planned transport would warrant access inside the palace grounds. The same logic told her waiters would not pay for expensive taxis into the city when cheap public transport was available. Her trawl through McBride's briefing had also thrown up Tinman's knowledge and passion for trains.

"It's worth a shot, Jack," Emily said. "Lots of waiters will head for the station. There's safety in numbers, that's what Tinman may be thinking."

"What time's the last train to the city?"

"Twenty-five past eleven."

Easton glanced at his watch. 11.18pm. Hence the need to jog.

When he arrived, the lights of the station hall burned bright as a beacon in the darkness. A homeless man with matted locks, his long-haired dog curled up on a sleeping bag, having clocked off for the night, argued with a member of the station staff at the entrance, accusing someone of having stolen his belongings as he begged. He implored the station worker to call the police. Easton recalled his year on the streets, the memory of the cloying cold and impenetrable boredom making him shiver. If he'd had time to hunt for change, he would have handed the man some. A few guests and waiters hurried through the ticket barriers, the mechanical grumble of a train trundling into the station, prompting haste.

No time, no ready cash to buy a ticket, no staff around as the only one on duty was attending to the beggar, Easton vaulted the barrier, ignoring snooty looks from some of the dinner jackets.

Waiters lined the platform, standing in a row, so close that if one had fallen the rest would have toppled like dominos. As the train slowed to a stop it became clear it was already populated with day-trippers returning to the city for work next morning. When the doors opened, the waiters pressed forward, filling most of the remaining seats in the five carriages.

Easton leapt onto the last carriage. The air was warm, stuffy with stale sweat and dog odour. The ride to the city would take around half an hour, plenty of time for him to check out each carriage. For several minutes he stood considering his options, working out how best to sweep the train. The more he absorbed Emily's theory, the more it made sense. All those black suits and white shirts looked the same. Hell, he was wearing one himself. The thought provided the same comfort camouflage affords a soldier in the field. But he was tense, too. He was alone, without the back-up of loyal colleagues. He contemplated doing nothing until the train reached its destination when gendarmes rallied by Macca and JJ would almost certainly be waiting. That may be too late, too many opportunities for a fugitive to flee as the train trundled slowly towards Paris. The image of Cam with a knife in his neck made up his mind. That, and the fact he could almost smell Tinman's presence.

Easton concentrated on remembering the details of Antoine Dubois, the waiter, the image eventually assembling in his mind. Long face, receding hair, red neck rash, the hint of a smirk as he proffered his ID papers. Shouldn't be hard to spot. He gazed down the carriage, eyes narrowing as he scrutinised each passenger facing him in a black suit. When he eliminated them all, he reached to check his weapon and started edging his way along the aisle, focusing only on those in black suits facing away from him.

Passengers paid him scant notice, assuming he was searching for the lone toilet, the train conversation animated, dissecting the events of the evening at the palace. As he passed each row he glanced around, expectation growing as he ticked off black suits carriage by carriage. One waiter in the third carriage, black fedora tilted over closed eyes, almost prompted him to draw his gun, but the man stirred in time, revealing silver hair and a distinctive hooked nose.

Easton's heart rate quickened, hand fingering his weapon again as he reached the final carriage. Packed with suits, several standing in the aisle, making an overview sweep of the carriage impossible. Where would Tinman sit? Almost certainly at the front in a seat facing backwards where he could survey any danger arriving from afar. If he was there, he had probably clocked Easton already. A disconcerting gripe gnawed in Easton's stomach. He edged his way along the carriage, muscles tense and alert, anticipating an imminent lunge from each row. The standing suits exchanged puzzled looks as he brushed past, but at least the crowded aisle disguised his pedantic progress.

Thirty seconds later, Easton reached the front of the train. Every suit checked. No sign of Tinman. His body relaxed, relief that the threat of mortal combat had dissipated, fighting with disappointment and irritation that Tinman had escaped. He worked his way back along the carriage, but while sliding open the connecting door his body braced as he heard a call from behind.

"Antoine, Antoine, it's me, Pierre."

Easton pivoted in the narrow aisle, turning to see Pierre Laurent, the chef from the palace who had recognised Antoine Dubois, gesture across the aisle. Not to a black suit, but to a man in a tattered grey overcoat with the collar turned up. The sort a homeless man may wear."Antoine." The chef called again and this time Easton detected recognition, alarm contorting the face of the overcoat man.

Easton fumbled inside his jacket but before he had drawn his gun the man had pushed the woman sat next to him out of the seat and stood behind her, using her as a shield, his right arm around her neck, left hand brandishing a knife, the point resting under her ear. He dragged her back along the aisle to the end of the carriage and Easton tracked them, his pistol aimed at the man's head. Easton could hear screams behind him as passengers ducked below seats or tried to squeeze their way through the narrow door into the next carriage. Some watched bemused and transfixed, too scared to move.

"It's over, Andrei." Easton spoke in English, using Tinman's real Christian name, his voice composed although blood pounded in his ears, his knees felt wobbly and a light-headed tingle accompanied the rush of anxiety.

"Maybe not," said Tinman, sounding equally calm. "If you know who I am, as I'm sure you do, you know what I'm capable of. You know I won't hesitate to slice this woman's throat. Put the gun down, or I'll kill her here and now."

The French woman was petite with wavy blonde hair, a porcelain complexion and wide brown eyes exuding innocence. She whimpered as Tinman reinforced his threat, pressing the point of the knife against her neck, bright red blood trickling immediately, staining her white collar. A pungent odour filled the air as her sphincter opened and her face crumpled in a fearful grimace, her lips imploring Easton to do as Tinman said. "Please," she mouthed in English. Easton did not blink, training his gun with both hands on the small portion of Tinman's head he could see behind the woman. For several moments they held their ground. Tinman desperate, but inured to the prospect of death by years existing on the dark side of humanity. Easton, uncertain of the outcome, but driven by the desire to end the killing spree of a man who had eluded all attempts at capture.

"Aren't you tired of killing?" Easton said, in an attempt to reason. "Let her go. Surely the great Andrei Reblov doesn't have to hide behind a woman. Do you have no shame?"

Tinman laughed. *The great Andrei Reblov.* Easton's description sounded like one of the novelty acts Tinman's mother took him to see as a young boy at the Moscow State Circus. A lifetime ago, before the excruciating loss of his parents and a twisted sense of loyalty to a brutal ideology had led him to murder and vengeance. The laugh morphed into a scowl.

"Shame? Shame is for those who doubt their purpose," Tinman snarled. "If you have a just cause, there are no means that can induce shame."

"Does that include poison, smeared recklessly so innocent lives may be lost, not just politicians and soldiers, but waiters, cooks, and God knows who else?"

THE HIT LIST

The realisation that Easton knew the details surrounding Tinman's objective earlier that evening stung. Tinman's jaw jutted and a momentary glint of piercing hate confirmed he was not for surrender. Easton had seen such a visage before, in the eyes of one of the British terrorists he hunted following the war in Iraq. Seconds before he blew himself up. Like a firework burning brightest just before it dies.

"There's collateral damage in every war," Tinman said, his delivery cold and even.

"This isn't war. What you're doing is murder, plain and simple."

The train lurched as it braked on its approach into the city. Out of the window, life rolled by in all its routine mundanity. Lights shimmered on the River Seine and in his peripheral vision Easton caught a glimpse of the Eiffel Tower, lit up like a Christmas tree, in the distance. Time seemed to stand still. Then Tinman, steadying himself against the train's movement, readjusted his choking hold on the woman. A mere fraction, no more, his arm so tight around her neck that her eyes bulged. In his readjustment his head turned marginally to the side and he muttered, "Three seconds, you have three seconds to …"

Tinman never finished his sentence. He had relied on Easton's innate decency to spare the woman's life, not realising Easton's next decision was instinctive and rooted in his father's sage advice from years past. The greatest natural advantage is for an enemy to underestimate your will.

Easton pulled the trigger. The bullet caught Tinman squarely in the temple, blasting out brain and skull fragments. The woman fainted, collapsing together with Tinman in a tangle of limbs as rivers of red chased their way like mountain streams down the carriage bulkhead.

51

It was nearly five o'clock when Emily received the summons to McBride's office.

On his orders she had taken a few days off to recover from her ordeal and with Al she had motored down to their seaside hideaway. She paddled in the ocean, soaked up some sun, sank a few beers, trying to think of anything other than the events of the last few weeks. Of course, it didn't work. There were too many unanswered questions, but at least she relaxed as usual in Al's attentive company.

They read about the aborted dinner at the Palace of Versailles in the Guardian. It was blamed on climate-change protesters who had somehow gained access, forcing security to evacuate leading politicians. Officials denied rumours of an assassination attempt, pinning a shooting on a Paris train that night on a drug gang.

Emily wondered at the skewed morality masquerading as protecting national security, as well as the rich invention of the appropriate media teams.

As she entered McBride's office her spirits lifted. The presence of 'C' on a corner chair by the panoramic window gave hope there may be some answers. Sitting at the conference table were McBride, Scafell, Stephens, Savage, and Jack Easton. Easton smiled. A compassionate smile, Emily thought, as if he was the only one who truly recognised the trauma she had endured.

She returned his smile and McBride said, "Good to see you looking well, Emily. We thought it only right you should be here after your interventions proved so valuable." Easton nodded. Scafell looked uncomfortable. Emily clocked the use of her Christian name. The first time McBride had used it. Acceptance of sorts.

"I can second that." Stephens wore his most avuncular expression.

McBride warned Emily that everything she heard was highly classified, covered by the Official Secrets Act she had signed on joining the Service, before going on to supply some explanation. He confirmed that Easton shot Tinman on the train to Paris after acting on Emily's information, and one of Easton's men had sadly been lost in the operation.

"Sorry." Emily aimed her condolence at Easton, who bowed his head.

"You should be proud, Emily," said McBride. "Your work here this last month resulted in one of the world's most dangerous and ruthless men being brought to justice. The kind of justice he understood."

The words droned in Emily's head. Despite listening intently, the phrases may as well have been Mongolian. They didn't make sense. All she could think of was Leanne pointing a pistol at her and the sound of two shots. Not knowing if she was about to die. And looking up to see Scafell's face, a smoking gun in his hand.

She looked across the table at Scafell and something flickered on his face. A twitch of regret? A flicker of compassion? Difficult to tell, but the question squirmed somewhere in Emily's gut. She had to know.

"Why did you kill Leanne?" The same question she'd asked when they had embraced in the mud of Epping Forest. Nothing he said that day had made sense, although at the time her brain was bruised and nerves shattered.

McBride glanced at 'C', received an affirmative twitch of his eyebrows, and took a long breath, his deep brogue guaranteeing an added gravity. "For twenty years or more Luke here has been a vital, perhaps the most crucial, cog in our fight against Russian Intelligence. He has helped save many hundreds of lives. Perhaps thousands. I don't think it too melodramatic to say that on occasion he has turned the course of history." McBride paused.

"How?" said Emily, eager to learn more.

"For twenty years he fed information of our choosing to the Russians while collecting information to bring to us. We saw the opportunity when he was in the Moscow bureau. It became clear the Russians had planted Leanne, subtly and delicately. She and Luke met in a Moscow bar. Both young and naïve. There was an instant attraction and Luke had no idea she was the daughter of a former KGB officer.

"For months they did what young people do, hung out in bars, went to the cinema and theatre. Leanne even dragged him to the ballet. When the relationship became more serious, the Service did some checks. Everything appeared innocent until a memo, a message of no real merit and little accuracy, was discovered on Leanne's computer in 2002, documenting incidentals about the search for weapons of mass destruction in Iraq."

"Why was that significant?" Emily was intrigued.

"Everyone knew the Service was tasked with supplying the intelligence for the British government. Unknown to Luke, we had planted the memo on his hard drive. A short time later it turned up on Leanne's machine, and not long after that we discovered it had made its way to the FSB. Someone had gained access to the memo without Luke's knowledge. It didn't take a rocket scientist to put two and two together. No harm done, but the sequence of events was indisputable."

"So when did Luke know about it?" Emily glanced at Scafell. His head bowed, eyes dull and vacant, as if the burden of his 20-year secret weighed heavy. He showed no inclination to tell his own story, happy for McBride to supply the explanation.

"It presented us with a wee opportunity, one that it would have been remiss of us not to take. While Luke was reluctant at first, we encouraged him to nurture his relationship. Over time he gained Leanne's trust, persuading her that he held anti-American, communist leanings. It allowed us to drip the odd morsel of intelligence Moscow's way, while collecting vital information about the growing threat from the Kremlin. Luke and Leanne became quite a partnership. Moscow thought they were working for them. Leanne was, but Scafell was always working for us."

"A double agent." Emily's eyes grew wide with respect. She had no experience but instinctively understood the risks involved in living a lie amid the enemy, especially during the uncompromising regime of Putin, when life was cheap, opposition ruthlessly eliminated and even loyal oligarchs met untimely ends for speaking out of turn.

McBride pulled a concerned face. "Not exactly a double agent. It was more complex than that. The Russians were delighted to believe they had a source at the heart of British Intelligence HQ, but nothing, I hasten to stress, was leaked or fabricated without our consent. It was vital that the Russians believed he was one hundred per cent committed to them. His life depended on it and so did many others. I can confidently confirm his actions in recent times saved the lives of many Ukraine soldiers as well as civilians. Part of the reason Russian generals were falling like autumn leaves when Putin invaded Ukraine is down to the information Luke gleaned from his Russian contacts. At great risk. Intelligence that always proved reliable. But he had no prior knowledge of Jones's assassination. That I can confirm."

Emily's misgivings were beginning to make sense. Her mind went back to Scafell's house when he had discovered Mason Jones's letter in her possession. He must have known Leanne was watching him. That's why he had reacted as any other Russian agent to preserve his cover. Why his speech was loud and forced so Leanne could hear. Why he argued the case for Russia against Ukraine, criticised Britain's role in Afghanistan and brought up the sinking of the Belgrano. The ideology that the West was evil was paramount, the one thing keeping him alive and his role intact.

"So he was prepared to do anything?" Emily's voice faltering.

"Except kill you, my dear." Stephens had been gauging Emily's mood and her appreciation of the truths she was hearing. "The life of an agent is pretty bloody at times. They have to cheat, mislead those they love, turn a blind eye to torture and hate. Sometimes kill or be killed. Yes, sometimes they have to be wicked and to do so not knowing exactly whether they're right or wrong. It would be wonderful if none of this were needed, of course it would. But the world's not like that, Emily. Tyrants flourish when good men drop their guard. And intelligence, reliable intelligence, is the best guard we have."

All Emily truly heard of Stephens's words were the first five, "Except kill you, my dear." Once again, they jerked her mind back to Epping Forest. She could smell the mud, feel the cold and rain running down her neck. She shivered, but now she understood.

Scafell had attempted to protect his identity to the last moment. She could vouch for that. He had gone along with the pre-determined plan. Yomped to the isolated killing spot, all the while sifting his brain for an escape route. He had jeopardised his cover trying to persuade Leanne that murder was not required. Only when the talking stopped and Leanne's gun hovered moments away from blasting a hole in Emily's chest did Scafell's 20-year cycle of apparent deceit and counter-deceit reach its inevitable crossroads.

Stephens's honeyed tones somehow seemed inappropriate as he put Scafell's stark choice into sharp focus. "Kill Emily and protect his identity, perhaps saving many lives in the future. Or save Emily and forever be mindful that one day the debt must be paid."

For the first time Emily truly appreciated Scafell's tangle of thoughts. She glanced across the table at his concerned expression and mouthed, "Thank you."

Scafell returned a weak smile and spoke for the first time. "I loved Leanne, truly I did. She was a kind, decent, resourceful woman, with a great sense of humour. We got on well. She listened to me, but there was one subject on which she wouldn't budge. She was her father's daughter. A child of the KGB. Wedded to the Kremlin ideology. In thrall to Putin. She would have done anything to please her father's old bosses. And they will stop at nothing to avenge her death."

"But why did she kill Mason? It wasn't necessary."

"She was smart." Scafell licked dry lips for a few moments. "I must have mentioned something, perhaps the way Mason looked at me sometimes. He was a canny guy, great with computers, and suspicious of everyone. He seems to have been fixated on some missing files, but they had nothing to do with me, although I always wondered if he knew who I really was. Leanne must have altered the files, especially the risk assessments, using my clearance code. She was tech savvy. My computer was protected with a biometric sensor, but the chances are she found a way around that. Maybe she lifted my fingerprint from a cup or glass and arranged for it to be cloned in some way. We'll never know, but someone, probably from the FSB, must have told her Jones was on to me and was about to expose me as a Russian spy."

"Why didn't she tell you? That would have been the logical thing to do."

Scafell shrugged. "We were together 20 years, but there was always part of her I couldn't fathom. Maybe she never totally trusted me. That's par for the course in our game, as I'm sure you'll discover."

A sadness engulfed Scafell, while Emily still required more evidence. "Are we sure this was all conceived in the Kremlin?"

"The fact that an SPS pistol killed Jones, the same gun Tinman used, confirms the FSB were involved," said Scafell. "Blaming the shooting on Tinman, known to be on a tour of vengeance, was the perfect smokescreen. To them it was nothing personal, merely good business, designed to protect me, in their minds their long-standing and valued agent at the heart of British Intelligence. It makes sense." He bowed his head.

McBride cleared his throat. "Other information has come to light in the last few days. Our technical department have recovered files from Leanne's computer and retrieved the sim cards on her phones. One word crops up on numerous occasions. Koshka."

"That's Russian for a cat. A female cat, I think," said Emily.

"Correct. From the dates and times, we believe Leanne used the code to communicate with Tinman before several of the assassinations. Whether she knew it was him is uncertain. Chances are, probably not. She may have believed it was a generic Kremlin operative, a handler used to pass on information. We'll never know."

McBride swapped glances with 'C' before sitting back in his chair, a silence descending on the room for many seconds as if honouring the memory of Jones.

Stephens was first to speak. "We have arranged a posting, and organised the necessary identity. It's a position of some importance but low profile in Central America, I won't reveal the exact destination, only to confirm it is minus Russian involvement and will suit Luke's talents."

"What's the time frame?" McBride was renowned for his practical mind.

"Time is of the essence," said Stephens. "The longer we wait the more likely Moscow will fit the pieces together. A flight leaves Heathrow later tonight. Luke is booked on that flight under a new identity. He is fully briefed."

'C' stood. "That all seems in order." He walked over to Scafell who also stood. 'C' offered his hand and they shook. A little stiff, but 'C''s tone was warm. "Good luck, Luke. We won't forget your sacrifice. The Service is in your debt." Scafell nodded and 'C' departed.

The meeting broke up, McBride, Savage and Scafell staying to chat informally about the impending arrangements while Easton ambled out of the office with Emily.

"Tell me, Emily, what made you think of shellfish?" Easton asked as they shared the lift to the ground floor.

"Pardon?"

"When you asked about seafood on the menu at Versailles, I thought you'd lost the plot, but it was the key to finding Tinman."

"A lucky guess, I suppose."

"Something tells me you don't do guesswork, Emily." There was respect and gratitude in Easton's tone. Emily's cheeks burned with pride.

The lift opened and they went their separate ways.

52

Emily drained her glass, sucking crushed ice, delighting in the contrast of the chill on her lips and the warm feeling the alcohol aroused in the pit of her stomach.

She had needed little persuasion when Al suggested a trip to the cocktail bar in Soho. The last time they visited Gin's Joint, they saved Wilson from a beating. Tonight was quieter, a few couples sharing intimate conversation, a television flickering high on the bar, set to the rolling news, sound turned down, subtitles trawling across the screen.

"It's good to see you smiling again." Al finished his pint and motioned to the barmaid, requesting another round.

Al knew Emily had faced life-threatening danger. He could only imagine what traumas she had undergone. But even though he had raised the alarm, alerting Wilson, security protocol precluded explanation over Emily's missing hours. He accepted that. Secrecy formed the essence of her job. As she had reminded him on countless occasions, it was for his own protection.

He had ventured to ask whether the *Sheeran* clue discovered at Portland Place delivered anything useful. Emily's answer, a coy smile, eyes wide and appreciative, followed by a nod of assent. A mere crumb of truth, but Al accepted it gratefully, his heart lifting with pride.

He also asked about Imelda Jones. When Emily left HQ that evening she had taken a detour to visit Imelda. Emily now knew Mason Jones's suspicions had been misplaced. That was understandable considering he was not privy to Scafell's status. Jones appeared convinced Scafell was a Russian spy. But in his attempt to discover evidence he had become a target. None of which Emily could divulge, but she wanted Imelda to know Jones had been doing his job, following his instincts, and the Service regarded him as a valuable asset. She told Imelda about the moment that afternoon at HQ, the silence honouring Jones's memory. Tears rolled down Imelda's cheeks and they hugged once more in the lounge, surrounded by miniature tipper trucks.

"That was nice," said Al, when Emily finished recounting her visit. "It must be hard for Imelda. It's one thing not understanding exactly what happened, Emily, but at least I know you're safe and well, and I thank God for that. It's quite another grieving for the love of your life when you've no idea why he was killed."

The barmaid arrived with drinks, a pink gin with lemon and ice for Emily and another pint for Al. Emily took a sip through a long straw, watching Al slurp his pint, at the same time wondering how she had the good fortune to meet someone as understanding. For the first time in weeks she felt safe, free of foreboding.

Her eyes wandered to the television. There were pictures of planes taking off and an aerial shot of an ambulance at the entrance to what appeared to be a car park. The location prompt in the top left corner read *Heathrow Airport*.

The tickertape crawling its way along the bottom of the picture seemed to take an age to explain the details of the story, but then Emily's mouth dropped open and Al detected concern in her eyes.

"Turn the sound up." A tremor distorted her voice and at first the barmaid did not appear to understand. "Please, put the sound on." Emily repeated the request, her agitation obvious as she pointed at the television. The barmaid lazily waved the remote.

"At this stage it isn't known if it was an accident or a suicide attempt." The reporter signalled behind him to the upper floors of a concrete multi-storey car park, his voice eager but devoid of emotion. "The man's body was found earlier this evening by a fellow passenger. He is thought to have fallen from the top tier of the multi-storey car park behind me, here at Terminal Four. The victim's name has not yet been released, but he is thought to be in his forties. A ticket found on his person suggests he was due to travel on a scheduled flight to Panama."

Al looked bemused. "What's going on, Emily? What is it?"

Emily tried to speak. Her lips moved but no sound came. She sucked a deep breath. Her mind tracked back to that afternoon in McBride's office when Stephens had described Scafell's dilemma on reaching the crossroads in his career of deceit.

"Kill Emily and protect his identity or save Emily, and forever be mindful that one day the debt must be paid."

This was the day. This was the hour, brutally sooner than expected, an unknown avenger had chosen to call in the debt. Of that Emily was certain.

She turned to Al, hugging him tight, seeking comfort, burying her nose in his chest, lost in a blizzard of unconnected thoughts and conflicting emotions. In that moment, she felt impossibly sad for Scafell, the man who had sacrificed his career and now his life to save her, yet she had never felt closer to Al, the man she loved for his uncomplicated charm and unwavering loyalty. Another realisation surfaced, too, so thrilling and unexpected that it flew into her mind accompanied by a vapour trail of guilt.

For the first time in her life, she felt she belonged, certain she was suited to the Intelligence career she had never sought, but which, by some complex twist of destiny, had found her. None of which she was able, or allowed, to explain.

Instead, when they separated, Emily lifted her glass, discarded the straw, sinking the pink spirit in one calm-inducing swallow.

"Are you okay?" said Al.

Emily closed her eyes and hugged Al once more. "Not yet, but I will be."

FRANK MALLEY

Acknowledgements

When I started researching this book it struck me how Britain's Intelligence services, such as MI5 and MI6, were often referred to as 'opaque organisations', as if somehow that was a criticism. Surely the whole point of services dealing in secrets, subterfuge and matters of national security is that they are not always totally transparent. Not so much an aim in an increasingly violent and uncertain world, as a requirement.

In the main, such organisations are manned by ordinary people, commuting each day to mundane jobs in administration, technology, and analytics. Men and women who must, via the Official Secrets Act, sign away their right to discuss work and emotions outside their workplace, even with those closest to them.

The characters in the book are not drawn from comic strip fiction, but from real life, largely anonymous, rarely flamboyant, but with all the flaws, fears, nerves and courage of the Ordinary Joe or Jane. As Roger Moore, of James Bond film fame, said, "You can't be a real spy and have everybody in the world know who you are and what your drink is."

Many thanks to the team at Sharpe Books for their faith in the project.

Most of all, love and gratitude to my family. To Michael, for his encouragement, and to Carole for her constructive feedback, her welcome cups of coffee and zeal in tracking down those misplaced apostrophes.

Printed in Great Britain
by Amazon

32050630R00138